CHRISTO|
THE CASE OF THE
KIDNAPPED COLONEL

CHRISTOPHER BUSH was born Charlie Christmas Bush in Norfolk in 1885. His father was a farm labourer and his mother a milliner. In the early years of his childhood he lived with his aunt and uncle in London before returning to Norfolk aged seven, later winning a scholarship to Thetford Grammar School.

As an adult, Bush worked as a schoolmaster for 27 years, pausing only to fight in World War One, until retiring aged 46 in 1931 to be a full-time novelist. His first novel featuring the eccentric Ludovic Travers was published in 1926, and was followed by 62 additional Travers mysteries. These are all to be republished by Dean Street Press.

Christopher Bush fought again in World War Two, and was elected a member of the prestigious Detection Club. He died in 1973.

THE LUDOVIC TRAVERS MYSTERIES
Available from Dean Street Press

CHRISTOPHER BUSH

THE CASE OF THE KIDNAPPED COLONEL

With an introduction
by Curtis Evans

DEAN STREET PRESS

INTRODUCTION

A Myster y Writer Goes to W ar

Christopher Bush and British Detective Fiction' s Fight against Hitler

After the Francophile Christopher Bush completed his series sleuth Ludovic "Ludo" Travers' nostalgic little tour of France (soon to be tragically overrun and scourged by Hitler's remorseless legions) in the pair of detective novels *The Case of the Flying Donkey* (1939) and *The Case of the Climbing Rat* (1940), the author published a trilogy of Ludo Travers mysteries drawing directly on his own recent experience in British military service: *The Case of the Murdered Major* (1941), *The Case of the Kidnapped Colonel* (1942) and *The Case of the Fighting Soldier* (1942). Together this accomplished trio of novels constitutes arguably the most notable series of wartime detective fiction (as opposed to thrillers) published in Britain during the Second World War. There are, to be sure, other interesting examples of this conflict-focused crime writing by true detective novelists, such as Gladys Mitchell's *Brazen Tongue* (1940, depicting the period of the so-called "Phoney War"), G.D.H. Cole's *Murder at the Munition Works* (1940, primarily concerned with wartime labor-management relations), John Rhode's *They Watched by Night* (1941), *Night Exercise* (1942) and *The Fourth Bomb* (1942), Miles Burton's *Up the Garden Path* (1941), *Dead Stop* (1943), *Murder, M.D.* (1943) and *Four-Ply Yarn* (1944), John Dickson Carr's *Murder in the Submarine Zone* (1940) and *She Died a Lady* (1943), Belton Cobb's *Home Guard Mystery* (1941), Margaret Cole's *Knife in the Dark* (1941), Ngaio Marsh's *Colour Scheme* (1943) and *Died in the Wool* (1945) (both set in wartime New Zealand), Christianna Brand's *Green for Danger* (1944), Freeman Wills Crofts's *Enemy Unseen* (1945) and Clifford Witting's *Subject: Murder* (1945). Yet Bush's three books seem the most informed by actual martial experience.

Like his Detection Club colleague Cecil John Charles Street (who published mysteries as both John Rhode and Miles Burton), Christopher Bush was a distinguished veteran of the First World War (though unlike Street his service seems to have consisted of administration rather than fighting in the field) who returned to active service during the second, even more globally catastrophic, "show" (as Bush termed it), albeit fairly briefly. 53 years old at the time of the German invasion of Poland and Britain's resultant entry into hostilities, Bush helped administer prisoner of war and alien internment camps, initially, it appears, at Camp No 22 (Pennylands) in Ayrshire, Scotland and Camp No 9 at Southampton, at the latter location as Adjutant Quartermaster.

In February 1940, Bush, now promoted from 2nd Lieutenant to Captain, received his final, and most controversial, commission: that of Adjutant Commandant at a prisoner-of-war and alien internment camp established in the second week of the war at the recently evacuated Taunton's School in Highfield, a suburb of Southampton. Throughout the United Kingdom 27,000 refugees and immigrants from Germany, Austria and Italy (after the latter country declared war on Britain in June 1940) were interned in camps like the one in Highfield. Bournemouth refugee Fritz Engel--a Jewish Austrian dentist who in May 1940, after Winston Churchill became Prime Minister and inaugurated his infamous "Collar the lot!" internment policy, was interned at the Highfield camp--direly recalled the brief time he spent there, before he was transferred to a larger camp on the Isle of Man, for possible shipment overseas. "I was first taken into Southampton into a building belonging to Taunton's School," he wrote in a bracing unpublished memoir, "already surrounded by electrically loaded barbed wire. . . ." (See Tony Kushner and Katharine Knox, *Refugees in an Age of Genocide: Global, National and Local Perspectives during the Twentieth Century*, 1999.)

Similarly, Desider Furst, another interned refugee Austrian Jewish dentist, wrote in his autobiography, *Home is Somewhere Else*: "[Our bus] stopped in front of a large building, a school, and the bus was surrounded by young soldiers with fixed bayonets. We had become prisoners. A large hall was turned into a dormitory, and we were each issued a blanket. The room was already fairly crowded. . . . We were fed irregularly with tea and sandwiches, and nobody bothered us. We were not even counted. I had the feeling that it was a dream or bad joke that would end soon." He was wrong, however: "After two days we were each given a paper bag with some food and put onto a train [to Liverpool] under military escort. The episode was turning serious; we were regarded as potential enemies."

Soon fi ding its way in one of Bush's detective novels was this highly topical setting, prudently shorn by the author of the problematic matter of alien refugee internment. (Churchill's policy became unpopular in the UK and was modified after the *Arandora Star*, an internee ship bound for Canada, was torpedoed by the Germans on July 2, 1940, leading to the deaths of nearly 1000 people on board, a tragic and needless event to which Margaret Cole darkly alludes in her pro-refugee wartime mystery *Knife in the Dark*.) All of Bush's wartime Travers trilogy mysteries were favorably received in Britain (though they were not published in the U.S.), British crime fiction critics deeming their verisimilitude impressive indeed. "Great is the gain to any tale when the author is able to provide a novel and interesting environment described with evident knowledge," pronounced Bush's Detection Club colleague E.R. Punshon in his review of one of these novels, *The Case of the Murdered Major*, in the *Manchester Guardian*.

For his part Christopher Bush in August 1940 was granted, after his promotion to to the rank of Major, indefinite release from service on medical grounds, giving him time to return full throttle to the writing of detective fiction. Although only one Ludovic Travers mystery appeared in 1940, the year the author was enmeshed in administrative affairs at Highfield, Bush published seven more Travers mysteries between 1941 and 1945, as well as four war thrillers attributed to "Michael Home," the pseudonym under which he had written mainstream fiction in the 1930s. Bush was back in the saddle--the mystery writer's saddle--again.

The Case of the Kidnapped Colonel (1942)

The secretive scientific researcher who is working on a startling invention of incalculable value to the war effort and is thereby beset at his country house by ruthless Nazi spies and insidious fifth columnists was, during Britain's life-or-death martial struggle with Germany in the years 1939 to 1945, a staple of fiction, stage and cinema. The first espionage story performed on stage during the Second World War, Geoffrey Kerr's *Cottage to Let*, debuted in July 1940, prompting theatre reviewer Herbert Farjeon (a brother of thriller writer Jefferson Farjeon and children's author Eleanor Farjeon) in his rave notice to observe, "It is a tribute to the serious nature of this war that we should have had to wait eleven months for the first spy play." The next year *Cottage to Let* was adapted under the same title as a film, directed by Anthony Asquith and starring several of the same actors from the play, including Leslie Banks as the reclusive inventor and the late George Cole as Ronald, the evacuee cockney boy who to the surprise of everyone around him reveals that he possesses the deductive faculties of an embryonic Sherlock Holmes.

Some of the more notable British detective novels (as distinct from thrillers) which draw on similar surefire mystery plot elements to those found in *Cottage to Let* are Mary Fitt's *Death on Heron's Mere* (1941) (*Death Finds a Target* in the US), G.D.H. Cole's *Toper's End* (1942), Christopher Bush's *The Case of the Kidnapped Colonel* (1942), Miles Burton's *Dead Stop* (1943) and Patricia Wentworth's *The Key* (1944). The basic plot had become commonplace enough by the time Christopher Bush's *The Case of the Kidnapped Colonel* was published that the author's Detection Club colleague E.R. Punshon, reviewing the book in the *Manchester Guardian*, was moved to query, "Does Mr. Christopher Bush . . . tell of yet another of those stupendous war secrets which enemy agents so persistently and so unsuccessfully try to secure?" Punshon's answer provided full encouragement to doubting detective fiction fans: "Well, perhaps, but with a difference. No wonder [Bush's sleuth] Ludovic Travers is puzzled, and so will be the reader in this amusing variety of the orthodox detective story."

The mystery opens in April 1941 with Ludovic Travers (who narrates the novel, as he will all the future ones in which he appears) learning that he is being transferred from No. 54 Prisoner of War Camp at Shoreleigh, where he had been Commandant since the exciting events detailed in *The Case of the Murdered Major* (1941), to Camp 55, near the city of Dalebrink in Derbyshire. There he is to take charge of guarding "two highly important factories, two vital tunnels, a bridge or two and a certain hush-hush establishment"—Dalebrink Park, a long-ago playground of the Hell-fire Club and now the private domicile of Colonel and Mrs. Brende. At Dalebrink Park the Colonel and a trio of experts in physics--including Professor Heinrich Wissler, a refugee from Prague who resembles Einstein as a young man --are conducting nationally vital research on defenses against the Nazis' night-flying aircraft

Assisting the experts at their important tasks is the Hon. Penelope Craye, a second cousin or thereabouts of Mrs. Brende and Colonel Brende's well-born and alluringly lovely private secretary. ("She looked Garbo and Hedy Lamarr all rolled into one.") As seems his habit with the beautiful and all-too-often calculating women who cross his path, Ludo gravely doubts the personal motivations of the Hon. Penelope Craye. Recalling those notorious fascist-loving Mitford sisters, the Hon. Diana and the Hon. Unity, we learn that before the war the Hon. Penelope had been the subject of much speculation in society "that she was one of the set of Hitler's apologists" and that "some would not have been surprised if she had been clapped in clink at the time of the Fifth Column round-up" (as in fact were Diana Mitford and her husband, Sir Oswald Mosley, leader of the British Union of Fascists). Why on earth, Ludo wonders, has so dubious a personage as Penelope Craye, if not "clapped in clink," been allowed free passage over a place as important to the anti-fascist cause as Dalebrink Park?

Also of concern to Ludo and others in the military administration is the presence, in Dalebrink's progressive "garden suburb" (home to "all the cranks in England") of the pacifist and leftist New Era Group (N.E.G.). Led by Sir Hereward Dove, "a man of some wealth and a dabbler in architecture and spiritualism," and local Anglican minister Rev. Lancelot Bennison (suggestive names both), the idealistic N.E.G. recalls the real-life Peace Pledge Union and the Anglican Pacifist Fellowship, both of which were founded in the 1930s in response to the deteriorating political situation in Europe as Adolf Hitler took power in Germany and made ever-mounting territorial demands of his neighbors.

Christopher Bush's son, the distinguished composer Geoffrey Bush (who sadly was never acknowledged by his father), was himself a member of the Anglican Pacifist Fellowship and a conscientious objector during the Second World War, which began when he was only 19 years old. Although he had been admitted in 1938 to Balliol College, Oxford, Geoffrey Bush spent his war years at the Hostel of the Good Shepherd at Tredegar in Monmouthshire, Wales, looking after "difficult evacuated children—rather more challenging charges one gathers than cheeky young Ronald in *Cottage to Let*. Although the mystery-writing Christopher loved classical music and the music composing Geoffrey loved detective fiction (he co-wrote the crime tale "Baker Dies" with Oxford classmate Edmund Crispin, himself a future composer and mystery writer), the father and son never met during Christopher's life and there is no doubt that Christopher would have looked askance at Geoffrey's pacifism (had he followed his son's activities at all), given Ludo's dismissive comments about the movement in *The Case of the Kidnapped Colonel*.

When Colonel Brende vanishes from Dalebrink Park, presumably having been abducted, some suspicion is cast at the N.E.G.—members of which, so the thinking goes, might have been crackbrained enough to have resorted to drastic criminal measures in pursuit of peace. Yet there also is the matter of come-hither Penelope Craye, whom George Wharton from Scotland Yard, having arrived to investigate the matter, suspects might have been carrying on an affair with Colonel Brende. "He was a man and she was a woman," Wharton coarsely observes to Ludo, "you're a man of the world and you can put two and two together." Was Mrs. Brende, the Colonel's elder by a decade or more, jealous of her husband's relationship--whatever it was--with the Hon. Penelope? And what about Mrs. Brende's dubious Mayfair nephew, Howard Craye, "a lounge lizard in uniform," and mysterious Major Passenden, recently returned to England from Europe, where he was thought to have died during the retreat to Dunkirk? With a missing notebook, a haunted summer-house and a poisoning in the offin as well, Travers and Wharton find themselves confronting one of their most challenging cases yet, with the security of the very Empire at stake.

Curtis Evans

CHAPTER I
FRESH WOODS

IT was at about nine o'clock on a morning of April of this year when a call came from the War Offic It was a Colonel Billow speaking, and he said he understood my Camp was being closed down. How was the job proceeding?

I said it was proceeding very well, whereupon he wanted to know if my adjutant was sufficient competent to finis it up on his own. When I said that he certainly was, I was told to report at the War Offi   the following morning at eleven hours, at Room 365. It was a question of a new appointment.

I knew he was about to hang up so I got in my question very quickly.

"Do you mind telling me, sir, if I shall be able to get back here again, or had I better assume that I shan't?"

That was a bit off his line of country. He told me to hold on for a minute, and I knew his hand was cupping the receiver while he asked an opinion of someone else. It was a couple of minutes before he spoke.

"That you, Major Travers? About that question you put. I think you'd better assume you'll be leaving for good."

So that was that, and to tell the truth I was by no means sorry to get a change of job. It is melancholy work clearing up, or well and truly interring, a biggish concern like ours which has been one's whole life for a matter of eighteen months.[1] Also we had been pretty well blitzed, and I was rather hoping for a job where the bombs might be of some less irritating kind. I was hoping, too, that the new job might be the least bit more active. Twelve hours a day and seven days a week in an offi   never was my idea of soldiering.

It was not till late afternoon that I was able to get away. I had managed to get hold of my wife at the hospital where she was nursing, but all she could say was that she'd do her best to get off but they were frightfully understaffed She was not at the station as we'd tentatively arranged, so I went on to the hotel. It

seemed as queer as ever not going to the old fla in St. Martin s
Chambers, but that had been closed down for the duration and
my man Palmer had been pensioned off

When I registered at the hotel the clerk said there was a
message for me. It was from Bernice, to say that she would be at
the hotel at as near nine o'clock as possible. I told the clerk that
I'd risk whether my wife had dined, and wait dinner till then. By
the time I'd cleaned up generally and had some tea, there were
still three hours to wait. In the old days they would have been
easy to pass. Now I was feeling somewhat restless, and loafin
about the lounge or strolling aimlessly about the streets had no
appeal whatever, and then it suddenly came to me that I might
do worse than walk the few hundred yards to the Yard and fin
out the whereabouts of George Wharton. If he happened to be in
town he might dine with Bernice and myself.

The last time I had been on leave, which was at the
Christmas, George had been out of town, and they told me at
the Yard that he had been for some time engaged on special
hush-hush work. Since I am one of those unoffici   so-called
experts whom the Yard frequently employs, though in my own
case the former ownership of an uncle as Chief Commissioner
made my employment perilously near simony, no bones were
made about telling me just what the hush-hush work was. As
I very well knew, from Dunkirk time till the utter collapse of
France, an enormous number of refugees had managed to reach
this country. Among them were undoubtedly enemy agents,
and so Superintendent George Wharton had become a kind
of scrutineer-in-chief, and was working with both the Special
Branch and Military Intelligence, not to mention the Home
Offic   But wherever he was working, the right man was for once
in the right place, for George is one of the few men I've ever
come across whose French is definitel as good as his English,
moreover he has up his sleeves tricks that would have made Bill
Bye and the Heathen Chinee look like amateur conjurers at a
children's party.

But I had no luck at the Yard that evening. There was no
one there whom I knew particularly well, though I learned that

the General—at the Yard they know him as the old General, and the adjective, I may tell you, is one of affection—wa still on special duty. Then someone turned up whom I knew, or who knew me, a little better, and he told me that George was at the moment in Derbyshire. When I asked for his address, he pretended there was no late information, and he looked sorry for mentioning Derbyshire at all. Then I actually wormed out of him that George's temporary headquarters were at a place called Dalebrink, about which I'd faintly heard. No sooner had he told me that than he was qualifying it by insisting that George wasn't really there; it was merely a species of operational centre.

As if to make up for the paucity of information, he told me quite a lot about Dalebrink. According to him it appeared to be divided like all Gaul into three parts: a small area where there were two mightily important factories, the town itself with its residential portion which made it a caravanserai for Lancashire, and a Garden City part by itself which was a cranks' home.

"Ah ha!" I said. "So the General's doing Buchan stuff is he?"

"Buchan stuff? he said blandly.

"That's right. *Thirty-nine Steps, Mr. Standfast,* and so on."

He smiled at my childish chatter, but there was something in his eye which told me I had not been so far out. Still, I did no more winkling out of information, and after I'd stood him a drink at a nearby hostelry, I made a slow way back to the hotel. Bernice actually turned up a quarter of an hour before time.

She was as sorry as I was that I had not been able to get hold of George, and during the meal we fell naturally to talking about him, for George is one of those people about whom one simply must talk as soon as their names are mentioned. George has *it,* and that little something the others haven't got, and though I am not modern enough to know the nature of its ingredients— he doubtless has considerable quantities of oomph. But the best thing about him is that he is fully aware of his own gifts and qualities. Bernice loves him and describes him consistently as a darling. As for my own opinions, the fact that he never ceases to be a source of delight does not alter the other fact that I have for him a tremendous respect and affection even if I have concealed both under the remark that if ever anything happens to him I shall insist on having him stuffed

Since George is going to be the major part of the queer things which I hope to relate, perhaps you would like to meet him well beforehand. George is a subject ripe for the brush or pencil of Belcher, in fact he bears some resemblance to the gent whom Belcher has immortalized with the cornet. But George is a walking paradox. His vast weeping-willow moustache gives him a henpecked look, and when he puts on his antiquated spectacles, he assumes at the same time an old-world, disarming simplicity. He believes himself that the Yard robbed the stage of a great character actor, and showmanship is the sap of his very vitals. Women, as he has boasted in his expansive moments, are as putty in his fingers, and he can smell a liar quicker than the devil can catch the whiff of holy water. His snorts, his grunts, his little hypocrisies, and even his sudden and terrifying assumptions of dignity and wrath, are merely the rich colourings of a ripe and fruity personality. George can dance, and who more deftly, with them that dance, and as for weeping with them that weep, he could make a crocodile blush for its puerile efforts Both his memory and patience are prodigious, and while he has made enemies enough in his time, I have never known him lose a friend.

As I neared the War House the following morning, I felt the approach of the usual depression and with it an apprehension. Many other men have told me they always feel precisely the same way. And in case you may ask why this holding-up of a story because of what may sound like a private vendetta, let me hasten to say there is no private vendetta, and that some little knowledge of, say, the whimsicalities of the War Offi may be most important in its bearing on the queer story I hope to relate.

Not all departments of the W.O. are daubed with the same brush. There are some to whom I am always ready to present arms, since they know just what they want, say so in the fewest possible words, and go the right way to work to get it. As to others, some pretty damning accusations have been made in the House. I doubt if it can be denied that an enormous number of us have come to regard the W.O. with feelings compounded of maddening rage, sardonic despair, and a helplessness utterly without hope. Sum it up by saying that if I make a slip of utter unimportance compared with the muddle, contradiction, waste and ineptitude of which the W.O. is freely and frequently capable, the same W.O. will rear in wrath and threaten to treat the wretched delinquent as if he had virtually lost the war.

Still, to get back. It was not my fault if I felt depressed. After all, I was about to interview someone who, for all I knew, would be the usual specialist in putting round pegs in square holes, and who had the authority to send me forthwith to Fiji or the Outer Hebrides. Argument would be out of the question. If there was a gap in the department's private jigsaw, in I would go, fi or not.

At the War House I signed the usual chit stating my business and with whom. A careful eye was run over me, and when it was apparent—regretfully, let's hope—that I was unlikely to assassinate any of the more decrepit colonels, I was handed over to an orderly and taken upstairs. In the corridors were wandering from department to department aloof young office who in the Great War could have been found at the business end of a feeding-bottle, and everywhere was decorum amid a slightly mouldy smell as of new distemper. I was kept under observation till ten minutes past eleven when I entered Room 365.

Colonel Billow was an agreeable surprise, because in under fiv minutes I was out of that room again. He was elderly but very, very brisk, and if I had wanted to say anything beyond a "Very good, sir," I'd have had no chance. He said I was on loan, as it were, from my old department, and was to take on the job of Commandant at a brand new kind of camp, known merely as Camp 55. The personnel were mixed and the duties were merely those of guarding various points. Camp 55 was near Dalebrink in Derbyshire, which was its address.

When he said that, my eyes popped. Instead of a "Very good, sir," I so far forgot myself as to say, or begin to say, "Did you say *Dalebrink,* sir!" Before the firs words were out, he was waving an impatient hand for silence, for he had picked up the local receiver and was about to speak.

"Is Major Splint there? Send him in, will you?"

The receiver was replaced and I was asked if I needed a railway warrant. I said I had one I could fil in, and then the Major Splint was shown in. He was told that I was Major Travers who was taking over from him, and would we have a talk about things as arranged. That appeared to be all. We saluted and out we went.

I liked the look of Splint, and I liked him still better when he said at once, "Let's get out of this goddam Zoo and fin a drink."

"I don't think I'd care to drink," I said, "with a bloke who speaks so disrespectfully."

He shot me a look, then grinned. Inside fiv minutes we were having some really excellent coffe and he was telling me all about Camp 55. Not that it was necessary, as he said, because down there I should fin the very prince of adjutants who could make me conversant with things as we went along. What we talked therefore might be classed as generalities and scandal.

The Camp was a hutted one, he said. Some of the troops were permanent, but two Companies stayed for about three months and were then replaced. All did guards and at the same time carried on training, for which there were facilities, including two excellent ranges. What had to be guarded were two highly important factories, two vital tunnels, a bridge or two and a certain hush-hush establishment.

As for the lie of the land, I should soon pick it up, he said. No map was required, for most things were along a line running north-west to south-east. Start north-west and there were the two factories, both well camouflaged Proceed south-east along the line for a mile and there was the town of Dalebrink—what might be called the old town with its shops and the residential area of the *hoi polloi*. Another half-mile and one came to the Garden City, small and well spread out, and occupying the slopes of some attractive hills. Another half-mile and there was Dalebrink Park, as it was known—a private estate on which was situated the hush-hush affai that had to be guarded.

"And where's our Camp?" I asked.

"Half-way between the Garden City and the Park and just off the main road to the north," he said. "There's transport, by the way, to take your men, and there's a special car for your own use."

"It sounds a cushy job," was my opinion.

"It is," Splint said. "It's a comfortable Camp, and the country's lovely. In the summer it'll be paradise. Still, you know what that part of Derbyshire's like without my telling you."

"And what's my own actual work?"

"Just being chief executive. I used to pay surprise visits to the guards at all sorts of hours. Harrison, the adjutant, is kept pretty much to his offic   so I used to take that load off his back." Then he smiled. "Honestly, I think it's a job you'll like. Or won't you?"

"I'm wondering," I told him. "Aren't there any snags at all?"

"Frankly," he said, "I can't think of any. Mind you, it isn't a job where you'll win any medals. Also you may expect to get more heavily raided than we've been up to now."

"No flie   in the ointment at all then?"

"Just one little one," he said, and smiled. "There's one young offic   who'll probably annoy you considerably–a chap called Craye. He's a kind of lounge lizard in uniform, and with any God's amount of sheer cheek. You may have to jump on him with both feet. He's only just turned up or I should have had him well in hand for you."

"I'll remember Craye," I said. "But what's the famous Garden City like?"

"Gawd, what a place!" he said. "It's a regular last ditch for all the cranks in England."

"What sort of cranks?"

"All sorts. I don't mind the arts and crafts gang and the long-haired poets and authors and so on. What I don't like are the Neggers." He caught my questioning look and explained. "We call them the Neggers from their initials—N.E.G., which is the New Era Group."

"A pacifis   show?"

He frowned. "It's more tricky than that. The Neggers are planning a New Order and they're a wily lot. It's a pretty good camouflag to pretend to be planning the future while you're doing underground work in the present. There's some very bad blood between the City and the town. People want to know why the whole collection of Neggers aren't under lock and key. You hear no end of talk about influence."

"What about the hush-hush place?"

"That's a differen proposition," he said. "I believe there's research being carried on in connection with the fighting of night bombers. There's a small gang of experts living in the Hall. Harrison will give you a special hush-hush document about it. I paid the usual courtesy call when the show started, but I haven't been inside the place since. I don't think one's made any too welcome."

"I suppose," I said with a vast assumption of indifference "you never ran across a man called Wharton down there?"

"Wharton?" he said. "What's he like?"

"A civilian. Biggish chap with an overhanging moustache."

He shook his head and I left it at that. In fact, the only other thing that happened of consequence was that he gave me the telephone number of Camp 55 and assured me there was an excellent train leaving at fourteen-thirty hours. I took him along to my hotel to collect my baggage, and before lunch I got hold of Harrison and arranged to be met at Dalebrink station.

Splint was on short leave before going out East, so he disappeared after lunch and I rang Bernice to give her the news, the address and the telephone number.

"Derbyshire!" she said. "My dear, what a dreadful distance away!"

"Inverness would have been farther," I said cheerfully, and before I could come in with other consolations, she was all agog with something she had suddenly remembered.

"Dalebrink, darling. Don't you remember? That charming Mrs. Brende."

"Mrs. Brende?"

"You must remember. She was at our wedding. You know. Her husband was in India. He was a gunner or something. A dear old soul about sixty."

"Oh, yes," I said diplomatically, and still unable to recall the lady. Fancy a man remembering people with whom he's barely shaken hands on his wedding day.

"You must look her up," Bernice was going on. "It will be lovely for you, darling, having a home from home."

"You mean, she lives at Dalebrink?"

"Darling," she told me in a rather hurt voice, "haven't I been telling you so all the time?"

It was a good train as Splint had said, and on that comfortable journey two things happened. Strictly speaking, one was a happening and the other was an idea.

With regard to the idea, it came at the tail end of a line of thought. As I lay back in the corner seat of the empty compartment, I began naturally to wonder about the new appointment. It is all very well for us old-timers to ape the fire-eate and to pray to be sent where the shells fall thickest, but there is something singularly attractive about a job where the Hun is not, and the voice of the turtle is heard in the land. While conscience therefore told me that though I was Category B Permanent, I ought to be a fighting man, something that I was pleased to regard as common sense assured me that I was about to do a job that someone had to do, and that they also serve who only stand and wait. The same insidious voice said it was humbug for me to regard myself as a real soldier. That tooth-brush moustache I flaunte in the world's face was a pathetic camouflag for my bat eyes and horn rims, and six foot three of gauntness, let alone the grey hair that has long spread abroad from its once distinguished siting round my temples. Then an apt quotation came to my mind, from old George Peele:

His helmet now shall make a hive for bees.

And as I thought of that, I thought of George Wharton, and I suddenly knew why I was being sent to Dalebrink!

Perhaps you don't get it, as our American friends say. Well, I have a flibbertigibbe sort of brain. I suppose, like everyone else, I have a small repertoire of things that I really know well, but for the rest I fear I have dabbled in an incredible number of things and gathered a junk-house of information which find application principally in the more abstruse cross-words. George Wharton gets exasperated by it because it serves to prompt me with an immediate theory to satisfy any problem. The fact that I am right only once in say, every four shots, does not discourage the furtive inner voice that prompts the said theories. George, as I said, becomes annoyed, sarcastic, and even epigrammatic about it all, but that hasn't deterred him from profitin in the past from my more successful efforts

When I thought of that quotation then, my thoughts went like this. George Peele—George Wharton—bees—bees in the bonnet—theories—coincidence: and there it was. It could not be coincidence, I said, that I was going to Dalebrink to do a job that Harrison could do far better than I and where the few talents I have would be wholly unused, and where at the moment was mysteriously lurking George Wharton with whom I had always worked in the old days at the Yard. George, I said, must have approached the Powers-that-be and have asked for me to be sent to Dalebrink. In that case something mightily strange was going on down there. The warrior's helmet, in fact, would not be a hive for bees. The warrior, for all he knew, might fin himself in false whiskers, with a truncheon concealed under his armpit.

As for the thing that happened, it seemed less than unimportant at the time. I had bought *The Times* to do the cross-word, and when I had finishe it my eye caught an advertisement. It was for something I rather wanted, so I began cutting it out neatly with my penknife. Then I wondered, since I still wanted the paper, if I was spoiling something on the other side, so I had a precautionary look, and I then saw a paragraph which I had missed at my fi st discursive reading. Mind you, I saw no importance in that paragraph. It had a certain interest in the adventurous train of thought to which it naturally led up, but it did not stay docketed in my mind. There was no reason

why it should. I even forgot straightaway the name of the offic
it mentioned.

This was the paragraph.

DRAMATIC ADVENTURES OF OFFICER

News has come from Lisbon of the arrival there, after
incredible adventures, of Major Passenden, R.A., who
was reported as killed near Tourcoing during the retreat
to Dunkirk. Major Passenden, it appears, was slightly
wounded and he shammed death till after the enemy
column had passed, and then tried to reach the coast. He
was captured and escaped, and was sheltered at the risk
of their lives by a French household. Two months later
began the Odyssey which ended yesterday at Lisbon.

CHAPTER II
A LOOK ROUND

I FOUND Harrison   the very good fellow that Splint had
described, but as he enters very little into this story I shall not
introduce him further. What I should say is that if Harrison
hadn't been capable of running that Camp blindfolded, then I
should never have been able to take the part in this story which
circumstances, and George Wharton, forced upon me.

Camp 55 also requires no description. It was situated in
parkland with its hutments on the gentle slopes of the sheltering
hills, and everywhere were trees to camouflag from bombing.
A large stretch of level grassland lay beneath, which was handy
for training of troops, and quite a good road led out to the main
highway.

There were about a dozen office   in Mess, but young Craye,
over whom I was anxious to cast an eye, was off duty and dining
probably in the town. I'd like to be clear, by the way, about Craye.
I had no intention of coming the martinet or schoolmaster. All
the same, if the young feller-me-lad had anything in him that

was worth the findin I flattere myself that I could lick him into shape without his being too aware of it.

At breakfast the following morning I spotted him at once, but as the more senior of us sat in somewhat awful state at one end of the long table, and the smaller fry had lumped themselves for their own comfort at the other end, I had no word with him. But in appearance he was just what I had imagined—tall, rather pallid, very languid and with a kind of petulant aloofness. There was breeding enough about him even if the whole man did seem in process of going to seed. The dark circles under his eyes were evidence of the thoroughness of the night's festivities.

There were three standing office in the Camp, of whom Craye was one. I had already met all the office of the two movable Companies, and the Warrant officer including my own, but as the standing office were not all in Camp overnight, Harrison was bringing them to my offi for introductions immediately after breakfast. I had a general word with him about them beforehand, and all sorts of interesting things emerged about Craye.

The three office worked on what might be called three-day shifts. On one day an offi was on duty for twenty-four hours, visiting and inspecting guards, including night visits at surprise hours, and since the distances were large, each used a motor bicycle. On the second day he was off duty altogether, but was not allowed out of Camp till sixteen hours. On the third day he was Camp Orderly Office and an important thing about the arrangements was that he was never allowed to change duties with another offic without the express sanction of Harrison or myself. In my old days as a subaltern I should have considered the job of standing offic as something definitel cushy.

"Craye's got a relative living quite close," Harrison told me. "At the hush-hush house to be exact. Mrs. Brende, wife of the Colonel Brende who's the head man there."

"Good Lord!" I said. "I'd been meaning to ask you if you'd heard of a Mrs. Brende in these here parts. She's an acquaintance of my wife who asked me to look her up. And she's actually living at Dalebrink Hall, is she?"

"She's young Craye's aunt," Harrison said. "Putting it another way, I rather fancy he's her favourite nephew. There's talk of his coming into her money."

"Craye," I said reflectively "I seem to know someone else named Craye."

"There's a Miss Craye—Penelope Craye—there too," Harrison said. "She's a very distant relation. Second cousin or something. She's Colonel Brende's private secretary."

There was a mightily curious look in his eye as he told me that, and then it changed as he saw the look of perturbation on my own face.

"Oh, my hat!" I said. "Penelope Craye!"

"Not an old flam of yours, sir?" he said, and grinned.

"In that respect thy servant is as a dead dog," I told him fervently. "But how the devil did that woman get into that particular galley?"

He shrugged his shoulders.

"Ask the War House. Or put it this way, sir. Why shouldn't she be there?"

"You're getting too deep for me," I said. "You tell me the details in words of one syllable."

So he did, and the facts were as follows. Harrison knew them well enough because he'd been at Camp 55 since the word go. In spite of his smashed shoulder and crippled arm he was a very presentable bloke, and I was rather of the opinion that he'd fallen under the spell of Penelope and knew in consequence more than anyone else about the hush-hush affair

Mrs. Brende was a Craye. She had the money and Dalebrink Hall was hers. She was much older than Colonel Brende, to whom she had been married about fiftee years. Harrison put her age as sixty, and the Colonel's at forty-nine or fifty but the trouble was that whereas he looked forty, she was looking well over her age. Rumour had it that she controlled the purse-strings pretty rigidly.

As soon as the Hun began night bombing, Camp 55 was formed. Since Colonel Brende, a gunnery expert, was in charge, and Dalebrink a highly convenient place for the research work, what more natural than that Mrs. Brende—directly or through her husband—should offe Dalebrink Hall and its grounds? Why shouldn't it be wangled that young Craye should be one of the Camp's standing office   and near the doting aunt? And since Colonel Brende had to have an amanuensis, why not Penelope?

"Now, now, young feller," I said to Harrison. "I can swallow a lot, but I'm not a python. Penelope Craye a friend of yours?"

"I loathe the woman," he said.

Just then the R.S.M. reported that the office   were waiting outside, so Penelope was left for future discussion. In came the three and were introduced. Craye's salute was most puzzling. The hand went none too briskly to somewhere in the region of the right eyebrow, and his back arched at the same time as if he had changed his mind and was about to kiss my hand instead. When after our brief and friendly chat he gave the same weird salute on dismissal, I really had to do something about it.

"Oh, Mr. Craye, just a minute."

The two went out and his eyebrows rather rose as he looked at me.

"What is the peculiar disability you suffe from with regard to your back?" I asked him sympathetically.

"My back, sir?" Craye, by the way, never really smiled. The corner of his mouth would twitch upwards a little, that's all. Now there was something condescending in the twitch.

"Yes, your back."

"There's nothing wrong with my back, sir."

"Then I'm glad to hear it," I said. "You're not carrying a lot of worries on your shoulders either, by any chance?"

He just twitched and said nothing. His look was a bit wary as if he were wondering—naturally, I admit—with what queer fis he had to deal.

"Since everything seems to be normal," I said, "I shall expect you to salute like a young offic   who has respect for his own bearing and for the example he gives his men. Salute again please.

"A bit better," I told him, "but it still won't do."

I didn't want to labour the point, and after a moment's silence Craye's voice came with a rather peculiar quality of veiled insolence.

"Is that all, sir?"

I swivelled round in my chair.

"Yes, Mr. Craye, except for one thing. If that salute of yours isn't what it ought to be next time you give it, I shall make no bones about putting you under the R.S.M. to learn saluting by numbers."

"I'm sorry about that," I said to Harrison when he'd gone.

"I'm very glad you did jump on him, sir," Harrison said. "I've had him on the mat for the same thing before. I think he gave that Mayfair salute of his to annoy me because he knew I shouldn't speak in front of you. Also he's one of the kind who just flick up a finge instead of returning the men's salutes."

"What is it?" I said. "Just damned superiority?"

"That's it," he said. "It isn't really an aggressive superiority— at least not always. He's grown up to lounge his way through life, and he's the grandson of a peer, and thinks he's got plenty of influenc behind him, and now he's got a uniform on he doesn't see why it should make any difference.

Harrison had spoken feelingly, and I was making up my mind that if there was any genuine trouble with Craye I'd have that gentleman shifted elsewhere, even if I had to fight whatever influenc he was supposed to have. Harrison and I were going the rounds of the guard posts that morning, and while I waited for him to clear off the routine essentials of the morning, I was thinking not of young Craye but of the distantly related Penelope, for her presence at Dalebrink Hall had come as something of a startler.

She would be, I thought, about thirty, and since Penelope Craye and racing parlance seem to have much in common, I might describe her as a fin mover and a good looker. Her poise was an insolent cock-sureness, and her patrician beauty has been described in detail and viewed in an ironical setting of repose by the readers of face-cream advertisements, for Penelope is none too well blessed with cash and was one of the firs to realize that features have an investment value. Always in the forefront of the more dubious of the Smart Set, and a standby of the snobbish illustrateds, she had the deft knack of getting kudos from various activities while others did the work. Her name had been connected with a man or two, and she had that kind of notoriety which takes the form of furtive whispers and hints at the unsavoury. My opinion of her—and I had run up against her many times—was that she was as hard as they make them, absolutely unscrupulous, a thruster of the firs order, and an expert in making use of an easily summoned charm.

But all that doesn't really matter compared with the mystery of Penelope Craye at Dalebrink Hall. There she was apparently as private secretary to the head of an important secret research department, but what was she actually *doing* in terms of sheer honest-to-God work? She could be gushing, plausible and cajoling, but to think of Penelope as taking down notes in shorthand, using a typewriter, filin correspondence and drafting letters was as fantastic as seeing the languid Craye in navvy's get-up sweating at an electric drill in a road-repair gang. Who then was actually doing the real work while Penelope got the credit?

But more staggering still was the wonder why she of all people should be entrusted with the secrets of a hush-hush establishment. Before the war it had been hinted pretty openly that she was one of the set of Hitler's apologists, and some would not have been surprised if she had been clapped in clink at the time of the Fifth Column round-up. And since publicity was the breath of her nostrils, how was she existing without it? I'd seen the weekly illustrateds regularly, and I hadn't seen a picture with the wording—*The Hon. Penelope Craye with Colonel Brende and a friend. The Hon. Penelope is doing very secret war work somewhere in England.* Then if she wasn't getting publicity, just what was she getting?

The whole thing was a mystery, even if I did fin some sort of a theory to account for things. Penelope, I told myself, was probably blitzed to blazes in London. The experience scared several kinds of hell out of her, and she was glad to work the ropes to get the job in the sylvan security of Dalebrink. Money perhaps was tighter than usual, and she was glad of the cash coupled with a free home. And if there could be no publicity, she could at least let all her pals know that she was a highly important cog in the war machine.

I thought no more about Penelope Craye when Harrison and I started off on that visit to the guard posts. I had a private map and could follow all routes and sitings, but what interested me most was the beauty of the country-side in that belated spring. The car, official   known as mine, had pre-selection gears so that Harrison could drive it, and that gave me the chance for a good look round. I had never visited the Peak District, and these outlying spurs of it were something quite new to me. In the sun of that cold April morning, the hills had the most fascinating colourings that shifted with the clouds that crossed them, and the detour road we took, that often overhung a sheer drop to the dale below, was a real switchback.

We took in a tunnel and a couple of bridges before coming out at the two factories. When we turned for home it was along that line of main road that Splint had mentioned. We inspected another tunnel and in a minute or two were at the town. Its population was about eight thousand and was far more pastoral than I had imagined. The shops were good and there were quite a lot of hotels. As it was near midday we halted at one for a drink. When we came out I noticed the police-station opposite. Something told me to go in and ask if they had any information about George Wharton. Then I foresaw complications— proof of identity, for instance—and changed my mind.

Harrison suggested that I should drive from then on so as to get used to the gears. The road was dead straight to the Garden City, but before reaching it I had to turn right if I wanted to see it, as it lay on a kind of by-pass.

"Splint was telling me a little about the Neggers," I said. "An interesting collection of coves, and I wish he'd told me more."

Harrison didn't smile. He just frowned and gave me a sideways nod.

"I think they're a damn dangerous lot," he said.

When in Rome, believe what the Romans, do, so I frowned portentously too, and at once Harrison was getting everything off his chest. The Neggers, it appeared, had been very active in pacifis palaver and propaganda for months after the outbreak of war. When the Government instituted the campaign against loose or defeatist talk, they at once lay doggo. When the campaign petered out, they emerged from the long grass, and were now as active as ever.

The main plank of their platform was that the war was caused by man's inhumanity to man, in other words Versailles. A just peace was still perfectly possible, and every death from an enemy bomb added to the blood guilt of the Government. There should be redistribution of Colonies, and so on. Nothing very new, as you can see, but there were brains in the Garden City who could make the hackneyed and illogical look mightily attractive.

The President of the Group was Sir Hereward Dove, a man of some wealth and a dabbler in architecture and spiritualism. The moving spirit was, however, the Rev. Lancelot Benison, the incumbent of St. Luke's, the church of the City. According to Harrison he was a menace. He had split the church by pacifis sermons, and so could be certain that the substantial floc that remained were Neggers dyed in the wool. The town and the factories had been at times seething with rage. After a speech made by Benison at a Neggers' meeting a very ugly situation had developed. A gang had been organized at the factories to smash up the vicarage and the building known as Neggers' Hall, but the police were tipped off just in time.

Benison thereupon organized his own defence body and threatened retaliation if necessary, and the police were afraid to take action because they had very much played into his hands through their ignorance of the factory plot.

"But isn't there anybody of sufficie drive and standing to organize local opinion and get something done?" I said.

"The town bigwigs are nearly all tradesmen," Harrison said. "Think how much money goes into their pockets from the City. The local paper does smite 'em good and hard. Oh, yes, and there's Colonel Brende. At least it's supposed to be Colonel Brende."

He explained. Letters written by one *Patria* had appeared in the local paper, showing up the Neggers and demanding action. Colonel Brende was supposed to be their author, perhaps because his wife was a Dalebrink notability, and because the firs letter had blasted hell out of Benison for demanding an immediate ceasing of night-flyin planes over the area. The research work at Dalebrink Hall required co-operation of that kind, and it guessed that nobody but Colonel Brende could have been in possession of the material for that devastating reply.

"What did Benison do then?" I asked.

"He hinted at retaliation."

"But surely that was pure hot air?"

"I don't know," he said. "Curious, wasn't it, that Haw-Haw should have the whole thing at his finger-tip inside a week?" He gave that same ominous sideways nod. "I tell you Benison's a dangerous man. He's a fanatic, and he's got a following. The sabotaging of Dalebrink Hall isn't as fantastic as you might think."

Then he suddenly broke off and his hand was on my arm.

"Slow down a minute, sir. There're our two coves. Those two at the church gate."

I not only slowed down—I drew the car to a halt about forty yards away. Two men were in earnest conversation and with them was a third—a burly man with slightly stooping shoulders, and this burly man was evidently the life and soul of the party, for as the car stopped he was all at once giving a mighty guffa and digging the more elderly of the other two in the ribs. Both laughed as if the joke were a vintage one. As for me, my eyes were popping clean out of my head, for the life and soul of the trio was none other than George Wharton!

Harrison noticed nothing of my surprise, and we sat there for a couple of minutes with our eyes on the three at the gate. Dove was a huge old man of about seventy, with a monstrous paunch and a patriarchal snowy beard. Benison was tallish too, four-square on his pins and hard as nails. Dove I had mentally classed as a William Morris run to fat and foolishness; Benison's vicious mouth and beetling eyebrows made him John Knox with his whiskers off And in case you may think I was regarding the whole thing as a joke, let me say at once that I hated the sight of both Dove and Benison, and when the three moved on towards the church and our car got going again, I said to Harrison that they looked a highly unpleasant couple.

"Wonder who that other fellow was?" he said.

I changed the subject with what I hoped was adroitness. In the afternoon, I said, I would finis the tour by going to Dalebrink Hall, calling on Mrs. Brende and combining business with duty. At once Harrison was off again.

"Benison actually accused Colonel Brende of organizing that factory gang, by the way."

"Surely that was nonsense," I said. "Brende's on the Active List and he wouldn't risk his career like that."

"Benison's usually sure of his facts," Harrison insisted. "He has to be if you come to think of it. At any rate, as I said, he told Brende that he had his own way of putting an end to Brende's activities, and Brende himself, if it became necessary."

I didn't want to hurt Harrison's feelings by even the most modest show of incredulity, so once more I changed the subject. We had turned into the main road again, which gave me some sort of excuse for saying that I'd do two surprise visits per week to night guards. Harrison promptly said he'd like to do a third and we fixe details then and there. When we got back to Camp it was just a quarter of an hour before lunch.

I thought that an excellent opportunity for ringing up Mrs. Brende. A man's voice, with a slightly Cockney accent, answered the phone at last. I could hear it buzzing for at least two minutes after Exchange had got me through.

"Who's speaking?" I said.

"Corporal Ledd, sir." I didn't know till afterwards, when Harrison told me Ledd was on our strength and loaned to Brende as batman, that he spelt his name like that.

I said who I was and asked for Mrs. Brende. For some reason or other that knocked him off his perch.

"You want Mrs. Brende, sir?"

"Didn't I just say so?"

"Yes, sir. And it's Mrs. Brende you want."

Before I could ask what the devil was the matter with him, he was asking me to hold on. Three good minutes went by and then came a feminine voice.

"Is that Mrs. Brende?" I said.

"No, sir. This is Mrs. Brende's maid. What was it you wanted?"

"I want to speak to Mrs. Brende," I said patiently.

"Oh, yes, sir; Mrs. Brende. Would you mind holding on?"

This time it was four minutes that I had to wait. I know, because my offi   clock was bang in the line of my eyes.

"Yes?" a gentle voice said, and there at last was Mrs. Brende.

I explained that I was Major Travers, Commandant of Camp 55, but known to her perhaps as Ludovic Travers, husband of Bernice Haire that was. At once she was asking if I would come to tea that afternoon. Not the main door but the one at the left-hand side by the stone pergola. Fourish was the time, and I said I'd be delighted.

When I hung up I was in a much better temper, even if the gong had gone long since for lunch. I forgot the wonder that had come to me of why Mrs. Brende was so hedged about with unapproachableness, for the simple reason that I liked her voice. Mrs. Brende, I somehow knew, would be someone nice to know.

After lunch Harrison gave me the necessary information about Dalebrink Hall and the hush-hush work that was going on there. The Park was about forty acres. A main drive led to the front door, and was some three hundred yards long. There was also a back tradesmen's road of about fiv   hundred yards, according to the large-scale map. Each entrance gate had a day and night guard furnished by us. Most of the park was enclosed by a wall, and it was very well wooded. In view of each of the three doors of the house—front, side and rear—we had a standing guard by day and at night the whole house was patrolled.

Thanks to the fact that every inmate of the house, and every caller, had to have a pass furnished by us, it was fairly easy to tell by our records something of what was going on. The important inmates were as follows:

Colonel Brende, R.A., D.S.O.
Francis Newton—Professor of Physics at the University of X.
George Riddle—research student at Y College, University of X, specially released by military authorities.
Heinrich Wissler—formerly Professor of Physics at the University of Prague; Nobel Prize-winner, etc.
Squadron-Leader Pattner, D.S.O., D.F.C.

There were also two maids and a cook; Lance-Corporal Ledd and two other men furnished by us, including a man cook.

Of Brende I had never heard, but Harrison told me he was brilliant but temperamental. He admired his brains but didn't care a lot for the man himself, though he admitted he might be prejudiced. The other inmates were, of course, Mrs. Brende and the Hon. Penelope Craye. No stenographer, you will note, and so I could pat myself on the back for having wondered whom Penelope was findin to do the actual work.

As for the research that was going on, it undoubtedly had something to do with the location of night-flyin aircraft, and Harrison believed it was the show that influence all those optimistic remarks spoon-fed at intervals to the public, that night bombing would soon cease to be a menace, or the menace that it had been, which is a subtle difference

When I had finishe work in my offi that afternoon and was waiting for the time to move off to Dalebrink Hall, I was in a mood both anticipatory and complacent. Life at Camp 55 had begun well, and it looked more than ever as if Wharton had wangled my appointment. I admit I'm always ready to scent a mystery, but think of the headlines if a go-ahead reporter could spread himself on the front page of a popular daily with the information I already had!

SCOTLAND YARD SUPER HOBNOBS WITH FIFTH
COLUMN SUSPECTS.

WHY IS SOCIETY DAME IN HUSH-HUSH CAMP?

and, as I suddenly remembered—

WHO DOESN'T LIKE THE COLONEL'S WIFE TO
PHONE?

CHAPTER III
I BEGIN TO WONDER

My wife is often telling me that I have the annoying habit of
being flippant and she should know. If I have been flippan about
that hush-hush work that was going on at Dalebrink Hall, let
me hasten to apologize for something unintended. Undoubtedly
the work that was being done there was of supreme importance
and in need of implicit secrecy, which was why our instructions
were to maintain such a close guard. If the experts working on
schemes for destroying night bombers could save the dropping
of only a few hundred bombs a year, then I for one would not
have grudged all night and every night on guard.

The drive to the Park took a very few minutes. I was glad the
sentry at the main gate would not let me through till my pass
had been inspected, and I was held up again fift yards short of
the front door, outside which I left the car. The house was early
Georgian of the best type, and I guessed there would be three
or four large downstair rooms and a dozen good bedrooms.
The gardens were not extensive but of the firs quality, and for
the terraced lawns and rock gardens use had been made of the
falling ground. I was particularly attracted by an early Georgian
summer-house of local stone that overlooked two grass tennis
courts about a hundred yards from the door whose bell I was
ringing. The whole place had neatness and charm, and I don't
know when I have seen anything that had for me so immediate
an appeal.

The door was opened by an elderly maid, whom her mistress
was later to address as Annie. From her age, her self-possession
and the smile she gave me, I judged her to be an old servant of

the family, and as soon as she spoke I knew she was the one to whom I had talked over the phone. The hall I entered was small and rather bare, and facing it was the door of what was known as the morning-room, into which I was shown. I remembered Mrs. Brende as soon as I saw her again. She also claimed to remember me, and she had seen my wife again since our marriage.

As a young woman she must have been a noted beauty, and at sixty she was still remarkably handsome. The quality about her on which I would like to insist, and which made the charm of her gracious personality, was her utter sincerity. There were no aids to beauty, no apologies, no affectations and none of those kittenish sallies which one often suffer from those who would proclaim that there is life in the old girl yet. Edwardian was her period as it was of the delightful room where we sat, and those of us whose memories run back to those years and whose young lives were moulded in them, fin   more than a gratifying of sentiment in such an hour as I spent that afternoon.

A faint scent of musk was in the room and the heavier smell of jonquils that still flowere   beneath the spacious window. My collector's eyes goggled at the Queen Anne silver and the Worcester china of apple-green, and I simply had to be roguish.

"It's very wrong of you," I said, "to use those lovely things. If they were mine they'd be popped into a cabinet, and I'd have the key."

She smiled. "I don't think your wife would be pleased with you then. These are really all I have now. Practically everything of value has been sent away for storage. After all, we must expect to be bombed here."

There was a London house, it appeared, which was being used for the bombed homeless.

"Conscience disturbs me terribly sometimes," she said. "If I am living here in comparative safety, I feel the house should be full of refugees."

"Yes, but the work that's being done here is just as important, surely."

"I suppose it is," she said. "But conscience is a queer thing. You never know where and when it's going to attack you."

Already I felt we had known each other for years. That was why I said she was being swindled. It wasn't conscience that was at her but a highly bogus impersonator known as introspection.

"Well, hospitality's in my blood," she said, and laughed. "Who are we to know what's bogus? There's still such a thing as entertaining angels unawares."

Then she was explaining what she had said about hospitality. The family fortunes had been ruined by it in the eighteenth century, and it was her grandfather who had restored them, and the Hall. At one time there had been fin   goings on; the kind of thing one associates with Medmenham and the Hell-fir Club. Where the tennis courts now were there had been an artificia lake, and it and the large summer-house that overlooked it had added much to the hilarity of the night revels, in which I gathered that the nude had taken no small part.

We talked about heaps of other things, and I found her both witty and tolerant. I could have stayed on well past the courtesy hour, and then just as I caught the time by the French clock on the mantelpiece and was preparing to rise, she mentioned young Craye.

"My nephew is with you, I'm pleased to say. Perhaps you haven't met him yet."

"But I have," I said, and at once began a gentle easing aside of the subject. "If you'll pardon me, he hasn't got your features."

She seemed quite concerned. "You think not? And I'd always flattere myself we were so much alike."

"It's nice for you having him here."

"I don't see much of him," she said regretfully. "He's always claiming to be on duty. But he's a dear boy, and my only nephew."

I was rather at a loss at that, so I was suddenly horrifie at the lateness of the hour, and began making apologies as I rose.

"Next time you must stay much longer," she said. "But for the cold wind we'd have gone round the gardens. And now you'd like to see my husband."

Does that strike you as a rather curious procedure? It did me, even at the time, in spite of the implied question. Before I could speak she was pushing the bell and Annie came in almost at once. The two smiled at each other.

"Annie," she said, "will you take Major Travers to see Colonel Brende?"

"Yes, ma'am," Annie said, and gave the beginnings of an old-fashioned curtsy.

"And, Annie, I'm always at home to Major Travers, whenever he'll be good enough to call."

"That's uncommonly charming of you," I said. "I hope I shan't outwear my welcome."

She merely smiled as we shook hands. Annie was smiling too as I followed her out through a side door to a corridor. It opened into a wider corridor, now absolutely bare, though the floo showed where furniture had stood and there were picture marks on the walls.

"The mistress is looking well, sir?" Annie suddenly said.

"Very well, Annie," I told her.

She looked pleased at that.

"If you'll wait here a moment, sir, I'll fin Ledd."

So I waited, and in a minute I could just hear her speaking to Ledd in the main hall just off where I stood. It was Ledd who came, and I gave him my card. He was a stocky, snub-nosed fellow of about thirty, with the badges of a famous London regiment, and I guessed he'd been a footman in civil life. He looked intelligent and cheerful and I liked the cut of him.

"This way, sir," he said. "I'll see if the Colonel is free."

Just off the main hall was a room empty of everything but two chairs and a trestle table. On the table was a pile of newspapers.

"Part of your salvage scheme?" I said, and pointed.

"That's right, sir," he said. "Once a week they call for them. Tomorrow's the day. I'll see if the Colonel's at liberty sir."

I've already told you of one bad habit I possess according to my wife, and there are doubtless others you have discerned. Here are some more. I have an insatiable curiosity. Even though I'm only in a minor way an antique collector, as soon as I enter a habited room my eyes are round it, and my mind is assessing the desirability and value of its contents. I talk to myself a good deal, though most decidedly not because I like to make a good speech or listen to a damn-fin speaker. I am also a restless individual who cannot sit still or slack except when there is need for concentrated thought. That was why I did not take one of the hard wooden chairs but began fingerin and reading the newspapers instead.

The pile consisted of *The Times* and *The Telegraph* only; three copies of the former for each day and two of the latter. As I turned them idly over, reading a paragraph here and there, I suddenly saw a page of *The Times* from which a paragraph had been neatly cut. Something came back to my mind. I took from my notebook that paragraph I had cut out myself, and it was the same one. You remember it perhaps: that one about a Major Passenden who had arrived in Lisbon after what were hinted at as incredible adventures in France. Then I looked at the other two copies of the paper, and they had the paragraph intact.

Just then Ledd came back.

"This way if you please, sir."

We went up a wide staircase, along another corridor, and then I was being shown into what had been a bedroom, but was now Colonel Brende's private offic He rose from the chair where he had been reading and came to meet me, hand outstretched.

"How are you, Major Travers? You've taken over from Splint, I believe?"

I would like to say here that I hate to be prejudiced. Proof lies in the fact that I refused to believe the warnings of my friends about Penelope Craye. According to them she was a heartless, self-seeking, over-sexed menace. Metaphors about her were always feline, how she could purr till she had the particular milk she was after, and how she could spit and scratch. To my mind all that was very overdrawn, and when she wrote to the London Hospital Committee of which I happened to be chairman, about the organization of a big charity concert, I took her at her face value. Till that concert was over we were pretty close friends. Then I began to discover that artists had been shabbily swindled and the private expense account nicely swelled; that

Penelope, in fact, had dipped her finger in the till. There could be no public scandal, but I took certain private steps to make her disgorge, and after she had tried the womanly helplessness defence and followed it up by a naive attempt to bribe, then she spat and scratched with a vengeance. After that we were deliciously polite, but I doubt if there was anything on two legs that Penelope hated half as much as my careful self.

My old father used to say that only a fool never makes mistakes, which in itself is a kind of argument against prejudice. Splint had spoken none too warmly of Colonel Brende, nor had Harrison been too enthusiastic when we had firs discussed him. Later Harrison had told me some more. He had all sorts of sources of information and was usually extraordinarily well informed, but I still refused to take Brende on other than my own judgment. Harrison said that Brende was ambitious and that even before the outbreak of war he was spoken of as a certainty for a move up to Brigadier, and then on. But something had gone wrong, as it had done in the past with Brende, and in France he had been in charge of an Area Air Defence Group. Brende was a mystery, according to Harrison. There was a streak in him somewhere and the War Offi had rumbled it, but it wasn't his brains and it wasn't his bravery. Harrison thought it was just a shade too much cunning, and a certain unscrupulousness, even amounting to ratting, when promotion was at stake.

I was conceited enough to have other ideas even before I had clapped eyes on Brende. If the man was a genius, then he was entitled to eccentricity. If his promotion had been blocked, then some gent at the War House had been at the old game of putting square pegs in round holes. Though I was not thinking about all that at the time, it does explain why I gave Brende an answering smile and took a pleasure in the handshake. In fact, as far as one can like at a second's acquaintance, I liked the man.

He was in mufti, of course, or perhaps I should call it *négligé*. The old gold of the pullover and the warm tweed coat went superbly with the deep tan of his face, and even in that get-up you'd have spotted him for a soldier and very pukka at that. He looked somewhere about fifty, full of blood and life, and though he was on the thin side, it made him look the more alert and tough.

"Can I get you anything?" he said. "A cup of tea or Sherry?"

"Thank you, sir," I said, "but I've just had tea with your lady."

He gave me the queerest look. It wasn't, in fact, long enough to be a look, but I saw on his face a flas of wonder and even dismay, then it was gone, far more quickly than I can write, and he was smiling.

"You know my wife?"

I explained and he was nodding quite friendlily and with no special interest. Then he began asking me about my previous job, and then, with a really disconcerting suddenness he said: "By the way, I haven't any real proof that you're what you ought to be. I suppose I ought to have had a look at your Military Identity Card."

I had the B.2606 in my pocket-book and smilingly handed it over. To my surprise he made no bones about taking it, and when he handed it back, all he said was. "Good." I didn't like it. Perhaps I've described the brief episode badly, but what he did was not prudent or careful, and it savoured of the officio and unnecessary. It changed the whole man and gave a glimpse of someone who had the capacity for making himself damnably unpopular. I think I must have shown something, for at once he was going out of his way to make himself most friendly and informative. Naturally one had to be most careful at the Hall, and he was sorry he couldn't tell me just what the research was out for.

"Things going well, sir?" I said.

He shrugged his shoulders and gave me a little smile.

"Can't grumble," he said, and it was easy enough to tell that things were going uncommonly well.

Then he got to his feet and was saying that there were some things he could show me, if I cared to look. I was hopping up at once, and just then there was quick tap at the door and in walked Penelope Craye. She was carrying some papers, apparently for signature, but she had on a tweed costume and her hat as if she were just going out. I told you, didn't I, that she was a pretty woman? I apologize for the understatement. That afternoon she looked Garbo and Hedy Lamarr rolled into one.

As soon as she saw me, she gave a little "Oh!" and followed it up with, "I beg your pardon. I'll come back again."

"Not at all," said the Colonel, and at once went across to his desk. "You don't know Major Travers, do you? This is Miss Craye, my secretary."

"Heavens!" she said, and stared. But she wasn't swindling me with those airs of surprise. I'd have betted all I have in War Loan that she knew I was in Dalebrink as soon as Brende knew, and that if the door through which she had come was that to her offic   then she had been listening ear to keyhole.

"You two know each other?" Brende said.

"We've met in town," I said, and, with my very best smile: "We've worked together on Hospital Committees as a matter of fact. You like it down here, Miss Craye?"

She didn't bat an eyelid. Even during the fiv   minutes she was in the room I could tell that a remarkable change had come over her. There was a certain demureness, and whenever I caught her eye there was a look in it that was trying to assure me that the past was over and she was a reformed character whose only wish was to be friends. Her keynote had changed too. The clothes she was wearing might be first-class but they were quieter than the paradisal adornments she had affecte   in the old days, and her manner was that of a high-class secretary— quiet, knowledgeable and unobtrusive.

"I think I would redraft this," I heard Brende say from the corner to which I had withdrawn. "It won't take you fiv   minutes to knock it off on your typewriter. And perhaps you'd better take down that chit for Department Q/Z."

She picked up a slip of paper from the desk and took down the dictated note in shorthand.

"Sorry to be all this trouble," Brende smiled at her when she had finished

Her eyes fell demurely.

"Not at all, I've heaps of time before I need go out."

"How is your wife?" she asked me as she passed.

"Very well, and very busy," I said.

"She's an absolute dear. I do admire her so."

Before I could recover from that, she was gone. Her look had had the same appealing quality of forgiveness, and Bernice might have been the friend of her bosom, and while I was wondering what was this new scheme she was planning, and its significance Brende was rising from the desk. He drew back an etching from the wall and disclosed a hidden safe in which he put some papers.

"Have you a dislike for working upstairs, like me, or don't you mind not working on a ground floor?

Before I could answer, he was saying that convenience was everything. There was the secretary's room, and that other door opened into his own bedroom.

"There's some pretty dangerous stuff here," he said, and waved at where the safe had been. I had the idea that after the unnecessary way he had inquired into my credentials, he was now trying to show me how completely he trusted me.

"Now what about a look downstairs?" he said briskly.

Two rooms were given up to research work, but I was allowed in only one, which was the old music-room, and a big one at that. Nobody was there at the moment as it was used principally at night, but I caught sight of various contraptions and machines. The other big room had most of the experimental gadgets, and there was also an offi in the old billiard-room. The servants' parlour had been taken over for a lounge, and the breakfast-room was fitte with forms, folded flat and tables, trestle folding, and used as a dining-room.

In the offi he introduced me to three of the staff The fourth, Squadron-Leader Pattner, was hardly ever there except at night, and I gathered that he was principally liaison between the research group and the R.A.F. The other three looked most interesting, even if the haphazardness of their clothes and the general untidiness might have made one tremble for the efficien of their labours.

Newton, the greatest living authority on acoustics—as I was told later—was a mousy little man wearing the baggiest flannel

I have ever seen, and an aged pair of tennis-shoes from which protruded a big toe. He looked about fifty and might have been taken for a down-at-heel clerk.

Riddle, who looked about twenty-five was tall and bony, and had the most carroty mop of red hair I have ever seen. He had a comical face, by which I mean that it had the most cheerful and friendly grin, and he looked the sort of chap who'd be still grinning if he fell off a sky-scraper, being certain in his mind that a few elephants had passed that way. One day, according to Brende, he was going to make Einstein look like a quack.

And talking of Einstein brings me to Heinrich Wissler, who was a Czech, for he looked much as Einstein must have looked as a young man. If Riddle's hair was a mop, then Wissler's was a super mop, and it looked as if he had long since given up hope of getting out the tangles. He was fattish and his face very red, and though he looked well over forty, they told me he was a terror at table-tennis, which, with darts, was the hobby of the gang in its leisure periods. Wissler cast on me a look of extraordinary apprehension as soon as he saw me come in. I don't know why, for I am a harmless-looking cove even in war-paint, and it couldn't have been his English which made him nervous of meeting strangers, for it was as near perfection as can be.

They were a friendly three and looked happy as sand-boys. Naturally we talked about everything but the job in hand, and I promised to come along some time and take on their best man at darts, a game to which my elongated form makes me peculiarly adapted. When we got outside Brende told me about Wissler, whose name was also one to conjure with. Some said already that he was the greatest living physicist, and Brende admitted that he had a staggering brain. He had clung on at Prague till after the German occupation, and had then managed to do a bolt. His wife was still there, and his son had died in a concentration camp.

The evening was still young and I had nothing, as far as I knew, to recall me to Camp before dinner, so I thought I would drive through the Garden City again in the hope of catching George Wharton. When I had driven a few hundred yards I came to a place where the woods made a fin shelter against the cold wind, and then the sun felt absolutely warm, so I pulled up the car and stoked my pipe, and did a few minutes' basking.

Naturally also I did some thinking. I told you of that unfortunate habit of mine of staring at other people's private and valued possessions, and here's yet another peculiarity of mine, which has arisen through a few years' work at the Yard. I have got into the regrettable habit of treating the ordinary meetings, happenings and circumstances of life as if they were those connected with a Yard case. I try to deduce things about people, and nose out mysteries, and if there are no mysteries, that worries me little for I can always imagine them.

So as I pulled at my pipe, here are some of the things I was thinking and wondering. In that side hall to which I had been admitted there was no telephone, and there had been none in Mrs. Brende's room. But there had been one in the main hall. with mysterious extensions to the main offic Colonel Brende's room and doubtless to the offi   of Penelope Craye. It seemed, therefore, that Mrs. Brende was something of a recluse who rarely phoned or received calls. When she did they were transmitted to her through the liaison of Ledd and Annie.

Penelope had not taken tea with us, perhaps because she was busy, but it was strange that Mrs. Brende had not mentioned even a distant relation who was living in the house. Colonel Brende had also not been mentioned till in that queer way at the very last moment, and it seemed reasonable therefore to draw certain conclusions. Mrs. Brende was a recluse, though an active enough woman mentally and bodily, and the reason perhaps was the nature of things, by which I mean that she was rather out of place, though the house was her home, in a station of highly secret and important research. When she offere the house to the Government she had probably made it a condition that she should still be allowed to keep her own rooms, and the Government had countered with the insistence that she should keep to those rooms.

Mind you, I did think to myself that Brende might fin the situation quite bearable. To be candid, his wife was of an age and temperament to offe him little physically, and he looked as full-blooded as they make 'em. Shakespeare may talk about the woman always taking a younger than herself and so wearing *to* him instead of still further *from* him, but the Bard is not infallible and I have known many such marriages that were as near perfection as may be, except perhaps for the physical side, and even there one can imagine toleration and latitude. People like the Brendes don't wear their affectio on their sleeves, and for all I knew the two might have settled down to an affectio the more deep since it was altogether unobtrusive.

Very woolly, all that thinking, wasn't it? But the problem of Penelope was clear cut enough. I'd never credited her with lack of brains. Carelessness, over-confidenc and trusting too much to luck, perhaps, but I'd never doubted that she had a brain both cold and calculating, and talents enough for the using. But it had never occurred to me that she could have endured the slog and grind of learning typing and shorthand for the sake of serving anyone else but the Hon. Penelope Craye. Why then the change of heart and outlook? Why did she want to be friends with me? Where was the catch in it all?

Just then a low, scarlet sports car flashe by me, and I caught a glimpse of Penelope at the wheel. I was certain she had not spotted or suspected me, so I moved my own car on in steady and wary pursuit. We passed the smaller houses of the City, then the church and the Neggers' Institute, and as we came to the larger houses with the spacious gardens, Penelope's car slowed down considerably, and I followed suit.

She went on at a crawl like that till the last house had been passed, and even then she didn't quicken speed. My car was now a hundred yards behind hers, and I was wondering if I ought to overtake her, for by now she was surely aware that I was on her tail. Then she rounded the bend where the road turns to rejoin the main highway. I still crawled on, and as I came round the bend, my eyes were once more goggling. Standing on the verge path and in earnest talk with Penelope was George Wharton!

Then he was replacing something in his breast-pocket and getting into her car. On it shot, and at the main road turned left.

Then it fairly hummed along and I lost it, but when I reached the shopping centre of the town, there it was drawn up outside what Harrison had told me was the only high-class tea-shop left. And there my nerve failed me. Much as I should have liked to stroll carelessly past the table where the two were undoubtedly sitting, and to bestow a knowing wink on George, there was Penelope to consider, and the last thing in my thoughts was to let her know I had been on her tail. As for George Wharton and the rest of it, in the words of Samuel Weller, latter adopted by George himself, the whole thing fairly beat cock-fighting

CHAPTER IV
ENTER WHARTON

WHEN I came in to breakfast the following morning, Harrison told me that there would be night flyin by our planes. It was usual for us to be informed by the Hall since an alert would alter the disposition of the sentries. The local civil authorities were also informed.

"Isn't that unnecessary?" I said. "Surely if the local siren doesn't go, everyone must know the planes are ours?"

"You'd think so," he said. "It's all the result of our friend Benison's mischief-making. He said the fact that the sirens didn't go wasn't enough, and nervous people wouldn't sleep unless they were dead sure whose planes they were."

"Many planes, are there?"

"It varies," he said, "but never more than a few. Sometimes they're on for an hour, and they have been on most of the night."

After the offi work was finished that morning I made a routine inspection of Camp with the R.S.M., and when I returned there was an offic in battle-dress waiting outside my door. He turned out to be a Captain Cross, commander of the local platoon of the Home Guard, an old-timer who had been on retired pay for the last six years and now was back in harness again.

Reminiscence is a vice among us old-timers, and we settled down to comparing experiences in the last war and findin mutual acquaintances. Then at last we came to the local Home Guard, and he told me it was well up to strength and keen as mustard.

"Where do most of them come from?" I asked.

"Oh, the town," he said. "The factories run their own platoon, also we don't get a lot from the City."

"And they're Anti-Neggers," I suggested.

He smiled. "They've put you wise about that then, have they?"

"To a certain extent," I said guardedly. "But what's the actual position at the City? Most of the young men called up?"

He said they were, though people considered there had been a surprising number of exemptions. Also the City had been accused of dodging the taking in of evacuees by importing their relatives and friends from bombed areas. Though those that had come forward for the Home Guard were the very best type, the City was lousy—his word and not a bad one—with slackers. If they could floc to join that fake defence body which Benison had started, why couldn't they be doing work of national importance?

"What's your genuine opinion of the Neggers?" I said. "Ought they to be taken seriously? Are there any really dangerous characters?"

"You're not for them in any way?" he said, and gave me a sideways look.

"God forbid!" I said hastily.

He smiled. "Then I don't mind saying they're a collection of bastards. Excuse my language, but that's plain talking."

"By Hitler, out of Wedlock," I said, but as it was a very bad joke he naturally didn't see it.

"I don't know that it's quite Hitler," he said frowningly, "but some of it is. Where does Benison get his money from?"

"Where indeed?" I said, not knowing what he was getting at.

"The living's four hundred a year," he was going on, "and he lives up to it. Indeed I've heard there used to be trouble over tradesmen's bills. Now he's got a fin car and he's spending money hand over fist And what about Haw-Haw knowing all that's going on here?"

I frowned knowingly, though all the Haw-Haw business leaves me cold. Half the things he's supposed to say exist only in the minds of the self-important windbags who originate them.

"You regard Benison as a bad hat?" I suggested.

"I regard him as absolutely ruthless," he said. "I believe he's unscrupulous and I know he's vindictive, and he's as cunning as a pack of monkeys. He knows just how far to go. And he knows how to hint at things so that he can't be pinned down to words. If he was clapped under lock and key Garden City wouldn't stink the way it does. All this Negger business would go plumb to pieces."

Then he was smiling feebly as if he knew he had let his tongue rather run away with him, and it was he who changed the topic.

"Still, I don't want to take up your time with those damn Neggers. What I really came to see you about was the question of co-operation."

"I'm rather in the dark," I said. "Perhaps Captain Harrison will come in and help us out."

Cross knew Harrison well enough. When the Camp had been temporarily short of guards owing to sudden changes over, the Home Guard had lent a hand.

"The position here is this," I said, "and Captain Harrison will correct me if I'm wrong. We don't pick men for guard. We have control over certain standing troops and personnel. The rest of the troops are ostensibly for training, and we call on their office   to supply so many guards by day and night. They make out the rosters, and once they're actually on guard, then they're under our control and supervision. What you're being good enough to suggest is that if there's a deficiency you'll continue to make it good."

"That's it," he said. "But what I would like are some co-operational exercises. Something on the lines of trying to enter certain spots which your men are guarding. Pretending to be parachute troops, in fact."

"That sounds good," I said. "What's your idea, Harrison?"

"I think it would ginger up everybody all round," Harrison said. "We'd have to have a big pow-wow with our people first You'd want one too, Cross. If your people didn't halt when challenged, for instance, they'd most certainly be fire on, exercise or no exercise."

"Why not?" Cross said cheerfully. "That's all part of the training. So what about it, gentlemen? Can we fi anything up?"

"No time like the present," I said.

In half an hour we had a scheme. Allowing two days for the two pow-wows, zero night would be on the Monday. The factories' platoon would not be asked to co-operate at the moment, but every other place we guarded would be considered liable to sham attack. One only per night was to be an objective, and that objective would not be settled on till the morning, and then by arrangement between the three of us over the phone. The scheme might be an elastic and continuous one, starting from the firs night, and we all thought it a really first-clas piece of training, Not only would it keep the guards on their toes but it would relieve all monotony. I was so pleased about it that I made up my mind to give a hundred cigarettes—if obtainable—to the one who captured most of Cross's parachutists, and Harrison was so pleased that he took Cross off for an immediate drink in the Mess.

After lunch I settled down to a study of the confidentia and secret files, which as far as they concerned Camp 55, were all new to me and I was particularly interested in the instructions for the absolute security of Dalebrink Park. There was also a memorandum from Command through district H.Q., making virtually the actual disposition of guards which we were maintaining.

"That lets us out," I told myself. "If anything does go wrong at any time then we pass the buck to district H.Q., and what they do with it is their business."

The buzzer went. Harrison was asking if I wanted to see a Mr. Jenkins who was claiming that I would like to see him.

"Jenkins?" I said. "I don't remember anybody of that name. What's his business?"

"He won't tell me. He merely gave me his card and said you'd see him."

"Be a good fellow and send me the card in," I said.

In it came by an orderly, and this is what it looked like.

MR. G. JENKINS
HIGH CLASS SECOND-HAND AND OTHER CARS
33 Copse Lane
Tel. Dale 721

As soon as I read it I thought I could explain Jenkins. I have a car which has been laid up since the outbreak of war, and though now a few years old, it is good enough class. Cars I knew were well up in price, and doubtless Mr. Jenkins had got wind of mine and wanted to do a deal.

"Perhaps I'd better run my eye over him," I called to Harrison, and then made a quick calculation of what my Rolls should fetch. Feet were heard on the duckboards, and voices at the door. There was a tap and the door opened. Who should walk in but George Wharton!

"Good God!" I ejaculated blasphemously, and then my face was wreathed in smiles. George's smile was more sheepish than anything as he held out his hand.

"Well, how are we?"

"Fit and fine, I said. "But how in heaven's name did you know I was here?"

The last thing I intended was to let him know I was aware that he had wangled my appointment. George wallows in stratagems, and nothing pleases him better than to have something up his sleeve, and, if he wanted to have his little secret, well, who was I to be a spoil-sport?

"Oh, we have ways and means," he said airily as he began taking off his heavy overcoat. I rang hastily through to Harrison and said I was on no account to be disturbed. By that time George had drawn up a chair to the electric stove and was stoking his pipe. I had to smile as I looked at him. There he was complete—moustache vast as ever, top of the spectacle-case protruding from the breast-pocket, and the creases on his forehead all a-quiver as he thought out some new subterfuge.

"What's this Jenkins business?" I said.

He chuckled. "Pretty good, eh?"

"Good?" I said scathingly. "'You may drive a car but you know as much about its insides as I do of the Archbishop of Canterbury's."

"I don't know." he said mournfully. "I've picked up a good few tips since I saw you last. Some would surprise you."

"I expect they would," I said. "All the same I'd love to hear you going over the points of a car with a customer."

He chuckled again. "I haven't got as far as that yet. Some might say it was all eyewash."

He looked round with an exaggerated caution, then he nodded, mysteriously. Next he shifted the chair still closer and his voice took on an asthmatic quality which was doubtless meant to be.

"I've been in the Garden City here for the last month!"

My eyebrows raised. "Negger hunting?"

That rather punctured the balloon.

"So you know all about that." he said regretfully. "Still, I don't know that you're right. All sorts of things had to be looked into, so it was arranged I should stay as her nephew with the mother of one of our inspectors. My business in town is supposed to be bombed out. The car idea allows me to get round the countryside a good deal."

"Found anything out?"

He leaned forward again.

"Picked up a couple who were wanted. Got 'em safely where they'll do no harm tor a bit."

"Really? That's good work. George. Neggers, were they?"

He gave a look of pain, and when he spoke again, his voice —thank heaven—was free of asthma.

"Neggers!" The tone was one of unspeakable disgust. "You've got Neggers on the brain. What's wrong with the so-called Neggers?"

"Good Lord, you're not serious!"

"And why shouldn't I be?" he asked virtuously. "Look at it the right way," he said, and poked the stem of the pipe at me. "What are we supposed to be fightin for? Liberty and freedom. Freedom of what? Freedom of speech, and a free Press. Fighting to keep it for ourselves and to get it back for those Hitler's taken it from. A fin collection of hypocrites we'd be if we said all that and then went and denied freedom to our own people? Am I right or wrong?"

I stared, then smiled rather wryly.

"George," I said in sorrow, "you've been nobbled!"

He chuckled, and out went his hand to give an avuncular pat to my knee. To George I'm still the fledglin on whom he firs clapped eyes fiftee years ago.

"My boy, you've got a lot to learn. You've got to trust the old stager for one thing. I've never led you far wrong yet, have I?"

"I'm not so sure," I said. "But if you've called to see me on pleasure, let's adjourn to the Mess for a refresher, and I'll see about an hour or two off If it's business—well, what about it?"

"No tea for me," he said, and shook his head. "I'm here strictly on business. You've got a car, haven't you? Well, I'm angling to buy that hell-wagon of yours. You tell anyone concerned that you're holding out for a certain price. That'll explain any future visits. And you've got my telephone number there."

"Good," I said. "Now, as the talkies have it, we're going places. What's the business?"

"You're responsible for guards at Dalebrink Hall?"

"Yes," I said, somewhat taken aback. "Why do you ask?" He told me, and what he told me explained a lot and left a lot unexplained. Most of it sounded genuine, but there was a streak of the bogus. Also, when one is dealing with George, it is hard to be sure whether he isn't being bogus himself for his own mysterious ends. Still, this is what he told me, from his own words and his own point of view.

He had originally been sent to Dalebrink after a Nazi agent— an Alsatian Frenchman, who, after an inquiry into his credentials and a brief period of observation, had been running loose ever since Dunkirk, when he landed with a boatload of refugees. He had been tracked to the Garden City where lived one of the people who had vouched for him, and Wharton had been able to collar both the agent and the guarantor. He was now on the point of roping in a Communist agent suspected of being in German pay, who also was at the City, though working at the larger of the two factories.

"About a week ago I thought my job here was as good as over," he said, "and then—"

"The town doesn't think the job's over," I said dryly.

Wharton gave a prodigious snort. "I know. They're clamouring for someone to arrest Benison and old Dove. And the so-called Neggers. And what are they—these Neggers? Cranks and intellectuals—God help us!—who think they can blackmail the country now it's up to the neck in trouble, to let them get on with all the cock-eyed theories they've been spouting about for years. Blether! I know. I've listened to it."

He gave another of those elephantine snorts of his, ran his huge handkerchief across his moustache, and went on with his story.

A few days before he had received instructions to contact a certain lady. She turned out to be a regular stunner, and the private secretary of the Colonel Brende who was working at Dalebrink Hall. Absolute class from top to toe, Wharton said she was, and an example of what a society lady can do when the old country wants help. Highly efficie too. One of her jobs was to open all correspondence except that marked Private or Secret. In the course of her duties she opened a letter with the Dalebrink postmark.

"Here it is," Wharton said. "Everything about it quite normal, except the writing, and our experts say it was printed by alternate hands for alternate letters. What do you make of it?"

This was the letter.

Dear Colonel Brende,

I beg of you to take this letter seriously. A dangerous scheme is on foot against the great work you are doing, and even against yourself. Those in it are high up and quite unprincipled. See that the Hall is better protected, and keep an eye on all who come in and out, even those you think you trust. I beg of you not to disregard this.

A Friend.

The only comment I could make was to raise my eyebrows, but I did ask what Colonel Brende had thought of it.

"He's never seen it," Wharton said as he replaced it in his wallet. "I told you this lady had sense. Well, she got in touch with the Bigwigs—she's one of 'em herself—and had instructions to get in touch with me." He had been adjusting his old-fashioned spectacles, and now he peered at me over their tops. "And if you want to know why she didn't let Colonel Brende see the letter, this is why. The Colonel's up to the ears in worry and responsibility, and the last thing she wanted to do was give him something more to worry about. And she was right."

"What do you think about the letter yourself?"

"You mean, do I think there's any truth in it?"

"In so many words—yes."

"Then I do believe in it. Why shouldn't I? Germany's just as anxious as we are about night bombing, and they're working like hell to stop our planes. You bet your life that's the firs thing on their espionage agenda, and they'd stick at nothing to get an inkling of what we're up to. They know there's something big going on at Dalebrink Hall. Of course they do. What they'd give their ears to fin out, is just what it is."

"Yes, there's quite a lot in that," I said. "And was that the only letter?"

"Oh no," he said. "There were two more, and both are now with the experts. The second one said the writer had still more information, and asked if the Colonel had taken the firs letter's advice. Yesterday morning another one came, and the writer said it was probably the fina warning. I met this Miss Craye by arrangement yesterday afternoon, and I sent off the letter the same night. The postmark was London, and it said that Colonel Brende knew the writer and had last seen him in France. Does that make you think?"

"Not unless it's another of your French Nazi agents writing it," I said. "If so he's either ratting on his pals or employers, or he's under some debt of gratitude to the Colonel. In the latter case the Colonel might be asked. He's got to be told about the letters some time."

Wharton shook his head. "My instructions are that he's to be told nothing. This Miss Craye and I are going to handle things. And you."

I stared.

"Yes, you. You've got to go into the question of those guards and tighten everything up."

"Just a minute," I said. "I take orders only from the War Office

He chuckled. "That's what you think. Before this day's out you'll be told to do what I've said."

"Good enough," I said. "But if I'm going into the question of guards, I've got to spill some of the beans to my adjutant. I'll vouch for him and let him know you're a Government agent. Anybody else can be told that yarn about my car." That brought something else to my mind. "By the way, isn't it dangerous your meeting Penelope Craye?"

It was good to see George's eyes bulge.

"You know her?"

"Good Lord, yes!" I said airily. "Bernice and I have known her for years."

"It's a small world," was all George could say as he began scrambling back to his perch. "But I'm supposed to be buying her car. She brought it along by arrangement the other day and I had an inspection bang in the middle of the road. I think I made an impression."

"I'll bet you did," I said, and then George was getting to his feet.

"Well, I'll be pushing along. You have my number, and if you do ring up, say you're not changing your mind about the car, but I can have another look at it if I come to such-and-such a place. If anything happens at my end I'll ring you in the same way."

And that was that. No sooner had he gone than a despatch-rider came in with a confidentia chit straight from Command. Not only was it smothered with red seals on both envelopes, but the actual letter was headed—*Immediate and Urgent.* I signed the receipt and called in Harrison. The result of our labours was that a letter was sent by us to Command, saying that in view of their previous instructions of so-and-so date, stated to be absolutely comprehensive for the guarding of Dalebrink Hall, we could make no possible further tightening except to double all existing guards by night. If sufficie troops were not available, we should call in the help of the local Home Guard unless otherwise instructed. Would Command please acknowledge and confirm

"That lets us out," Harrison said. "And when had we better start?"

"Well try and get a medal each," I said. "We'll have Company Commanders in as soon as we've had a spot of tea, and we'll get Cross. To-morrow we'll have the new scheme working."

It was late that evening when the whole thing had been worked out and settled, and I was pretty tired mentally when I got into my camp-bed. Then just as I was dozing off I heard the faint drone of a plane.

"Damn the planes," I said, and got my head further under the blanket. But round and round that cursed plane went, like an elusive mosquito, and it must have been another half-hour before I dozed off

Then there was a tremendous bump that rattled the windows of my sleeping quarters. I knew what that was, half asleep though I was, so I felt for my glasses, and slid out of bed. In a moment or two my bare feet were in the rubber boots and I in a British warm. Just as I opened the door there were a couple of terrifi thuds, and they were damnably close. Then there was the light of a flare and more heavy crumps.

Something appeared in the shadow where I stood. It was Harrison.

"That you, sir? The real thing this time. And Dalebrink Park by the look of it."

We had our dispositions in case of bombing, and we made our way at once to our posts. I was at the main telephone while Harrison saw the various squads at the ready, and then I stepped outside to watch. Since I'm no hero I also stepped elsewhere pretty often, for bombs fairly plastered down for best part of an hour. One fell within a hundred yards of one of our huts, and another spattered our covered trenches with earth. Then things quietened down, and before one could hardly realize it everything was as quiet as the grave.

Wires run from us to every one of our posts, so that in the event of parachute attack, troops can be rushed to a point. We got hold of the Park—by which name our Dalebrink Hall posts were known—and in half an hour we knew most of what had happened. The old coach-house had received a direct hit and the Hall no vital damage. Most of the bombs had fallen in the park itself, but a gardener's cottage had been demolished and there were casualties. One of our men had been blown off his feet and was sufferin   from shock.

In the morning, when the damage could be inspected, it was plain that we had all been lucky. Two houses bad been demolished on the fringes of the City and there were casualties, but those were the only important additions to the night report. I didn't actually see anybody at the Hall, though I had rung Mrs. Brende and, after the usual delays, heard from her that she was all right, but I saw for myself that the structure of the Hall was undamaged, though many back windows were broken and slates dislodged.

That afternoon Dalebrink had another sensation. It was a Friday, the day when the Dalebrink *Clarion* went to Press, and when it appeared that afternoon, it had a letter from Benison. I should say that the editor of the paper was quite impartial. Though he was doubtless as true blue as any of us, he printed anything that wasn't libellous and which kept up the circulation of a paper which the rationing had much cut down in size.

Benison   must   have   gone   straight   to   the   offi   of the *Clarion* that morning and written the letter in the white heat of rage. And I must say that the case he put up was one that took some refuting. Twelve people had been killed, he said, and some forty injured, and but for the practice flyin that had been announced, most would have been in their shelters, and still alive and uninjured. The authorities responsible had murdered those twelve souls as surely as if they had cut their throats. Protestations had been made and local opinion and judgment ignored. Now murder had been done. From then onward let Dalebrink take the handling of its own affair into its own hands.

That was the gist of the letter, and it was a minute or two after I had read it that I found counter arguments: that one can't have omelettes, for instance, without breaking eggs. But I had no time that day to spend on Benison, what with the new guard scheme to put into operation, and Friday pay-day and all the rest of it. What I did not know, or suspect, in spite of Wharton's revelations, was that zero hour was getting mighty close, and things were really going to happen. To tell the truth, I took those revelations of Wharton's with a very big pinch of salt. If he could swallow Penelope, hook, line and sinker, then he could swallow anything, and when it comes to patriotism, then any man can be incredulous. In fact I thought there was just a touch of the penny dreadful about the whole thing. And there I lost, not for the firs time, my sense of proportion. After all, there was quite a lot of good digestible steak mixed up in the old penny dreadful with the highly coloured gravy.

CHAPTER V
PRELUDE TO ACTION

Saturda y afternoon is supposed to be an easy one for administrative staffs Harrison was such a glutton for work and a stickler for duty that I had had to winkle him out of his offi and send him off to get air and exercise, and I was perfectly content to stay in because there was a long letter to write to Bernice. Only a clerk was in the adjutant's room, and it was he who rang through and said a Major Passenden, a gunner, would like to see me. The name conveyed nothing to me at that particular moment.

"What can I do for you, Major?" I said. He was a fine-lookin chap of about forty, and in mufti, which was either marvellously valeted or brand new.

"I really want permission to go to Dalebrink Hall," he said.

"I went there and your people said I couldn't get in without a pass." He smiled in the most likeable way. "So I wondered if you or your adjutant would give me one."

"I see," I said cheerfully, and was wondering how to put the matter to him. "The trouble is, it isn't quite so easy as that. There're all sorts of preliminaries and it's as much as this tunic of mine is worth if I don't take precautions."

"That's all right," he said, and smiled. "Red tape and the War House are the only two things you can't tell me about."

He was a quietly spoken chap, but alert enough and, I judged, a good man at his job. He had none of that God-Almighty-ness that you so often meet in gunners.

"Good," I said, and reached for pencil and paper. "Whom do you want to see?"

"Colonel Brende. He's an old friend of mine."

"Business?"

He shot me a look. "Oh, just a chat. I worked immediately under him in France, you know."

"Your Military Identity Card?"

He smiled ruefully. "No can do."

Then, thick-head that I was, I suddenly remembered.

"Good Lord," I said, and was fumbling at my horn-rims, which is a trick I have when I'm knocked off my perch or I have an unexpected brainwave. "You're the Major Passenden who had that little trip from Dunkirk to Lisbon."

He nodded. "The news was a bit gaudy—"

"I only saw a paragraph in *The Times*," I said. "Some day I'd like to swop a damn good dinner for the whole story."

"You'd lose over the transactions," he told me modestly. "Still, it does explain things such as loss of identificatio cards."

"Any proofs of identity?"

"Only these."

He hauled out of his breast-pocket a bundle of letters which had evidently awaited his arrival in England, and there was also a War House chit about a month's leave, and where subsequently to report.

"Good enough," I said, and handed them back. "How'd you know, by the way, that Colonel Brende was down here?"

He shot me another look.

"Learned it at the War House when I was reporting."

"And you now want to see him on business. We'd better say that as it may jerk things up a little. Important business, shall we say?"

"Very important," he said laconically.

I showed him the latest regulations and instructions by which I was strictly bound, and explained that the issue of passes had to be confirme by District H.Q.

"But why shouldn't the mountain come to Mahomet?" I said. "May I get him on the phone for you?"

"I'd be most grateful," he said.

I got through quickly enough, and it was Penelope who answered. I thought it would do no harm to appear friendly.

"Hallo, young lady," I said. "Why aren't you out getting into the fresh air?"

"I know," she said. "Dreadful of me, isn't it?"

"And is the Colonel in too?"

"I don't know," she said, "but I could fin out. What did you want him for particularly?"

"Just something private."

"It isn't private for me," she said, with just a touch of the girlish. "I've very strict instructions about bringing the Colonel to the phone."

"Have it your own way," I told her amusedly. "Tell the Colonel there's a Major Passenden here, wanting to speak to him on urgent business."

"Major Passenden," she said slowly, as if she were writing it down. I could imagine her being business-like for my special benefit "I'll see if he's in, but I'm pretty sure he isn't."

I told Passenden what was happening.

"You had a bit of a blitz here last night," he remarked while the wait was still on. "I saw a few useful craters near the park gates."

"It was a bit heavy while it lasted," I said. "I've been in worse, but I hate 'em all."

"Funny they should make a dead set at the Hall?"

"Yes." I said, and then as my fingers went instinctively to my glasses. "You knew what was going on there?"

"A friend of mine gave me some idea," he said off-handedly Then Penelope's voice came again.

"That you. Major Travers? Oh, this is Penelope Craye again. I'm frightfully sorry, but the Colonel's out. He may not be back till to-morrow."

"Can you get in touch with him?"

"Heavens, no!" she said. "I believe it's something frightfully hush-hush."

I repeated it all for Passenden's benefit and he merely gave a resigned shrug of the shoulders.

"Awfully good of you, taking all this trouble," he said. "What I think I'll do is put up at a hotel in the town and try again to-morrow. You don't happen to know a hotel you can recommend?"

I told him of one and suggested he could phone from my offic While he was doing it I took a turn outside, or the truth is rather that I had walked a yard or two outside when I fairly leapt in the air. Just round the corner of the long hut someone had started up a motor-bicycle, and it shot round within a couple of yards of me. It wasn't the nearness that startled me so much as the roar of its engine, which was as raucous as many a car I've heard snorting and snarling round the Brookland track.

"Hi. you there!" I hollered, and its rider drew it to a halt some fift yards along the tarmac. I recognized him as Craye, and he spotted me right enough and came paddling the bicycle back.

"Mr. Craye," I said, "is it necessary for that engine of yours to make that damnable noise?"

He looked the least bit sheepish for a moment, then recovered his usual aplomb.

"Sorry, sir, but you have to do it to get speed."

"Do it?" I said. "Do what? If you've been tinkering with the exhaust, see it's put right again. It's Government property you've been tinkering with."

"Very good, sir," he said, and still lingered. "But she doesn't run nearly so well, sir."

I could have exploded.

"Mr. Craye," I said, "don't argue with me about motor-bikes. I was driving one before you'd seen a scooter. Get that exhaust put right."

He looked so genuinely apologetic that I weakened.

"You're not the only one who's tampered with an exhaust in his time," I added.

He smiled, and rather stared at me as if unable to believe that it was I who had been so human. Then, and it took some doing, he gave me a first-clas salute.

"Very good, sir. And thank you, sir."

Off he cruised and I found myself smiling. There was something in Master Craye after all, I was telling myself, and then Passenden emerged from the offic   I strolled with him as far as the gate, and we both hoped we'd be meeting again in the near future.

I had just finishe   my letter and was thinking about tea when the buzzer went again. This time I had a real shock.

"The Rev. Benison is here, sir, and would like to see you."

There was a moment's hesitation before I asked for him to be brought along. What he wanted from me, official   or unofficiall   I couldn't imagine. The best thing was to wait and see and have no answers ready.

"Major Travers?" he said, and his austere lips had a thin smile.

"Come in, padre," I said. "May I send for some tea for us?"

"For me, no," he said, and gave a slight raise of the hand. "Part of my war-time discipline is to do without tea."

"Then tell me what I can do for you."

Now he was at close quarters he looked more like John Knox than ever, if his frame, perhaps, was sturdier. Given a battleaxe and a clear space, he'd have made a sorry mess of quite a lot of anti-Covenanters. As his eyes met mine, I saw, again with surprise, that they were an intense blue.

"What I've come about is this," he began. "When the Camp was firs started, the men used to come to my church on Sunday mornings."

"The usual church parade," I suggested.

"Yes. And then for no reason at all they changed over to the town. I approached Major Splint about it, but he said the matter was out of his hands. I wondered if you could do anything in the matter."

I leaned back, thinking hard. Our eyes met and it was mine that fell. Then I leaned forward.

"May I speak as a layman and entirely without prejudice?"

"Do, do."

"Well, rightly or wrongly, I've been informed that the parade is held at the parish church because of certain pacifis views expressed from your own pulpit."

His lips moved in the same thin smile.

"I thank you for your frankness. But, may I put a question and back it with a statement? What I preach is the Gospel. Can you fin anywhere in the Gospels a word in favour of war?"

"I'm no theologian," I said. "I do seem to remember something about not bringing peace, but a sword." He was about to cut in but I went hastily on. "You'll probably say that was metaphorical and that's where you've always got the stranglehold over us laymen. So let me speak official for a change. How could any responsible offic let his men listen to pacifis arguments when he can't give his own arguments there and then? A soldier is a fighter and in this war he's got to be a pretty grim one. And," I went on, getting it off my chest, "there were men of good sound religion in the past who fought pretty well. The Covenanters, for instance. Gort can preach a good sermon, for I've heard him."

He nodded benignly.

"Major Travers, I'd be delighted—genuinely delighted—if you'd come along to our little Institute and give us a talk one night. We might stage a little debate."

"No you don't, padre," I said. "I'm a soda-water bottle, not a fountain. The Regulations wouldn't allow me to make such a fool of myself in any case, thank heaven. But to speak absolutely officiall the matter of the church parade is definitel not in my hands. It's in the hands of the Colonel of the battalion which supplies the two Companies. My own few available men go with them for convenience."

Now I didn't want him using the Camp on any pretext whatever, so I didn't ask him to see the office concerned. What I did suggest was that he should write me a letter, which I'd pass on to the right quarter. He seemed grateful.

"Perhaps you'll drop in some time when you're in the City," he said. "I shall always be very pleased to see you."

"That's very good of you," I told him, and then I had to go and spoil things by saying that I had read with interest his letter to the *Clarion*.

"You disagreed?" he said quickly.

"Not at all," I said. "Speaking as a layman, and civilian, I saw your side of the argument. I admit I wish you'd been more explicit about the way you proposed that Dalebrink should defend its own interests."

Our eyes met again, and this time it was his that fell.

"I had an argument in this same room with your predecessor," he said. "It was when we at the City were threatened by a mob and I asked if he would affor protection. He told me he had no jurisdiction. I told him he couldn't equivocate. Either he was a man of peace or of war. Still, there it was. We took steps to look after ourselves then, and we shall do it now."

But when I shook hands with him at the main gate, he said a curious thing in farewell.

"I'm very grateful to you, Major. Don't believe all you hear, by the way. In my time I've made my own contribution to peace, and to war. My only son was killed at Messines."

That afternoon I had changed my mind somewhat about young Craye. Now I was thinking pretty hard about Benison. Where did rumour end and truth begin? Was the man all he had appeared that afternoon, or had his visit been one of pure design? Had he some scheme on hand the success of which depended on throwing the wool over as many eyes as possible, and if so, why were my bat eyes important? I had no answers. Somewhere in me I did have a sneaking respect for the man, and in the same deep places there was something of apprehension. While he was sitting in my offic where of all places I should have been cock of the roost, I had felt that it was he who had dominated both the room and the conversation.

Perhaps it was because of that uneasy feeling in my mind that I began thinking of Passenden instead, and almost at once I began to wonder something. Before I knew where I was, I had a theory, and an extraordinary one it was.

Passenden had said at firs that all he wanted with Brende was a chat. Then he had said with laconic directness, and now I came to think back, something of irony, that his business was highly important. He had been in France for months, and he had known Brende there, like the writer of the anonymous letters. *Was he the writer?*

The thought hit me like a sledge-hammer. In France, occupied and unoccupied, he might have come into contact with sources of information. That last letter had borne a London postmark, and he had been there at the date of posting. But what of the two earlier letters? There was always a queue a mile long for the Clipper service, I thought, and he might have sent the firs two letters by a trusted friend, with instructions to post in Dalebrink. I didn't like the argument, but there the possibility was. The letters were written by an educated person, and were quiet and direct, like Passenden himself. And if all that were true, then Passenden had come to Dalebrink as soon as he had ascertained Brende's whereabouts, to give him by word of mouth the truth about the warnings he had hitherto been able to write only guardedly.

As I sat over my tea in the almost deserted Mess, the arguments swayed me this way and that. There was the revelation that only when Passenden knew himself about to see Brende did he give a hint as to who the writer was, and as for arguments against, well, the fact that Passenden had apparently no reason for keeping back that information in the earlier letters, or being even more explicit in the last one, was only one of the things that came to my mind. In fact I thought so much about the whole thing that my brain went woolly, and I was glad when Harrison came in.

"You're early," I said. "I thought I ordered you to get out and stay out?"

He grinned. "So I did, sir, till I ran into Cross. He wants a stunt for his men to-night. It doesn't matter apparently how late they're up to-night because there's all Sunday to sleep it off.

"What'd you tell him?"

"Well, I told him that unless he heard to the contrary, he could make the Park his objective. I thought it would be a good idea to get the new patrols working keenly, and if we got the chance of mentioning it to Command, they'd simply wag their tails."

"Good," I said. "We'll get those medals yet. I think I'll be that way myself after dark and have a look-see. Did he give you an idea of how many men he was using?"

"About seven or eight picked men. He can't get any more because of the guards he's furnishing. I told him I thought that would be ample."

I quite agreed, and that we didn't want the stunt to go as far as actual holding up of sentries or patrols. If any of Cross's men could prove they had got through our lines, that was good enough.

I picked up *The Times* and found that some enterprising person had got ahead of me and practically finishe the crossword. Then as I began looking through the paper again, I remembered something, and about Passenden. Up to that moment everything in the relationships between Passenden and Colonel Brende had been vague, so to speak, and had consisted in nothing but Passenden's own statements and my own deductions. Neither had spoken to the other, and Brende had not spoken to me. What I recalled now was something definite that paragraph which had been cut from *The Times* in the pile of salvage at Dalebrink Hall.

Passenden's story was implicitly true then, though I had
never really doubted it, and someone at the Hall was interested
in him and his escape, and would therefore be glad to see
him personally. But who? Three copies of *The Times* daily, I
told myself, and two of *The Telegraph*. Why the differenc of
numbers? Probably because Mrs. Brende took *The Times* herself.
A copy of each of the other papers might be for Brende and
Penelope, and a copy for the Hall Mess. From whose copy had
the cutting been taken? Probably from Brende's, though Mrs.
Brende's was not out of the question.

The whole thing may seem unimportant, and I didn't
worry my brains over it much at the time, but what was
disturbing was the remembering of the tangible evidence of that
cutting as opposed to nebulous theory. Perhaps I don't make
myself clear. That cutting, in so far as it made Passenden's story
true, made my theories less presentable. Why should a man so
well known to the person to whom he was writing have to use
anonymous letters for communications? Why didn't he sign by
initials? Why not make an allusion to something of private but
mutual interest to reveal his real identity?

I suppose those thoughts made their contribution to my
restlessness of that evening, but somehow I could settle down to
nothing. At half-past six I had a bath and change, and was firs in
at dinner. Then during the meal I thought of something else. If I
was going to mooch round the Hall in the dark that night, then I
ought to make myself better acquainted with the lie of the land.
Round that garden were all sorts of paths and hedges, with steps
to rises of ground, and at least one ornamental pool of water,
and I was anxious to take neither a bad toss nor a ducking. Also
the more one knew, the greater the mobility, and I didn't want
to have to stand under a hedge while things happened in the
dangerous distance.

After dinner I slipped quietly away in the car. It was a clear
evening but very cold, with the wind settled in the north-east,
and I still had an hour of daylight before me. First I went round
the park for the preliminary survey. Some of it was walled, with
bushes and creepers growing over the bricks, and some of it

had tall hedges, in which were plenty of oaks. In the wall, about three hundred yards from the house, was a door. I got out of the car and tried it and found it locked. But it was evidently used by somebody, for there were fresh marks where the key had turned, and there were *faint* indications on the wide grass verge that someone had been walking that way. Then my eye caught the still fainter marks of tyres. Someone had been drawing up a car on the verge and then using that door. If for purposes of secrecy, the spot was perfect, for the door was well overhung by the low branches of a huge oak, and since there was a sharp curve in the road, a car coming by would be past before the hidden car could be seen.

I was looking at things from the point of view of some attack on the house, and at once I saw the unimportance of it all. Any active person could get into the park, not only over the wall, but through weak spots in the hedge. What was important for defence was the inner perimeter, as it were—the patrols that were maintained closely round the house itself by night. All the same, what I had seen was interesting. If nobody inside the Hall had been using that door, then someone outside had been using it to get into the grounds by night and make a furtive survey. Who that someone was I had no idea. I knew it would hardly be Cross, but I did think it might be a Negger.

That inquisitiveness of mine had wasted too much of my daylight, so off I went at once to main gate guard, and in case the reason for my visit should be suspected, I asked no questions, but drove straight through. When the inner sentry halted me, I left my car just short of him and went towards the house on foot. There was no reason why I should let the Hall know what was in the air that night, though it did occur to me that if I saw anyone connected with the house, I might give him a private tip in case there should be unusual noises.

Well, I had a good scout round and I got my bearings. I flattere myself that everywhere, including the kitchen garden, was clear in my mind, and then I came back by the rear of the house. Dusk was heavy in the sky, with dark clouds towards the west, and if it hadn't been so late in the year I'd have said we

were due for snow. Then I saw the stone summer-house against
the sky and beyond it could just make out the line of boundary
wall and the door, though they were three hundred yards away.

I took off my glasses to polish them, for the light was suddenly
none too good, and as I did so I was thinking that if I hurried
back to Camp there would be no need to use lights. Just then I
saw something move by the summer-house, and I hooked my
glasses on again In what I can only call a fraction of a second, I
saw a man standing by the summer-house, and I was dead sure
it was Colonel Brende.

Now I did not remember till afterwards that according to
Penelope Craye, the Colonel was away and would most likely
not be back till the morning. What I did think was that I'd just
give him the private tip that we and the Home Guard had a stunt
that night, so I made my way across the lawn. It was about a
hundred yards, and the light was getting no better, but I didn't
worry when the Colonel was not in sight for there was nowhere
he could go, and I guessed he'd be sitting on one of the teak seats
on the flagge surround. But when I got to the summer-house
there was no sign of him.

I thought that was extraordinarily odd, so I took a look
round. Behind the summer-house was nothing but the flagge
surround, and though there was a door at both back and front,
each was locked. The flagge surround was a good twelve foot
wide behind, then came a wide bed of wallflowers and then a
clipped yew hedge. The soil of the bed was undisturbed, and the
hedge had no gap. Where Colonel Brende had gone—if it had
been Colonel Brende—was a mystery.

I stood for a minute or two in the deepening dusk, and more
than once my fingers went to my glasses. Then I had to admit
that I had been mistaken. When I had hooked my glasses on
after cleaning them, my eyes had had no time—particularly in
that treacherous light—to get back to anything like focus. Of
one thing only was I sure. It had not been Colonel Brende I
had seen, but I must most certainly have seen a moving object
resembling a man, and what that object was I couldn't for the
life of me imagine.

CHAPTER VI
SATURDAY NIGHT

THE fun was not likely to start before the night was good and dark, which would be between nine and ten, or, to speak the lingo, twenty-one and twenty-two hours. I walked from the Camp and reached main gate well before that latter hour, and I gave the sergeant no hint of why I had come. The men on duty till midnight had already been posted, and so he could scarcely pass round the news that the Commandant had made an unexpected appearance and they'd better keep their eyes skinned.

The inner patrols moved on the gravel and lawns and the flagge walks round the main building, and through opened doors into the walled enclosure behind which are what are usually called the servants' quarters. Four men moved and four were standing. When a patrol reached a standing man, that man moved on. That kept them awake and keen, and it kept them reasonably warm on a bitter night. And since the movements were not strictly regular, it had seemed to Harrison and myself that anyone from outside had a mighty poor chance of slipping through.

I moved about well outside the patrols, and bitter cold I found it, though I had on gloves and an additional sweater, and the British warm well round my ears. Soon I was trying to get the lie of the land relative to both shelter and visibility, and all at once I had an idea. There were plenty of seats by the summer-house and the hedge behind it would make shelter. The floo level there was a good ten feet above the tennis-courts, and I ought to be well placed for hearing.

Well, I made my way slowly towards it, and as I did so I heard the challenge of a sentry far away to my right. Cross's men were abroad then, I thought, but though I strained my ears to listen, I could hear no more. That bitter north-east wind was now blowing, as I judged, at about thirty miles an hour, and the boughs of the trees soughed and creaked. I found my seat, which was one of a pair placed either side of the summer-house front door, and very soon I began to get used to the light. Considering I had had no vitamin diet, as I amusedly told myself, it was astonishing how much I could see. But it was only that the clouds had lifted somewhat, for above me I caught the twinkling of quite a number of stars. Where I sat was sheltered and comparatively warm, and I had a shrewd idea that one of Cross's men, if he were at all familiar with the Hall gardens, would try to use the summer-house as a kicking-off place for an attempt to get through the cordon.

But nothing happened. The luminous dial of my watch showed the time to be twenty-three hours. Things, I told myself, ought to be happening by now, and things, in fact, did begin to happen. But if you are expecting an Othello narration of moving accidents by floo and fiel or hairbreadth escapes in the imminent deadly breach, you are in for the anti-climax of your life. What happened firs was this. I had a tickling in my throat so I coughed very, very quietly into my handkerchief, and it was then that I heard a noise.

I couldn't describe what the noise was like, but something told me that someone was close, and had moved. I held my breath, and at the same moment I heard the distant drone of a plane. Then that damnable tickling started in my throat again. Slowly I got out my handkerchief, and as I bent my head forward for the cough, things really happened. What they were I didn't know, for the simple reason that I knew nothing at all. It was like that evening in the trenches when I was talking to my sergeant and we were laughing at some joke. In the middle of that joke, or so it seemed, I looked round, and there I was in a hospital bed at Étaples.

When I opened my eyes that night, quite a lot of things were happening, and I can't tell you the sequence in which I became aware of them, but at the same moment as I felt the pain in my head, I heard a tremendous crash, and a bomb fell some few hundred yards away. I didn't know where I was, but I remember saying to myself in my rude soldier's speech, "To hell with this. This is no place for me." Then I knew I was lying on the flagstones My finger went to my glasses, but by the mercy of Providence they were unbroken. Then I felt the pain in my head again, and on the top of my skull was a lump. Next I knew I was going to be violently sick—and I promptly was. After that I felt a little better.

Then I began to damn and blast Cross and his men, and tell myself that if I found the misbegotten son of Belial who'd knocked me out, I'd knock several kinds of hell out of him. Then I heard two more tremendous crumps, though farther away, and I was aware of excited voices from the men at the house.

"There he is!" a voice said excitedly. "Look. Over them trees. There's the parachute!"

Distant searchlights were weaving in the sky, and I rolled over on my back and stared at them. Then I hoisted myself up on my elbows. There was the drone of receding planes, a more distant thud, and then nothing but the same old sough of the night wind. I was suddenly icily cold, and I got somehow to my feet and to the seat. In a minute or two I could feel like walking, and I had a shot at it. A sudden wonder made me look at my watch. The time was just on one hour, and I had therefore been lying on those flag-stones well and truly sandbagged, for best part of an hour and a half.

I had a few halts before I reached the guard hut at the main entrance, and though I was still feeling groggy on my pins, I flattere myself that the sergeant noticed nothing unusual about me. I saw he was both pleased and excited, but I couldn't very well ask him what had been happening since he knew that I'd been on the spot. What I did ask him to do was to give me his version of the night's doings.

No wonder he was pleased. The Home Guard had tried to get through and three of them had been collared, including Cross himself. But for the raid happening and, as he said, spoiling things, they'd probably have collared more.

"Where are the Home Guard now?" I said.

He grinned. "Two men are here, sir. Captain Cross just went off to fi d the others, then we're making them a spot of hot tea."

"I think I'll have a cup too," I said.

I had come through the black-out screen to the light of his room, and he had a good sight of me.

"Excuse me, sir, but are you all right?"

"Not too bad now," I said. "The fact is I had a nasty fall."

"Sit down there, sir, and I'll get a cup of tea."

Off he went. Cross's two men were in the room, which was a kind of clink.

"You fellows had bad luck then," I said.

One of them shook his head and gave a wry grin.

"Your men were a bit too thick for us, sir. We thought we were all right when we got by a patrol, and then we ran clean into a standing sentry. You feeling any better, sir?"

I believe my face was rather green, and I still had the very devil of a pain in the head, but I was twice as good a man as had tried to get up from the flag-stone at the summer-house.

"Here is Captain Cross," one of the men said, and I heard him speaking to the sergeant outside. Then he came in, and fiv men with him, and he was taking the defeat of his attempt in an extraordinarily good spirit. His men said they had enjoyed nothing so much for a long time, and it would buck up the whole Platoon if every man could take his turn at such night operations.

"You're knocking off pretty early, aren't you?" I said.

"I ought to be getting back," he said, "and seeing what's being done about those German airmen. I hope they've been rounded up."

The sergeant had brought in tea and had gone out again. I thought the opportunity a good one.

"I'd like to ask you people a direct question, and it's a highly confidentia one. I must ask you to give me your word that you'll not mention the matter to a soul."

Cross said he could answer for himself and his men, so I asked which of them had given me that crack on the skull. Cross was horrified and his men were absolutely at a loss. Not one of them had been near the summer-house. If they had been near it, one said, they'd have seen me on the ground and would have gone for help. When Cross began introducing the men and telling me who they were in the town as proof that that kind of thing wouldn't be done, I told him their word was good enough for me, and I now had my own ideas on who had been responsible for the attack.

"One of the Neggers, I shouldn't be surprised," said young Holby, who was the son of a local solicitor and waiting to be called up for the R.A.F. I didn't tell him that as far as I was concerned he had hit the nail on the head, but I began asking about the raid.

"Just when I came to," I said, "I heard the very dickens of a bang—or I think I did."

"That wasn't a bomb," Cross told me. "That was one of their planes brought down by one of our night fighters At least we think so. We distinctly heard cannon shots."

"The crew baled out?"

"We saw a couple baling out," he said. "Holby says he saw a parachute coming down at about half-past eleven, but I tell him he must have been wrong. We only heard one plane then, and I'm sure that was ours. It was another hour before the raid got going."

"Heavens! that reminds me," I said. "I ought to have been back in Camp if there was a raid. Harrison will be wondering what on earth's happened to me."

The tea had been drunk and Cross said he'd take me back in his car at once. Two of the men were going with him, and the rest had their own transport. I was glad to accept the offer His car was along the road with two others, under the care of another of his men. Young Holby came with us, and he and I had the back seat. He told me he was very keen on night work and had been trying out a special vitamin course. In his view it had made a difference and he could literally see like a cat in the dark. His voice lowered when he told me about that firs parachutist he had seen. About two miles, so he judged, over to the south-east, was where he had caught sight of the something white in the sky, against the clear and the stars.

I felt rather uneasy about that. Part of our job was to be at the disposal of the Police and the Home Guard for the rounding up of any baling-out airmen, and I had the uncomfortable feeling that I had been letting Harrison down, so when the car stopped at our main gate, I asked Cross if he would be having any information within, say, the next hour. If he had, I'd arrange for the telephone orderly to bring it to my bedroom.

The telephone orderly said Captain Harrison had gone to bed about half an hour before. I asked what the raid had been like from his point of view, and he was rather contemptuous. Nothing had fallen near the Camp, and he reckoned there had been no more than twenty bombs in all, most of which, if not the whole issue, had fallen in open country.

I thought it might be a good idea to ring the local police and hear what they knew. The Superintendent was still out, the station sergeant told me. There had been no local damage, as far as could be at present ascertained.

"Rounded up any Huns?" I asked.

"We got the three that baled out," he said. "The pilot was dead in the plane."

"Heard any news about any others baling out, more to the south-east?"

"You've heard it then, sir, have you?" he said. "No, we haven't any more news about them. They're out of our district. They come under the Buxton rural area. What we have been asked is to keep a look-out. That's really what the Super's after now."

Young Holby had been right, then.

"Why did they come down?" I asked.

"Ask me another, sir," he said. "What we think is that the machine developed mechanical trouble and they got the wind up. After they jumped, the plane might crash fift miles or more away. All I do know is that there weren't any of our night fighter in the sky till half an hour later."

"Well, let us knew if you want any assistance," I told him and rang off

Somehow I didn't feel like bed. There were some biscuits and chocolate in my drawer, so I munched some and then stoked my pipe. After that I felt much better, and my brain began to function more clearly. I told myself that I'd make a full report to Command of the night's activities, and get Cross to make one too, to form an appendix. In the Service, as in a few other thing in life, it's always as well to get your blow in first Let Command get the idea that we were fine enthusiastic young fellows, and then, if the time ever came, they'd fin it hard to eat their own commendatory words. We might even be spared one or two brass-hat inspections.

The phone went. Cross was ringing, and he gave me much the same news as had come through the police. I ought to have known from the way he rattled it off that he was anxious to get something else off his chest. What he had to say was startling.

It appeared that one of the men who had been in the car with us lived on the south-east edge of the City, and he hadn't told me so at the time in case I should insist on taking that man home first before coming to the Camp. After he left me therefore, he turned back to the City. Not four hundred yards from the park, at the strategic angle of the side road and the main highway, he had come across a strong piquet of men sitting in the lee of the hedge.

The light was pretty bad, of course, and he had thought at firs that they might be some of his men whom his second-in-command—an elderly but bellicose retired colonel—had sent out scouting for Hun airmen. So he got out of the car and then found that they were a party of a dozen or so Neggers, all armed with stout sticks. They were a mixed lot, and the man in charge —a little fat futurist artist of a chap, about fifty—sai blandly that they were picnicking by way of experiment, and certainly they all seemed to have haversacks with food and thermos flasks

"Naturally I couldn't do a thing about it," Cross said. "They were on the public highway. What do you think they were up to?"

"Lord knows!" I said, and before I could advance a theory his voice was coming in again, and most impressively.

"I think it's Benison's idea, to do with training his gang. Also, do you think there's any connection with a certain affair?

I didn't gather what he meant: then I tumbled to it.

"You mean a certain crack on the skull," I said. "I certainly do. But not a hint to a soul. If those gentry are spying round the Hall at nights, we and your people will lay a nice little trap. Get 'em off the main road in a Government prohibited area, and we've got them where we want them."

"That'll be great," he said. "How is the head, by the way?"

"Heaps better."

"Good," he said. "Hope you have a fin night's rest. Good night then, sir."

"And to you, Cross," I said. "And I'm extraordinarily grateful to you."

Then I was suddenly feeling very sleepy, so off I went to my bed. By manipulation of the mirror I saw that the skin of my skull was unbroken and the swelling too had much gone down. When I woke at dawn, after a somewhat restless night, I was feeling fairly well in myself, except for a slight headache, and a couple of aspirins had eased that inside an hour. Then, with a restless fi on me, I got up. An early cup of tea was going in the cook-house, where they were pretty surprised to see me at that hour, and then I amused myself by getting out the preliminaries for that report to Command.

What was lucky about that was that I jotted down all times while they were fresh in my mind. At about twenty-three-thirty I had faintly heard a plane, and that was when the firs parachutists had been seen. Cross's men had then been inside the park and approaching from two differen directions so as to make a feint, if necessary, while the main attempt at penetration was made by way of the back. My crack on the skull was within ten minutes of that—though that was not going into the report to Command—and at about one hour or so I had come round and heard the crash of the plane our fighter had shot down.

Well, all these preliminaries have taken a long time, but I can honestly say that now you know as much as I do about every happening that has the least possible bearing on the extraordinary outrage that took place that night, unknown to myself, and on the tragedy that followed still later. You, perhaps, are in a much stronger position than myself, since you have more to suspect and something definit for which to look. To me, things were just happenings; queer happenings, I admit, but then I am always looking for queer happenings and imagining mysteries where there are none.

What I will say is this, and in some measure of self-defence. My job was to carry out efficient   the duties of my appointment as Commandant of Camp 55, and everything else was merely a persistence of bad—or good—habits. What my job most certainly *wasn't,* was to be a detective, either before or after the events that actually happened. If I hadn't got into my head that George Wharton had wangled the appointment for mysterious reasons of his own, I should never have noticed things, imagined them, or made deductions. After all, to do those things in Government time was taking pay and allowances under false pretences, though that point of view would never cause me many sleepless minutes.

But to get back to the story. It was still fiv minutes short of seven hours thirty, when the firs breakfasts are available in the Mess, and I was longing for a cup of coffe when an orderly fetched me to the telephone. Penelope Craye was on the line, and as soon as she spoke I knew something serious had happened.

"Major Travers, is that you? Can you come here at once?"

"Why? What's the matter?" I said rather blankly.

"I'm frightened to death," she said. "Something's happened to Colonel Brende. I think he's been murdered!"

"The body's there?" I said, and gaped even more blankly.

"No," she said. "I hardly know what I'm talking about. He isn't here, but—" She broke off and I could hear her making strange noises as if she had the words but they wouldn't come out.

"Listen," I said. "This isn't a matter for me. It's to do with the local police, or some higher authority."

"But I thought it was to do with you," she said. "You're responsible for looking after us."

That hadn't struck me. I gaped a bit more, then decided on a policy.

"You get hold of the local superintendent. I'll ring the guard to admit him. After that I'll see what I can do."

"I'm so grateful," she said, and from the wobble in her voice I knew she was crying. I waited a second or two, then hung up.

To say I was taken aback was putting it mildly. A dozen things then began to flas through my mind, and firs was the wonder how I stood in the matter. Whatever the delinquencies or neglect of any subordinates, I myself in the long run was responsible for the safety of the Hall and its occupants. How would Command take what had happened? But what *had* happened? I had gathered precious little from Penelope's incoherencies, except that Brende was missing and she suspected murder.

The bell shrilled again, and this time it was Wharton on the line.

"Get me Major Travers, will you? Very urgent."

"This is Travers."

"Didn't recognize your hallo," he said. "Now listen to this carefully. Something's happened at the Hall with regard to Colonel Brende. Miss Craye rang me about a quarter of an hour ago and I've been trying to get you ever since. I'm going along there and I'd like you to come. Be at the main gate in half an hour's time."

"Right," I said. "Did Miss Craye mention my name to you?"

"She did," he said curtly. "You're in charge of the place, aren't you? In half an hour then at the front entrance."

He rang off leaving me with cold comfort. I *was* in charge of the place and there was no denying it. Still, as I told myself as I hastened to the Mess for a quick meal, there was no use in getting flurried Even George didn't appear to know just what had happened, and I could also console myself with the knowledge that it was the nature of Penelope and her kind to talk in superlatives.

CHAPTER VII
THE MISSING COLONEL

Now though I had no idea what had actually happened to Colonel Brende, I did realize that it must have been something pretty serious, if only because Penelope Craye had been so obviously distressed and had mentioned the word murder. As I was driving towards the Hall, I naturally therefore wondered if there was anything I could contribute by way of information, and it seemed to me that there were three things I might have to tell Wharton. There was the man, or person, I had seen at the summer-house at about twenty minutes short of nine o'clock, there was the fact that the side door in the boundary wall, unguarded by us, had been in use, and lastly there was that crack on the skull which had laid me out at about a quarter of an hour before midnight.

I was early at the front gate, but Wharton was a few moments late. As we walked towards the house he told me he had been getting hold of someone whom he called "one of the Nobs." He loved little secrecies like that, and there was a wee, likeable touch of the snob in him, so that though he would use those derogatory terms for what he would also term "the Big Bugs," or "the High-and-Mighty," you could tell that he was always gratifie by even the most remote contacts with the great ones of the land. I rather guessed he'd got through to the Home Offic At any rate he told me his orders were that whatever had happened was to be kept secret.

"There's not to be a word to the local police," he said. "We don't want more than one cook at this pot of soup."

"Is that a hint to me?" I said, but George wasn't in the mood for flippan conversation. Also we were almost at the front door, and George marched straight on to it and only halted in the very act of ringing the bell. He also knocked to make sure. Ledd opened the door while George's hand still was at the knocker. There was something differ nt about Ledd that morning, and then I tumbled to what it was. He had assumed an expression of extraordinary gloom, but as that snub nose of his rather militated against the dismals, the effec was rather that of a determined scowl.

"Who are you?" Wharton fire at him as we stepped inside.

"Corporal Ledd, sir, Colonel Brende's servant."

Wharton grunted, and then Penelope appeared. Her nose had recently been powdered, but she had not quite eradicated the traces of many tears. She, too, was different If she had been quiet the last time I saw her, now she was positively subdued. The Quaker Girl to the life, I thought, what with the dove-grey frock and its white trimmings, the downcast look and the gentle voice rich with gratitude.

"So glad you're here. It's been awfully worrying for us. Will you come this way?"

"Where're we going?" Wharton wanted to know.

"I thought perhaps you'd like to see his room."

Wharton nodded, then glared round at Ledd.

"You'd better come too."

Ledd shot me a look of plaintive surprise, with, it seemed to me, a certain uneasiness. Up the stairs the four of us went, and past the door of Brende's offic and then Penelope was opening the next door to it. Wharton stepped in and fille the doorway. Over his shoulder I had a good view. There was a camp-bed which had been slept in, a couple of chairs, of which one was an easy one, belonging to the house, a trestle-table, a small table by the bedside with a carafe of water on it and a pad and pencil, and finall two chests of drawers, the drawers opened, some of the contents on the floor and all giving signs of thorough search.

"Who's been in here?" Wharton asked over his shoulder.

"I have, sir," said Ledd.

"I had to come in," Penelope explained. "And I thought I'd better bring Mr. Newton."

"Who's he?" Wharton wanted to know.

He was told, and that Newton was second-in-command, as it were, and therefore in charge when Colonel Brende was away.

"Well, thank God Lockhart's elephants haven't been in," Wharton said with his firs attempt at humour. "Not much point in worrying ourselves to death about foot-prints."

So we all stepped in, and then Wharton was once more rounding—I can only call it that—on the mournful Ledd.

"What did you touch in here?"

"Me, sir? Nothing, sir," Ledd said with injured innocence.

"Then where's the suit and so on he was wearing before he got into bed?"

Ledd stared, looked a trifl foolish, then took a step forward as if he were going to search the drawers. Wharton had a look instead for himself. Nothing was either in the drawers or on the floo but oddments of underclothing, and a pullover or two, a tunic and two pairs of slacks.

"What was he wearing when you saw him last?" Wharton asked Ledd, and Ledd described the very clothes Brende had been wearing that afternoon when I firs met him. Penelope put in a word.

"Men get very attached to their clothes. He simply loved that brown coat, and it really wasn't too untidy. Do you think so, Major Travers?"

I said readily enough that I'd have gone anywhere in it. Wharton chimed in by asking where the Colonel *had* been in it. Penelope repeated that she had no idea. He'd left a chit, which she'd thrown on the fire to the effec that he had gone out and might not be back till next day. Wharton wanted to know if he would have seen any important person in that easy-going rig-out. Penelope said he was very unconventional that way, and when a highly important person came down from town to review the research work that had been done, Colonel Brende had worn precisely the same clothes.

Ledd said the Colonel put his clothes on the bedside chair at night, and his boots or shoes on the floor He had been so astounded not to see the Colonel there that he had not noticed the slippers had gone too. What he had thought was that the Colonel had got up for an early walk.

"I'm not blaming you about anything," Wharton told him.

"I might have thought the same as you did. And now you, Miss Craye. Did you touch anything here?"

"I only touched that," she said, and pointed to a white something like a large rolled-up handkerchief that lay on the floo by the bed.

"Naturally you would," Wharton told her with an immense amiability. "It would offen your sense of tidiness."

He slipped on his rubber gloves, picked up the wad and shook it. I caught at once the sweetish scent of choloroform. Then he replaced it carefully and his eyes went slowly round the room.

"What's that?"

That was a fishing-rod tucked in the shadow beneath the open window along the wall. Wharton picked it up. Then he tried its length. When extended it reached well beyond the pillow of the camp-bed. The rod was replaced and he was looking out of the window. Through it I could see the trees that bordered the park and beyond them the greyish line of the hills.

"Fond of fresh air, was he?" Wharton was asking Ledd.

"Yes, sir. Always had that window open, no matter what it was like outside."

"What sort of a sleeper was he?"

"You couldn't move, sir, without him hearing you. Regular like a cat, he was."

Wharton was motioning for me to go over, but to keep clear of the window-sill. Along the wall beneath us ran an immense wisteria, as fi e a specimen as I have ever seen. Some of its trained branches were more than my two hands could have circled. Wharton grimaced at me, then sadly addressed the room.

"There we are then. If he'd sent out invitations on gilt-edged paper asking for the place to be burgled, he couldn't have done it better. He asked for service and he certainly got it."

Penelope clicked her tongue.

"I don't think you ought to say that, Mr. Jenkins. It's not fair to Colonel Brende. He was a light sleeper. You said so, didn't you, Corporal Ledd? I'm sure he'd have heard anybody at that window."

Wharton was at once his most gushing and apologetic self.

"You must excuse me. No fool like an old fool, and that fit me pretty often. But there's been just a little subterfuging— shall we say? The name's Wharton—not Jenkins." He had put on his spectacles, and now was roguishly regarding her over their tops. "Jenkins is on my mother's side. Superintendent Wharton of New Scotland Yard—that's me."

Penelope's face had flame   red and she was staring. Ledd also went a rich pink, and his lips were moving as if he were talking to himself.

"That's highly confidential of course," Wharton said. "And now where's the Colonel's offic   Through that door there if I remember rightly."

I didn't know till then that Wharton had ever met Colonel Brende, but I should have known that he must have met him, even if it was not in the Hall. At any rate he turned the key of the door through which we had come, slipped it into his pocket, and then was courteously opening the other door for Penelope to pass through.

The room was in much the same condition as the other. Every drawer in the desk had been prised open, and papers were scattered everywhere. My eyes went at once to the etching behind which was the safe, and as they left it I saw that Penelope Craye's eyes had been that way too. Wharton was across as soon as he heard about the safe. I guessed it was open since the etching was hanging crookedly, and open it was. Wharton had a good look inside and announced that it was empty.

"What was kept in it?" he asked Penelope.

"I don't really know," she said. "Everything that was secret and confidentia I know went in it. But I was never allowed to see them. Colonel Brende was most particular."

"He never even gave you a hint of anything extra special being in it?"

She shook her head. "Never. I did guess, though, that all his private papers were in it."

"You mean the results of his private researches?"

"Yes, of course. His private researches." She hesitated for a moment. "That's really why he slept in the next room. He used to say he was his own bulldog."

Wharton grimaced. "A pity the bulldog didn't have a burglar-proof kennel. That"—and he waved contemptuously at the safe— "I could make a mess of myself with a Woolworth screwdriver and a couple of hairpins. As for a burglar—"

He broke off and over his face came a look of what I can only call brazen roguishness. He swivelled the look on Ledd.

"I suppose you've never been a burglar?"

I expected Ledd to grin. He didn't. His face went crimson again and his tongue went round his lips. He heaved a breath or two, then sort of puffe out a "No, sir."

"Good," said Wharton. "You keep to the straight and narrow path, my lad. It always pays."

He gave Ledd a last look from over the spectacle tops, and Penelope Craye's voice came in after a premonitory cough.

"There's something I think I ought to tell you. Colonel Brende did have something really important in the safe." She smiled disarmingly. "I don't really know it, of course, but I think he had."

"Ah!" said Wharton hugely. "You tell us all about it."

"I think so, because that's the reason he came home."

"Just a minute," I said most apologetically. "I think I'd better tell Superintendent Wharton about Major Passenden."

Wharton made notes on what I had to say, but Penelope added nothing.

"I see," he said. "This Major Passenden wanted to see him but he was out. He wasn't expected back but he came back."

"Yes," she said. "At just about seven o'clock. I happened to be in my offic and I was simply staggered when he rang. I even thought to myself, 'Now who on earth can be in the Colonel's office and then it turned out to be the Colonel. I said I hadn't expected him, but he said he'd got the very idea he'd been hunting for for months. He looked simply delighted with himself."

Wharton turned to me, and his smile had a smugness that made me wince.

"That's what I call a first-clas witness. Miss Craye not only kept her eyes open; she knew how to put two and two together. And what else did the Colonel let out, Miss Craye?"

"Well, there wasn't much else," she said, all a-simper with Wharton's compliments. "He asked if I'd do a letter or two. I can show you copies if you like, but they weren't really important, and then he said he didn't want to be disturbed again as he would be working."

"And the last time you saw him was?"

She frowned and her lips moved with mental calculations.

"At about half-past eight. He'd had his dinner and was working here at the desk."

"Where'd he have his dinner?"

"Here, sir," Ledd said briskly. "I brought it up, sir."

"And when did you see him last?"

"When, sir? At about a quarter to nine, sir. I passed Miss Craye in the corridor when she was going to her room."

"Her room?"

"He means my bed-sitting-room," she explained. "It's the length of the house away, on the other side."

Wharton nodded his thanks, then was asking Ledd if it was usual for him to be dismissed so early.

"Well, sir, it wasn't all that usual," Ledd told him. "Sometimes it happened like that when the Colonel didn't want to be disturbed. Generally though, I used to look in at about ten."

While all that conversation was going on, I was feeling relieved that I had not had the opportunity of telling Wharton that at the time Colonel Brende had undoubtedly been in that very room, I had seen near the summer-house a someone for whom I had at firs mistaken him. Then while Wharton was making a note of the times as given by both witnesses, I did manage to get near the door and try the handle. Wharton spotted me.

"Locked, is it?"

"Yes," I said, "and there's no key this side."

"The Colonel kept it locked, sir, when he went to bed," Ledd told him.

"Then wherever the Colonel is, the key is," Wharton said, and rather obviously. "And what did you do with yourself, Corporal, when the Colonel said he didn't want you any more?" Once more Ledd's face flame crimson, and I wondered what the devil could be the matter with the man.

"Went for a walk, sir."

"Alone?"

There was a slight hesitation. "Yes, sir."

"Ah!" said Wharton, and almost wagged a roguish finger "Sure that it wasn't spring and thoughts of love? In other words, you hadn't a date?"

Ledd gave his firs grin, and it was a sheepish one.

"No, sir. Nothing like that, sir."

"And what about you, Miss Craye?"

"I didn't leave my room," she said. "I read a book and went to bed early. I was glad I did, because I slept through most of the raid."

"Your bedroom connected with here?"

"Oh, yes." The blush this time was what might be called a pretty one. "The room's really my sitting-room. The Colonel would often give me a ring if he wanted anything."

"And that pad beside his bed was for if he had any ideas in the night?"

"Yes," she said, as if surprised. "How marvellous of you to have noticed it!"

"We may be getting a bit old but we're not yet doddery," Wharton told her unctuously. "And now about the sleeping arrangements for the whole house. I think I'd better get an idea."

There was no difficul whatever about that. Colonel Brende's rooms faced west. Mrs. Brende's two rooms faced south, and her bedroom was actually over the front door. Penelope Craye's large room faced east, and the intervening rooms were all empty. As corridors ran completely round, communication was easy enough, and the head of the servants' stairway came out on a landing at the centre of the north corridor. As for the rest of the inmates, Newton, Wissler and Riddle slept in the old dining-room, which had been partitioned off and the two maids and cook in the original butler's pantry and its annexe. Squadron-Leader Pattner slept out, for his periods of stay were very occasional.

Wharton walked round the corridors to familiarize himself with the lay-out, but expressed no desire to see inside the rooms. Then he dismissed Ledd.

"Not a word of this to a soul. You understand, Corporal?" Ledd said he did, and Wharton's tone was so grim that he was once more nervously licking his lips.

"I hope for your sake you do," Wharton told him menacingly. "Any leakage traced to you and God help you. Colonel Brende's away on business. You understand that? Away on business, and you won't even say that unless you're asked."

Away went Ledd. Wharton's voice was as soft as butter again.

"I don't think we need keep you any longer at the moment, Miss Craye. Major Travers and I will just have a quick look round, then we might have a word with the others."

"Come on," he said to me. "We'll have a look at that wisteria."

He left the front door wide open, and round we went to the west wing. When we ran our eyes over the wisteria there was no need for more. There were the marks on the branches where feet had trodden. As Wharton said, it was easier and quicker than using a ladder. All at once he was grasping a branch and pulling himself up, and before you knew it he was six foot clear of the ground.

"There you are," he said, puffi   a bit as he reached the ground again. "Just what I said up there. The fool of a man might just as well have put an advertisement in the paper. *Nice commodious room. Full of secrets. Guaranteed easy to burgle.*"

"Just a minute, George," I said. "Are you looking at things from the right angle? Why all this harping on burglary?"

He glared at me. "Secret papers have gone, haven't they?"

"I know. But why not talk about the real happening? Why not say bluntly that Colonel Brende's been kidnapped?"

He rumbled on for a bit, then shrugged his shoulders.

"Well, perhaps for Ledd's benefit   That's why I harped on the burglary side."

"Good," I said. "Having got so far, let's go a bit farther. Frankly, I don't see how he could have been kidnapped. You know the disposition of the sentries and so on. Not only that, they were all keyed up to the highest pitch of alertness on account of that Home Guard stunt."

"What stunt was that?"

I told him, though I had to admit the sentries didn't know it was actually on that night. They had been previously warned, however, to expect a stunt any night and any place. In my judgment then, though the night was dark enough, the unconscious Colonel could never have been carried through the cordon. Two men would have had to carry him, and a quick dash through, after a sentry had moved along, would have been hardly feasible.

"I suggest you try it out," Wharton said.

I disagreed. What might happen on one night with one set of men was no real guide to what had happened last night with quite another set. But I did suggest an alternative to the carrying of the Colonel. His captors waited till the effect of the chloroform had worn off and then he went out on his own legs with the business end of a gun against his spine. But even then it would have been a difficu business.

"I don't quite see that," Wharton said. "Whoever held the gun at his back knew perfectly well that if a sentry challenged, then the Colonel—with the gun still in his back—would call out that he was Colonel Brende and everything was all right."

"We can argue till nightfall," I said. "We'd better build on facts. I claim the whole thing was incredibly risky, and yet the facts remain. Someone made him get out of bed and dress himself, and the somebody or somebodies took or made him take his pyjamas and slippers. That means he was being taken to somewhere for a stay, and to a place where it would be dangerous to buy pyjamas and slippers."

"We've been up against the impossible before," Wharton said with something of contempt. "Dammit, you wouldn't expect a job like this to be done by people who wouldn't face risks and who hadn't got brains."

Then he was shaking his head and scowling away to himself.

"What we've got to get into our heads is that this is a hell of a serious business. There mayn't be a whisper down here, but there'll be the very devil of a commotion in town. If he was the key man of all this research, there's likely to be an earthquake if we can't get hold of him. And that'll be another devil of a job if we've got to keep everything secret."

Off he stumped to the front door. Ledd was there, looking round for us. Before he could speak, Wharton wanted to know if anything of the Colonel's was missing from the bathroom. Ledd said he'd just looked, and nothing was missing. Shaving tackle and everything was still there.

"Good," said Wharton. "Looking for me, were you?"

"A Major Passingham is on the phone, sir, asking for the Colonel."

Wharton raised his eyebrows and gave me a look. I took the call.

"Yes?" I said.

"Hallo! Is that you, Brende?"

"No," I said. "It's Major Passenden, isn't it? Well, this is Major Travers. I just happened to be at the Hall. Colonel Brende, if you still want him, has gone away again. He may be away for a few days."

I was about to hang up when I caught his voice again.

"Did you say 'gone away *again*'?"

"Yes."

"But this is Sunday, and only yesterday afternoon I was told he wouldn't be back till to-day."

"I know," I said. "Apparently he changed his mind and came back last night."

"Oh," he said ruefully, and, "Sorry to be such a nuisance. Very much obliged to you."

Neither Wharton nor I saw anything important in that little talk, and there we were wrong. I was particularly to blame, for something had been clean under my nose. There was the vital clue, standing out a yard, and I missed it. And if you have missed it too, let me tell you here and now what it was. Perhaps you still won't see it, just as I failed to see it, and its implications. It was that Ledd reported that a Major Passing*ham*—not Passenden— was on the phone. That is what should have made me think back.

A tremendous change had come over the offi   where Wharton interviewed the three experts. When I had last seen them they had been more like three people having a brief, enjoyable holiday from a job of work which was even more congenial than the necessary leisure. Mind you, as Wharton and I well knew from experience, it is easy to imagine a strained atmosphere and suspicious words and actions. Emergencies and unusual happenings make for unusual reactions, and somewhere in the mind of the most law-abiding of us is a very definite uneasiness in the presence of the law. For all that, I would still insist that never had I interviewed three people who looked and acted in a more suspicious way. For one thing everything had to be prised out of them, and when they did speak, it was in frugal language more noticeable for what it obviously concealed than what it told.

Little mousey Newton was all a-dither. He had been upstairs and formed his own conclusions from what he had seen. He said so, but when Wharton asked what the conclusions were, he stammered and hesitated, and then from the mountain of thought produced a monstrous little mouse. There had been a burglary, he thought—*thought*, mind you!—and when asked what about Colonel Brende, he gave his opinion that the Colonel had gone after the burglars. Wharton's jaw sagged, and he stared, but he kept his patience.

"Did you see him last night?" he asked.

"Yes," said Newton slowly and dubiously, as if afraid of the evidence of his own eyes.

Wharton gave what I call his Colosseum smile—that of a lion who has missed his firs snap at a fat Christian.

"Well, what did he say? What was he looking like? And when did you see him?"

Imagine from now on the *ums* and *ers* and the way he kept looking round at the others, and this is what was winkled out of Newton. Brende had seen the three of them the previous night just before he had his meal, and he announced, diffidentl one gathered, and out of modesty, that he had got what he was looking for.

"And what was he looking for?" Wharton asked. "You needn't make any bones about telling me and Major Travers."

"Well, I can't really say. He was working on independent lines."

"But haven't you any idea on what lines?"

"No," said Newton, after due thought. "It's all highly technical."

"It certainly is," said Wharton grimly. I put in a helping oar.

"What was it, Newton? Problems in sound, or ballistics, or light, or what?"

"Well, a little of each. Problems in pure physics mostly."

"Ah, well," said Wharton resignedly. "And will you tell us when you saw him last?"

Even then Newton had to shuffl   Riddle had seen him last, or rather, hadn't seen him.

"What happened, Mr. Riddle?" Wharton asked with a new hope.

Riddle had been looking extremely uncomfortable, but when he began his story, he had no hesitations. When you've seen as many people under cross-examination as I have you'll know that what comes pat has often been rehearsed, and that when a witness is voluble, it is often out of relief at having been asked nothing about what he hopes to conceal.

Riddle said that when the bombing began the three used the presence of enemy planes to verify certain research results. One interesting thing was noticed—something highly technical, and to do with vibrations—and Newton thought Colonel Brende might like to have it at once, or confirm Like the others, the Colonel worked much at night, and Riddle—after what had been said—expected the Colonel to be working. But the offi   room was locked, so he gave a cautionary tap at the bedroom door. There was no sound, so he peeped inside. The bed, he could see, had been slept in and, though he had not registered at the time what he had seen, he now knew that the drawers were open and their contents scattered. Newton volunteered the statement that Riddle had that kind of brain, and could be implicitly believed. As for the time, it was exactly one hour thirty minutes when Riddle looked in the room.

"Now we're hearing things," Wharton said. "What about you, Professor Wissler? What can you tell us?"

"I can say nothing," Wissler said in his slow, precise English. "Everything happened as everybody says."

Wharton shrugged his shoulders, and I can swear that Wissler gave a sigh of relief. Wharton must have caught it, for he whipped round on him again.

"How did you spend your evening, exactly?"

Wissler had never left the house, as Newton could verify. Wharton turned to Riddle. Riddle said pat enough that he had been out a lot of the time.

"Out where?"

"Just walking round," he said, and he was doing his best to grin. "We don't get much exercise here, so I often walk for an hour or two."

"Well, when did you walk last night?"

Riddle pursed his lips and then said cheerfully enough that it was from eleven o'clock till about one. Those were his usual times when there was nothing doing. All the sentries knew him, he said, and they could confirm

Wharton had to be content with that. Riddle had seen nothing unusual during his walk, which had been out the back way and into open country. But he had at least established one thing—that the kidnapping of Colonel Brende had taken place *before* a certain time. When Wharton ended the proceedings by commiserating with Newton on the loss of all Brende's papers, and above all on the fact that Brende had gone before he could give details of the vital discovery he had made, Newton remarked surprisingly that everything would go on as before, and the loss might not be all that great.

It was not till we were outside the front door again that Wharton exploded.

"If those are your professors, give me the damn fools. What's the matter with them? What're they scared of?"

"Oh, it's just the way the mind of those fellows works," I said placatingly. "They're all geniuses in a way and you can't expect them to act like a man in the street. Where are we bound for now?"

"Nowhere," Wharton said peevishly. "I had to get outside here or bust."

Then he was screwing up his brow as if in tremendous thought.

"Something I want to have another look at. I know!"

Back to the house we turned. Up the stairs we went and to the door of Colonel Brende's bedroom. Wharton took the key out of his pocket. Out of the corner of my eye I saw Penelope Craye having a surreptitious look at us from round the angle of the corridor, but I said nothing to Wharton. After all, he was taking Penelope at her face value, and if there were things to fin out, I was rather wishing he would fin them for himself.

CHAPTER VIII
WHARTON INVESTIGATES

What Wharton wanted to look at were those marks on the stone window-sill. There were no finger-prints however, but merely smudges, and so many that one could imagine how they had been made. The abductor, for instance, must have rested his elbows on the sill while he manipulated the chloroform wad, and then he had knelt there while he deposited the fishing-ro and got into the room. Some of the marks may even have been where Colonel Brende himself went out.

Wharton did some measuring, and made notes. Then his eye fell on the fireplac in the offi and he went across to look at the ashes.

"It was cold weather," I ventured. "He'd want a fir here."

"I know," Wharton said. "It's always instinct to take a look at a fir in case anything's been burnt."

Then as we went back to the bedroom in came Penelope Craye, or rather she peeped in apologetically.

"I thought I heard you here. Is there anything I can do?"

Wharton pursed his lips.

"Well, as a matter of fact, there is. You might try to give us some idea of what's been taken from the safe, and his desk."

"But I told you I couldn't," she said, and then hesitated. "What I could show you is the list of incoming letters. I have to keep those for the postage book, you know."

"That'd be fine, Wharton said.

As soon as she'd gone to her offic he was whispering hoarsely.

"Keep her here. Don't let her get out on any account. Say I've gone to see Ledd."

I told Penelope that Wharton would be back in a minute, and I was carrying on, so we went through the book together and I took notes of dates on which documents marked Secret had been received. Then she opened the morning's mail, but there was nothing interesting. There was still no sign of Wharton, so I made more time by asking if she had any ideas. She said she had none. The only thing staring her in the face was that Colonel Brende had been kidnapped, and the thought of that sort of paralysed her brain.

"Kidnapped by whom?" I said.

"I don't know. How should I know?" Straightaway I was beginning to notice signs of returning distress, so I decided to use the soft pedal, but after a quick shake or two of the head, she was composing herself again. "I know it's all so incredible, but why shouldn't it have been enemy agents?"

"Yes, but why?" I said. "It may sound foolish to you, asking that question, but it's your point of view we want."

"Well, Colonel Brende was the brains of everything here, wasn't he? I mean, once he'd gone, everything went."

"Yes, of course," I said.

"And not only that. If enemy agents got hold of him, they'd try and force everything out of him. They'd make him tell what he knew. They'd give the world for that. They know we're miles beyond them in what's being done here."

"True enough," I said. "The trouble is that when we're up against what we've always regarded as fiction we can't accept it readily as fact. If the Hun has got Colonel Brende, then things are pretty bad."

"You saw *Bengal Lancer*?" she said, eyes popping. "Do you think they'd do things to him like they did there? Splinters under his nails?" Her face wrinkled in horror. "I can't bear to think of it all. It's too dreadful."

There was still no sign of Wharton, so I told her the offi room and the bedroom would now be sealed, so she would have to hand over any keys that opened the door from her offic She made no bones about giving me the only one there was, and we went out to the corridor. Wharton had considerately left the key in the door of Brende's bedroom, so I locked it.

"Is there anything else you have to do here?" she asked as we went slowly along the corridor towards the main stairs.

"We might have to see Mrs. Brende," I said, and then she caught sight of Wharton through the window.

"There is Superintendent Wharton just coming back. Isn't it curious that his name shouldn't be Jenkins?"

She was trying to pump me about Wharton, but I merely said we'd go downstairs and meet him in the hall. There I told him what we had been doing, and he was gushingly grateful. All that remained to do was, as I had anticipated, to see Mrs. Brende.

"I'll ring for Annie," Penelope said, and I caught Wharton's quick lift of the eyebrows. "You'll excuse me, but I'm so frightfully busy. I literally don't know if I'm on my head or my heels."

Annie appeared and took us towards Mrs. Brende's room. We waited while she made enquiries, then were shown in. I introduced Wharton, and it was plain from the look on Mrs. Brende's face that she knew all about things. She had been reading *The Times,* for there it lay and her pince-nez on it.

"A bad business and an extraordinary one," Wharton told her with a heavy shake of the head. "When did you firs hear about it, ma'am?"

He loved that old-fashioned method of address, which was part of his technique. I have told you that he always boasted that women were like putty in his hands, and he loved above all those of his own generation.

Mrs. Brende said that Professor Newton had given her the news.

"A very excellent fellow," was Wharton's surprising comment.

"He is," she said. "I like Professor Newton, and I admire him enormously."

I have also told you that the quality that struck me most about Mrs. Brende was her absolute sincerity. That quality was never more apparent than at that moment. That she might be making revelations about her private life was of no apparent concern. Very quietly and frankly she answered all Wharton's questions, and seemed unaware of his apologies for them. For instance, she had heard nothing in the night, she said, except the raid. Her bedroom door had been locked. She had not seen Colonel Brende that evening or night, and would have been surprised if she had seen him. Colonel Brende, she did say, had his work to do and his various interests, and all she was doing at Dalebrink Hall was living in her own house.

Then Wharton took an unexpected line. He even put words into my mouth, but I had long ceased to show surprise at anything George might say or do.

"I've no wonder you regard it as inexplicable," he told Mrs. Brende. "Major Travers here thinks just the same. If Colonel Brende was kidnapped—and, bluntly, that's what it amounts to —then he doesn't see how he could have been got through the sentries."

"That, of course, I can't give an opinion about," she said. "But I do fin it incredible." She smiled gently. "I suppose we oughtn't to be incredible, considering things that do happen in war-time."

"Exactly," said Wharton. "But Major Travers has a theory with which I'm inclined to agree. Colonel Brende wasn't carried unconscious through the sentries. He thinks—and I must say I'm inclined to agree—that after the chloroform was given, then a drug was administered that made him do what he was told. In other words he did what he was told and his bodily faculties were unimpaired. He got out of the window and walked somehow through the sentries. After that, getting out of the park was easy.

And I could tell you of at least a couple of drugs that would act as I've described."

She merely nodded gently, as she had been doing while George was spinning that plausible theory.

"Is your husband by any chance a local man?" he asked.

"A Derbyshire man, yes," she said. "There have been no connections now for a great many years, but the family used to live at a village called Sowdale, which is rather more north. It was my home too."

Annie came in to say I was wanted on the phone. It was Harrison reporting that Major Passenden was wanting to see me, and what should he say. I said Passenden might as well wait as I'd probably be along in a matter of minutes. Then I hurried back to the room, for I didn't know what new use George had been making of my name. He was just in the act of going, it appeared, so I mentioned Passenden.

"Passenden!" Mrs. Brende said. "A relation of Hugh Passenden?" Then she smiled. "I beg your pardon, but I knew a Major Passenden. He was killed just before Dunkirk. A very great friend, and of my husband."

Then it appeared she had missed that paragraph in *The Times,* and you can imagine her surprise. I said I'd certainly fin ways and means of letting Passenden see her, and she was most grateful. Then, I hope with a lot of tact and some more charm, I said I'd discovered that both Bernice and I knew the Colonel's secretary.

"Isn't it a small world," she said perfectly naturally. "She's actually—let me see, what is she? Well, we have cousins in common, so what does that make her?"

"That beats, me," I said, and was aware that Wharton was anxious to be on the move. Another couple of minutes and we were going. Wharton's last words were: "Delighted to make your acquaintance, ma'am, and I'm only too sorry it wasn't on better business. But, as I said, I'll keep you fully informed."

We didn't leave at once, however, for Wharton paid a visit to the Brains Trust and impressed on Newton the urgency of absolute secrecy about the kidnapping of Colonel Brende, and he minced no words. Also every scrap of information, or even of theory which might shed light on the mystery, was to be at once reported to him. Nothing, he insisted, would be too trivial. In the meanwhile Newton and the rest would carry on as normally as possible.

After that we at last went off to our cars. Wharton followed me in the direction of the Camp, but when we had got well round the bend he overtook me and signalled for me to stop. Then he got in my car, and I knew, not without pleasure, that I was about to hear things.

"A fine lady, that Mrs. Brende," he began. "No man would want a fine witness."

"You said that about Penelope Craye," I reminded him.

"Oh, her," he said, and chuckled. "No harm in a little soft soap. But about this Mrs. Brende. I'd heard a lot before I got here this morning. My supposed niece knows all the local history and gossip."

"And what did you know?" I asked, ready to be on Mrs. Brende's side.

"Only what you might have gathered for yourself the last few minutes," he said unctuously. "She and her husband go their own ways, don't they? Did she express any grief at what had happened to him? One of these May and December marriages, and he was the one who cooled off And that Craye woman is in it, or I'm a Dutchman. Why all that 'I'll ring for Annie' business? Why didn't she take us to Mrs. Brende? I'll tell you. Colonel Brende and his secretary have been seen in Dalebrink together."

"Wait a minute," said I, stemming the flood "Does 'seen' mean seen in compromising circumstances?"

He hedged at once.

"Well, not necessarily. But they've been seen. And"—he leaned over archly—"he's never been seen out with his wife. He prefers the company of the secretary."

"That's silly scandal, and dangerous," I said. "Why shouldn't he go out with his secretary? After all, she's a relation, however distant, by marriage. And another thing. What's made you change your opinions about Penelope? You were cracking her up to me as if she were heaven's gift to Scotland Yard Superintendents."

George merely chuckled.

"So she may be—yet. Know what I found in her room?"

"So that's where you were."

"The batman was just going in to clean up when I was that way," he said, "so I sent him to fin Ledd and I nipped inside. A thick wad of papers had been burnt in the grate, so I put what I could into an envelope, and they're going up to town straightaway."

"Papers?" I said. "Why shouldn't she burn papers? Why shouldn't they have been her own papers?"

"Why not?" he told me amiably. "Also, why shouldn't I fin out if they were? This is a queer business, isn't it? Why shouldn't there be something fishy?

"Why not?" said I, to be in the fashion. "Anything else did you fin out?"

"Nothing but what you know," he said. "But I'll tell you what I've already done. One or two of my men will be down here as quick as they can get. Everyone in the house is going to be tailed from now on, and every telephone talk is going to be listened to. I admit it doesn't look an inside job, but I can't affor to take chances. Now you tell me a few things for a change. About this Major Passenden, for instance."

I told him far more than that. I explained all about the Home Guard stunt, and when it ended. The importance there was that since it did end at about one in the morning, and Colonel Brende was kidnapped at some time before half-past, the job was most likely to have been done in that half-hour. The sentries would ease off then, and human nature being what it was, might even surreptitiously forgather for a chat about experiences. I admitted that nobody in the house knew about the stunt, but if the job were not an inside one, that did not matter. Cross, or his men, might have let all Dalebrink know what was happening at the Hall, and the news might have reached the necessary ears. If so, the kidnappers saw a chance, and took it.

"A bit highfalutin, don't you think?" Wharton protested mildly.

"Not more so than that theory you fathered on me, about the drug."

"That's where you're wrong," he said. "I believe that theory's correct. It's the only explanation there is."

"Have it your own way," I told him, and went on with my revelations. There was the crack on the skull, and the Neggers whom Cross had seen at the road junction that night, and lastly I told him about the side door to the park.

"Good God!" he said. "Why didn't you tell me that before?"

At once he made me turn back, and there he was inspecting the door and the grass verge, and I fretting about Passenden waiting in my offic   He even made his way through a nearby gap and had a look inside.

"Right," he said, when a good ten minutes had gone by. "Now we'll go and see this Major Passenden."

"You want to see him?"

"Why the surprise?" he was asking, almost aggrievedly. "If he wanted to see Colonel Brende on important business, why shouldn't he tell me what it was? And a bit apposite, wasn't it, him turning up yesterday? And where was he last night when you got that crack on the skull?"

"Now, now, George," I had to say. "Please don't take me for an utter fool. And for the love of heaven let's get back to the Camp. This head of mine isn't any too good. If you'd shown as much interest in my skull as you have in Passenden, it'd have been more friendly, and a damn sight more sensible."

He merely gave a silly chuckle. I shot my own car on, but he was at the Camp as soon as I. Passenden was with Harrison, who sent him in to me. When I introduced Wharton, he looked highly interested but no more.

"Do you vouch for Major Passenden as being a reliable person to whom I can talk?" Wharton asked, and in a humorous sort of way. Passenden pricked his cars at that, and no wonder. One doesn't walk into a Commandant's offi   and expect to meet a Superintendent of New Scotland Yard.

"Most certainly," I said, wondering what he was going to divulge and why.

"Then later on I'll tell the Major what's been happening," Wharton said. "But firs of all, sir, what was your, precise business with Colonel Brende?"

"Oh, just a chat about old times, and experiences," Passenden said off-handedly "We hadn't met since before Dunkirk, you know. I was working under him out there, and I was always a very close friend of the Brendes."

"You're a Derbyshire man?"

"Born and bred."

"You knew Dalebrink Hall before?"

Passenden looked rather surprised, but he said he had always known it well. He had known Mrs. Brende before her marriage and had often been at the Hall in her widowed mother's time.

Wharton nodded. "And so your business wasn't what might be called secret. Or, if it comes to that, urgent."

Passenden smiled. "Only in so far as I'd come all this way to see him. I had intended going to Scotland for my leave."

"And, if I may apologize both to you and Major Travers, what did you come here for this morning?"

He put the question with such obvious humour that Passenden took no offence

"Well, I came for two reasons. One was that I couldn't get hold of Colonel Brende this morning, but I got Major Travers instead, so I thought I'd call and see if Major Travers had any news." Then he smiled rather wryly. "The other thing's more serious. Last night I was collared by the police."

"Oh?" said Wharton, and smiled broadly.

"Yes. I put up at the *George* as Major Travers advised me, and just before I thought of turning in, I thought I'd stroll as far as the Hall. Sentimental reasons and—"

"At what time would that be?"

"Oh, I should say I left at about ten-thirty and I took my time. I had a good look all round, and then I got under a tree when the blitz started. Then I thought I'd walk back through the City, but when I got to the side road I saw some coves sitting under the hedge, and I thought: 'By Jove, these chaps are Home Guard! They'll ask me for a pass or something, and I haven't got one.' So I nipped through a gap to make a detour. I got out on a meadow and I ran slap bang into a couple of cops. They wanted to know who I was and asked to see my identity card." He shrugged his shoulders. "And that was that. They—or one of them—went back with me to the *George* and found me all right so far, and I also gave Major Travers's name as a reference. So I thought I'd better come here and explain."

Wharton nodded benignly. "And what time was it when the cops nabbed you?"

"Can't say. Probably well after one in the morning. I didn't mind how late it was because they gave me a key at the hotel. By the way, the cops were looking for baled-out airmen. Huns."

"And did you see anything else extraordinary? Or hear anything?"

Passenden rather stared, then shook his head.

"Not that I can remember."

"I see." Wharton nodded once or twice, pursed his lips, then leaned forward impressively.

"Major Passenden, I'm going to tell you a secret. You'll give me your word that it *will* be a secret?"

"Most certainly."

"You see," said Wharton as if to himself, "I can't handle you as I would an ordinary sort of person. I can't tell you that I have the power to take drastic action if a word of this gets out."

"All the same, you *are* telling me," cut in Passenden.

"Oh, come, come," said Wharton. "You mustn't take things that way. Still, there we are. The secret I have to tell you is this."

I said Passenden was a quiet sort of chap, who gave the impression that nothing would rattle him. He wasn't rattled then, but he was extraordinarily interested—up to a point, as I was later to recall. After that he tried to appear politely interested, and no more.

"Kidnapped. But how amazing!" was his comment when Wharton had finished "Someone didn't want him to go on with that job he was doing."

"Tell Major Passenden what makes it even more amazing," Wharton said to me.

I told him, and very fully. I showed him the lay-out of the sentries and patrols, and showed how the presence of Cross's men made an exit from the building even more difficul   It was then that once more he began to be less interested. It was his own thoughts that were worrying him, not my disclosures.

"And now do you recall anything strange you heard or saw?" Wharton wanted to know.

Passenden only shook his head again. Then the conversation came to one of those queer full-stops, and Passenden said he would be going. If he recalled anything he would let us know. I assured him that I'd clear him with the local police.

"And now you're bound for Scotland?" Wharton asked.

"I shall try to see Mrs. Brende first, he said. "I'll get her to meet me in the town. Probably to-morrow morning I shall start for Scotland." He gave a quick look. "I suppose there'll be nothing in the papers about this?"

Wharton's look was one of horror. Not a word would be let out to a soul, and heaven help any of the few who let out what they knew.

"Mrs. Brende knows?" Passenden asked.

"Yes," Wharton said. "But you're not to let on that you know. She knows the need for secrecy, and she's a woman of discretion."

No sooner had he gone than Wharton was asking if he might use my phone. I left him at it and went to see Harrison. He had various papers for me to sign, and then I had to swear him to secrecy and say that something had gone wrong with the guards the previous night, which was all I could let out. He must have thought me somewhat offhand but he said readily enough that he'd have assembled for me at eighteen hours that night every man who had been on guard at the Hall. I assured him it was a private affai and nothing for him to worry about. Then we discussed the report to Command on Cross's show, and I went back to the offic   Wharton was still phoning, so I strolled round the Camp. It was another quarter of an hour before Wharton had finished No sooner had he hung up than a call was coming for me. It was Benison. Could I see him that afternoon at any time to suit myself. I said would three o'clock do, and we agreed on that.

"What on earth does he want?" I said to Wharton.

"Ask him about that picket of his on the road last night," Wharton said.

"I will," I said. "And what did you think of Passenden?"

"Fine looking soldier."

"Dammit, George, can't you ever come straight to a point?" I said irritably. "What did you think of his evidence?"

"What's the good of my answering?" countered George. "When I hinted he might have given you that crack on the skull, you pooh-poohed the idea. Now it turns out he was at the right spot at the right time."

"Leaving that," I said, "what did you think of him?"

"Well, there was a discrepancy in his evidence. He told you he had urgent business with Brende, and just now he said he hadn't. Also he was more occupied with what he was thinking himself than what we were telling him. That chap knows something. I'd even go so far as to say he knows a lot."

"Funny," I said, "but I thought the same thing."

"He's one of those strong, silent men," George went on. "If he hadn't been what he is, I'd have said he was thumbing his nose at us, as much as to say, 'I know a hell of a lot, but I'm not going to tell you, and you can't make me.'"

"But can we make him—I mean, if what you think is true?"

"Within a very few hours there'll be a man on his tail," Wharton said. "That's as far as we can go at present."

I nodded. "Let's hope Passenden doesn't spot him. But about the whole affair George. Got any ideas? If you have, you're far ahead of me."

George was getting to his feet and saying that he would have to get home and do some real telephoning. He appeared to remember my question as an afterthought.

"Ideas, did you say? Don't know that I have. A couple of questions I'd like an answer to, though."

I knew I was expected to ask what they were, so I did.

"Well, you tell me this," he said. "Why should the drawers of the desk be prised open when Colonel Brende—unconscious, mind you—had the keys in his pocket?"

I could only say it beat me.

"And why should the safe be shut? I know it wasn't locked, but it was shut, and the picture put in front of it. If a person searching the rooms is in all that hurry that he throws everything about, why the sudden craze for neatness over the safe?"

"Don't know," I said. "Unless—"

George cut in hurriedly as he made for the door.

"Don't tell me. I know what your theories are. Not worth a damn. All the same, if you fin a real answer, let me know. And let me know what happens with Benison this afternoon."

Off he went. I heaved a sigh, then pulled out my pipe. Then the telephone went again. This time the police wanted me. Only enquiries about Passenden, so I soon satisfie them.

"Anything new about those Buxton parachutists?" I asked.

"We haven't heard any more," I was told. "We don't think they've been caught yet. This is fin country to hide away in for days."

"It certainly is," I said.

"Also we've been busy. What do you think the latest is, sir?"

"Lord knows!" I said.

"Only a burglary at the Institute—Mr. Benison's Institute. Someone broke in last night and he's raising Cain."

CHAPTER IX
SLOW GOING

AFTER an earl y lunch that Sunday I had a short nap, and when I woke, that head of mine was feeling better. A tepid bath and a change into civilian clothes helped still more, and I made up my mind that I would walk to the City to see Benison. As it was not yet time to start off I rang Cross and managed to get hold of him.

He gave me the information which I wanted. His men had entered the park at two points only: three men and himself through the hedge not far from the back entrance, and the others over the wall at a spot plumb opposite. These men were to make a feint, and generally create a diversion so that the four could penetrate at the rear of the servants' quarters. It was soon after midnight when the attempt had been made, with the disastrous results for them that you know. As for his men seeing or hearing anything unusual, Cross said he was sure they hadn't, since every man had made a report and the exercise and lessons to be learned from it had been thoroughly discussed that very morning, which was parade day for the Home Guard.

"Now a very ticklish question," I said, "and I'm sorry I can't give reasons for asking it. Are you dead plumb sure of the bona fide of every one of the men who were with you?"

He wasn't any too pleased, as I'd anticipated.

"Didn't we go into that last night? I'd trust any one of them with anything and anywhere."

"Good," I said. "You see, if I make a report on the stunt to Command, Command may ask me if I was sure of men who had been allowed inside a prohibited area."

"I get you," he said. "But they're good fellows, every one of them. Tell Command to ask me, and I'll tell them."

Well, that was that. Cross hadn't any fift columnist who'd used the stunt to facilitate the kidnapping, though one still couldn't be dead sure. After all, it's the primary duty of a Hun agent to get himself accepted as British to the marrow, and Cross might have been deceived. But what did rather depress me was the knowledge that Cross's men had been grouped and not strung out. You get the idea. They didn't form a cordon through which the kidnapper and Brende had to pass, and therefore they could be discounted as deterring agents. In fact, they might even have facilitated the kidnapping. That feint of theirs must have certainly succeeded to some extent in attracting the attention of sentries and patrols.

No church bell was ringing as I neared the City, but it seemed that Sunday-school was in session, for children were entering the church gate as I walked up to the vicarage door. Benison was waiting for me, and who should be with him but Sir Hereward Dove. I didn't like that old man. Physically his paunchiness repelled me, and there was a crumbiness about him as if a short inspection of his waistcoat would reveal the history of his recent meals. He had also the habit of making sucking noises with his teeth, as if those meals still lingered on his palate.

Benison was making himself most agreeable, with apologies for bringing me over and enquiries as to how I was settling down. Then at last we got to the matter in hand, which was the burglary. It appeared that the vicarage had been broken into as well as the Institute.

"Fortunately nothing was taken," Dove put in. He had a heavy, guttural voice and spoke slowly. "And I may say, for an excellent reason. There was nothing to take."

"Nothing?" I said.

"Sir Hereward means there was nothing here which they were looking for," explained Benison. "What they thought they'd find was subversive literature, or evidence to make our little movement into some traitorous organization."

"What leads you to think that?" I asked politely.

"Doesn't it follow?" Dove said. "The two burglaries had the same object. Neither the Institute nor here, if my good friend Benison will pardon me, contains anything to attract a burglar."

"And where do I come in?" I asked with a Whartonian attempt at humour.

"Of course, of course," Dove said. "Show him that message, Benison."

The message was a typewritten one, delivered through the post and reaching Benison on the Saturday morning.

Dear Sir,

I have information that another attempt is going to be made by a small body of roughs to set fir to your Institute, and to spread placards and posters about. To throw dust in your eyes, the gang is coming not from the town way but the other way from the direction of the

Hall. I cannot tell you how I got this information, but it is O.K., and I advise you to put a spoke in their wheel by collaring them before they do any mischief. Though you don't know me, I owe a good deal to you, and I am glad to repay you in this way. Good luck to you and your cause.

A Friend.

"So that was why you had that picket out last night," I said.

"Yes," said Benison, and looked more grim than confused. "We talked the matter over"—he and Dove, he apparently meant—"and we took the advice in the letter. And pretty fools we were to fall into the trap. While our men were out there, the burglaries were being committed."

"I don't know," I couldn't help saying. "It's a very plausible letter. It has just the right amount of flatter in it, and it reads genuine. But may I ask just where I'm personally concerned?"

"The local police have refused to give extra police protection," Dove said. "They've always been hostile and they say they're insufficient staffe as it is. So if we put in an application to the Military Authorities, should we have your backing?"

I ducked for the long grass at once. Dove's huge fish eyes were on me, and Benison's look was one of wary anticipation, and I had the sudden and certain feeling that the two were laying some snare for my trusting feet.

"But didn't I understand that you've nothing of value to protect?" I said.

"The Institute's valuable property," Benison said. "If it were burnt down—and this letter shows we've clever and determined men to deal with—then it couldn't be rebuilt in wartime."

I might have said a whole lot. I could have pointed out, for instance, the cool impudence of asking for military to protect peacemongers and mischief-makers, and allow them to continue their activities in security. What I did say was something different

"Sorry. I'm afraid I'm not with you. I couldn't do anything in any case till the authorities have asked for my views. Then I should say that I haven't the men available, and, frankly, I should hint at surprise that the military were about to be used to guard non-military objects."

"Somehow I thought you'd say that," Benison said. The suspicion of a smile went over his lean face, and I thought to myself that if he shoo'd the bees out of his cassock, he could be a very likeable man. "But one other thing. I suppose you get all sorts of men in your Camp?"

My eyes narrowed, and I saw what he was driving at.

"I'm afraid I can't discuss that," I said. "But we do have all sorts. If men are called up by ages, we not only get the law-abiding. We must get a few burglars."

Dove was looking at me in no approving way. There was the dangerous man of the two, I thought, and there was the money that had set Benison on his feet and bought his car. All the same I couldn't see old Dove climbing wisteria in the dead of night, even with a seven-course dinner at the top.

"Why'd you ask me that?" I went on. "Do you think the burglary was committed by my men?"

"Not at all," Benison said hastily. "It was just an idea that occurred to us. We've had no burglaries here before."

I had the idea that that was all, and got to my feet.

"One thing I would like to ask you," I said, "and it's if that picket of yours saw or heard anything unusual last night."

Then I had to explain guardedly what I mean by "unusual." Benison said he would enquire and let me know. I said goodbye to Sir Hereward, but before he could hoist himself out of his chair, Benison and I were out of the room.

"Sir Hereward's not so active as he was," I said.

"His principles are active enough," Benison said. "That man, Major Travers, is of the stock from which martyrs were made."

I nodded politely.

"If it comes to that," I said, "quite a lot of people nowadays are ready to die for convictions."

He shook his head over me rather than at me, as if I were a brand hard to pluck from the burning. I saw him still shaking his head as he turned back to the vicarage door, and I was soon doing a bit of thinking too. Was everything what it had appeared?

What was the trap those two had been laying for me? Whatever it was, I had the feeling that in having any dealings whatever with them, I was running grave risks. In the future I determined to have nothing to do with either of them except over the phone, and then I'd take an immediate note of what was said.

As for any connection between that pair and the kidnapping of Colonel Brende, the more I thought, the less I could see. Benison might have threatened in an angry moment, and egged on by old Dove, to take what action seemed to him necessary to stop the work at the Hall, but I never went so far as to imagine he would be concerned in a major act of treason. It was the old story of refusing to believe in the fantastic even in fantastic times, though I did admit that both burglaries and the anonymous letter might be Benison's own fabrications, and therefore that picket of his had been there for quite a differen purpose from the one which the anonymous letter made seem so obvious.

I had walked on through the City in the direction of the Hall, and I all at once made up my mind to have another look for myself at the grass verge by the side gate of the park. If Brende had been unconscious, he could hardly have been carried through a scarcely visible gap in a thorn hedge, or hoisted over the wall; and if that side door had been used, then the car by which his abductors had taken him away had been waiting there for him.

As I came round the bend by the gate, somebody tried to get out of sight. It was Wharton, and he was too late. He pretended that he didn't know it was I, and showed great pleasure at my appearance.

"Don't walk there!" he said, and grasped my arm. I looked down to see he had been making a plaster cast of some tyre marks, and the plaster was setting.

"Better go through here," he said, and, to my surprise, put a key in the door and opened it.

No sooner were we through, and peering under the hanging boughs to make sure we were unobserved from the house, than a car was seen leaving by the drive.

"A taxi," Wharton said. "Would that be Mrs. Brende going off to see Passenden?"

"That'll be it," I said. "There is a pass issued to a local fir   of car proprietors."

Then he asked me what had happened at the vicarage and I told him in detail.

"All seems open and above-board to me," he said. "I think I know those two gentlemen by this time."

Then he was shooting a queer look at me.

"What's up?" I said. "Thought of something?"

"Yes," he said. "That Major Passenden's a liar, and I can prove it. Of the two Brendes, it was Mrs. Brende he knew best, isn't that so? Right then. When he found Colonel Brende was away from the Hall, why didn't he ask to see Mrs. Brende? He told us this morning he only wanted a chat. Why didn't he want that chat yesterday? Because he had important business with the Colonel, and he didn't want Mrs. B. to know."

"Hold hard," I said. "I think I know why he wanted to speak with the Colonel sort of secretly. He'd got wind of the fact that the two were going their own ways. As a friend of the family, he was distressed, and he wanted to be tactful."

"You and your theories," Wharton said with the profoundest contempt. "If that's true, why couldn't he be as frank with us as we were with him? I tell you the man's a liar. I can smell him from here."

Another grunt or two and he was going forward. Before I could even wonder where, he was stopping and drawing something carefully out of the ground. It was another cast, this time of a heel of a woman's shoe.

"None too good," he said, having a close look at it. "Women's heels are all the same nowadays. I doubt if I'll ever be able to pin this on anybody."

"You've only two choices in the house," I said. "Mrs. Brende and Penelope Craye."

He glared. "What about that Annie? And there's a cook and another maid."

I had to agree, and, having Penelope in my mind, decided to confess something.

"George, I've been deceiving you about Penelope Craye."

He peered at me. "Deceiving me, or your wife?"

"Nothing like that," I said, and told him most of what I knew about Penelope in the past. It was also my opinion that she had wriggled herself into the Hall by means of influence dating from the days of the old Dilly-Dally Government gang who'd hoped complacently to win the war off their own private bat, and without folding up their sleeves.

"Now I'll tell you something," Wharton said. "The old man isn't napping all the time, though you appear to think so. That wad of papers in her room wasn't a wad. It was a note-book! Why was she burning a note-book?"

I didn't know, and George didn't want an answer in any case, for he was opening the door again and passing me through. The cast of the tyre had set and he regarded it with a certain pleasure.

"A pretty big car," he said. "Tyres well worn, and this rather nasty cut. Lucky I'm in the car business. Before to-night's gone I'll know a lot about that car."

He was going to the town at once, he said, so I thought I'd accompany him. Just as our car was creeping round that sharp curve, Penelope Craye's fast little car shot into the main road ahead of us. George, both hands grasping the steering-wheel like grimmest death, tried to catch her up or at least keep her in sight. Her car went straight on past the City turn towards the town, and then she outdistanced us. When we drew near that tea-shop, her car was parked outside. George said he had business through the back door of the police-station, so would I stay in the car and keep an eye on her. His gang of plain-clothes men were not due till a later train, which was really why he had come to the town.

George came back and she had not left the tea-shop. In fiv minutes, however, she was getting into her car again. Once more George moved ours off but a hundred yards down the road she turned sharp left. When we got to the turn, George had to wrench round his wheel and keep to the main road, for her car was outside a garage just round that corner, and she was going off on foot along the side road. George drew our car up at the kerb and hopped out.

A good quarter of an hour later a small boy came shyly to the door and gave me a note. It was from George, saying I was to take the car back to my Camp, and he'd call for it later.

You may remember that I was due to interview the men who had been on guard at the Hall the previous night. Harrison had them assembled in a dining-hut, and I told him I'd do the job myself. First I tried a liberal use of commendation, praising the whole bunch for their keenness and the way they'd scuppered the Home Guard, who, I revealed, had been all picked men.

Next I tried something more crafty. When they knew the Home Guard had been on a stunt and duly discovered, did they forgather round the house to compare notes and rejoice, as it were?

They were too wary birds to admit that, but I was told that two patrol men took the prisoners to main guard, and so the actual guarding of the building was weakened to that extent till they returned, which was in about ten minutes.

"Now another question," I said. "Naturally we all want to do this job as well as possible, and it's up to all of us to fin loopholes in the defence because the Home Guard might have another crack at us. So let's look at things from what we know ourselves and from their point of view at the same time. In other words, is there any man here who fancies his chance of getting through our cordon?"

There was a buzz of talk and then one stocky little chap got to his feet and said he could.

"Good," I said. "You'd be prepared to make the attempt, even if the guard knew an attempt was going to be made?"

"Yes, sir," he said doggedly.

"Even if the conditions were that you forfeited a week's pay if you lost?"

There was a laugh at that, but he held his ground.

"Right," I said, and dismissed the parade. But the volunteer I kept back, and we had a friendly talk. His idea was that he'd firs of all black his face and hands, and he'd wear rubber-soled shoes. In some places there was a lawn between the sentries and the house, and he'd choose one of them on which to slip across. I remembered then that there had been nothing but lawn beneath Brende's window, but the dry winds had hardened it so that it would have been wasted time to look for footmarks.

"And then what?" I said.

Then he would wait till a patrol moved along, he said, and in a flas he'd be across behind him. And he'd be fla on his belly at once, in case he showed up against the house.

Well, I thought I'd try him out, and that very night, so I asked if he'd keep a still tongue in his head till a quarter-past nine, when I'd smuggle him into the park in my car. If he got through he was on a quid, and if he failed he stood to lose nothing. He was all for it, so I told him to report to my offi at nine o'clock, his burnt cork with him.

On Sunday nights there was cold supper instead of dinner. I disposed of a meal and still there was no sign of Wharton. Nine o'clock came, and my volunteer, and Wharton had neither turned up nor phoned. Then by the time the volunteer was ready, Wharton was phoning. He hoped to be along at any minute, and he wanted to see me urgently.

I waited half an hour, then sent for the R.S.M. and explained all about the volunteer to him. Then I had a further idea, with which went the offe of a further quid. In fact, I wanted him to get through the sentries and then climb the wisteria into Colonel Brende's bedroom. Then I made it even more difficul Let both him and the R.S.M. get through into the bedroom and back again. The R.S.M. was keen as mustard. All he wanted was a few minutes to make preparations. I said he could take my car, and as soon as the stunt was over he was to ring me from main guard.

It was nearly ten o'clock when Wharton did turn up, and he said he could stay no more than a minute. What he wanted to see me about particularly was the conference which was on in the morning at eleven hours. At least three Big Bugs, he said, would be there, and I'd better be there too.

"We've got to put our heads together," he said, "and decide what to let out and what to keep under our hats. For instance, if I were you I wouldn't say a word about that crack on the skull."

"Why not?"

He looked quite hurt. "Well, it wouldn't look very well for the Commandant to be inspecting a stunt and to let himself get cracked on the skull. I'm only trying to do you a service."

"And I'm grateful," I said dryly. Then the phone went, and it was the R.S.M. In his tone were both satisfaction and regret.

"We pulled it off sir, and then went and got caught on the way back. Sheer bad luck, sir. We waited till a patrol went by and nipped back behind him, but he hadn't gone on. I reckon he was scrimshanking, but he says he was going back to tell the sentry something he'd forgot."

"Good enough," I said. "Tell me more about it later."

I told Wharton what I'd been up to. He didn't look any too pleased, and suggested I'd better keep that under my hat too at the conference. I had to smile.

"And what about you?" I said. "What are you keeping dark?"

"All about Major Passenden for one thing," he said. "What are you clicking your tongue for?"

"Forget it," I said. "I did have a theory about Passenden, but as it's only a theory, you wouldn't be interested."

"But why not?" he asked with virtuous indignation.

"Never mind," I said, and told him the theory about Passenden being the author of the anonymous letters that had so accurately predicted the kidnapping. George's look of interest was what I call his bellicose one.

"I get you. That's why he came down here instead of going to Scotland—to see Brende personally. Lucky I've got a man on his tail."

When I asked what had delayed him in the town, he said it was the arrival of his men for one thing, and preliminary work over the next day's conference for another. Then he was getting to his feet and grumbling about my having kept him.

"What about the lady you were following?" I asked as we went out to his car.

He did some tongue-clicking.

"Disappointing. Thought I was on something good. She's got a little fla quite near that garage. Had it only a week."

"Why shouldn't she have a little place of her own?" I said. "She must have been bored to tears at the Hall. But where did the disappointment come in?"

"I put a man on the job," he said. "Thought perhaps there might have been some carryings-on. Not a bit of it. Far as I can make out there's never been a man there. And she's using her own name."

He was in the car, so I thought comment would be unheard. Then, as he was ready to move off he put his head out.

"One or two other things I'm keeping under my hat, by the way. What's worrying those three brainy ones at the Hall, for instance, and how Master Ledd has something on his mind."

Then with a wave of the hand he was going. George, I thought, did certainly think of things. Those three at the Hall had struck me as being not only worried but somewhat scared. And yet, I thought to myself as I strolled back to the offic   there was every reason why the three should be alarmed. Perhaps the Hall would close down now as a research station. Even if Newton had so unexpectedly stated that things would go on as before, they just couldn't go on as before. And what about that discovery which Brende had made? Brende was not a loose talker. If he had announced he was at last really on to something big, then that something was lost for good and all if nothing more was ever seen of Brende.

I was rather depressed that night when I turned in. The seriousness of things had a grip on me, and I knew they must be worrying Wharton too. If Brende's discovery were lost, or if, worse still, it got into the wrong hands, then the consequences would be incalculable. The thought of that conference did me little good too. If the dear old W.O. was represented, anything might happen, and I might be the very scapegoat needed. One thing only did cheer me up: the thought that whatever it was, that conference would not be dull. Wharton would see to that.

CHAPTER X
BIG BUGS

I WAS ver y hot and bothered when I arrived at that conference, and this is why. Like many a better man before me, I trusted too much to the infallibility of my car. When I got into it, it was still a quarter to eleven, which allowed ample time to get to the Hall and be nicely early. Then something went wrong and she wouldn't start. I sweated and fussed for fiv minutes, and then young Craye happened to go by. I've no false pride, thank heaven, and I made no bones about calling him in.

He agreed with me that the trouble lay in the carburettor.

"Ten minutes and we can put it right, sir."

"Ten minutes is no good to me," I said. "I ought to be at the Hall in under fiv minutes' time."

"I'll fi that, sir," he said, and was off at the double. Next he was coming back in a car he'd borrowed from another office   I got in, and almost forgot my attaché case, and off we went.

"I haven't seen you for some time, Craye," I said, and then remembered. "You've been on leave, haven't you?"

"Long week-end, sir."

"Have a good time?"

"Very, sir."

He was a good driver and I told him so. Then he let on that he'd wanted to be a racing driver, and he'd put in spells at various works. As we came through the main gate I said I supposed he was often at the Hall. He grinned and was very frank.

"I generally see my aunt about once a week, sir, but I don't think the Colonel loves me very much. That's why I usually drive in the back way." He grinned again. "Rather one in the eye for him, sir, if he sees me acting as your chauffeur.

He brought the car round in an elegant sweep and we were at the front door. I told him I was very grateful as we'd made it with a minute to spare.

"That's all right, sir," he said. "If you ring up the Camp when you want to come back, sir, I'll come along for you. Your case, sir. You've forgotten your case."

So I had, and the grin I gave was a bit sheepish. Then I found I needn't have worried after all. Wharton hadn't told me that there was a preliminary conference at ten hours thirty, and it was still in session. It was a quarter of an hour later before I was called in.

Now I'm not going to bore you with details of that conference. There shall be no reports of speeches, no arguments, and no going over again of ground we have already trodden. As far as I can make it, everything shall be brand new, and with some bearing on the case.

Wharton had said there would be three Big Bugs at least, and there were actually four. In addition, Squadron-Leader Pattner was there, and a special stenographer. I daren't think what would happen to me if I divulged names, and some of the things that were talked about, but when I think of it I recall a picture I saw in my youth, with Dreyfus on his last ignominious parade and a fat French General ripping the buttons off his tunic.

Three of the four had handles to their names. There was a brass-hat—gunner—from the War House, a high offici of the Air Ministry, the head of a Government Research Department, and a Home Offi representative. I shall allude to them as Gunner, Air, Hush, and Home. In fact, when you come to think things over, I was very much the louse in that collection of Big Bugs, for George Wharton was a mighty important person, and Newton was even more so, even if one judged only by the deference the four paid him.

The headquarters of the conference, which was something of a Court of Enquiry, were in the downstair offic which had been swept and garnished, and the dart-board removed, though I was somewhat amused to see copious marks of darts on the wainscot surround. What I at once gathered was that visits had already been paid to the upstair rooms and the outside grounds, for almost the firs thing that happened was that Home read me the general conclusions at which the conference had arrived. These were that Brende had been kidnapped by persons unknown.

Pretty obvious, you may think, but after all, the enquiry was to establish itself on some sort of basis. The next thing was that I was called on to explain the steps taken for the security of the building and grounds. I was well provided with documents, thank heaven, and when I had finished Gunner gave me a clean bill of health on the spot. Home, with a humour of which I had not suspected him, said he'd probably be advising that the Royal Family should change quarters at once.

"Is that all, gentlemen?" I said, when I'd replaced my documents.

Wharton whispered quickly to Home, who whispered to Hush. Hush asked me to remain, so down I sat again at the side table from which I had spoken. Then Newton was called in. What happened was this, and if there is repetition of anything you already know, consider it deliberate on my part. There were certain nails in the case which cannot be hit too hard and too often on the head. I would like you to remember too that Newton —modest, shy and very human—had his opinions treated with enormous respect. As one of the most distinguished of living scientists, he was entitled to no less.

I can't breathe a word of his report on his work, in which Wissler and Riddle were closely collaborating, also I didn't even understand a quarter of the terms he was using, especially when he directed himself to Hush and Gunner. What I gathered generally was this. The original ideas, the importance of which had at the time been recognized by all concerned—and especially by the W.O.—had been put forward by Colonel Brende, who had frankly stated his inability, brilliant mathematician though he was, to carry on into what I term guardedly—and perhaps erroneously—the realm of pure physics. That was why Newton and his collaborators had taken over, with the Colonel as nominal head.

But the Colonel was far too restless a person, and with far too alert a brain, to remain inactive, or merely a nominal head.

He had other ideas, and he was working on them privately, in that upstair offi of his. What they were, Newton had no idea.

"He had a special note-book," Newton said, "and when he was very pleased with himself, he would come down here and wag it at us. He used to say he'd have us so-called experts all beaten yet. He did that on Saturday evening, only this time he hinted he really did have us beaten."

"In other words, he'd really discovered something big," put in Hush.

"Well—yes," said Newton hesitatingly.

"Did you ever have a look at that note-book?" asked Gunner.

"Well—yes," said Newton again. That hesitating manner of his was something of an irritation. "I mean, he once flippe the pages over in front of me, like this, and I saw he'd been going pretty deeply into—well, I hardly know how to put it. Advanced mathematics shall we say."

"He wasn't anything of a physicist?" asked Home.

"I don't know," said Gunner. "I came down here, as you know, to report progress, and Colonel Brende let me have a look at that book of his." He leaned forward towards Newton. "A brown book, something like the old Field Service book."

"That was the one," Newton confirmed

"Well, it had things in it that were far beyond me," Gunner said. "I could get the hang of some of it, but not much. I know there were some very interesting diagrams, and it struck me he'd been dipping pretty deeply into physics."

"I'm sorry if I gave the wrong impression," Newton cut hastily and nervously in. "After all, there is what I might call physics and physics. I mean, it isn't a closed book, so to speak. We all do some physics at school."

Then Home came in with a most unusual and, to me, unexpected question. Was Newton himself, from private observation and contacts, perfectly satisfie about Wissler?

Newton answered with no hesitation or nervousness. While he claimed no infallibility, he'd vouch for the genuineness of Wissler's feelings towards both this country and Germany, and his wholehearted desire to give this country the benefi of his knowledge.

"But this business of his visits to the man Benison," Hush said. "On two occasions he called at the vicarage, and the last time he remained there for over an hour."

That voice was the voice of Wharton, as I couldn't help guessing. One other person seemed highly interested, and that was Pattner, whom I was meeting for the firs time. He was a sturdily built chap of about forty, with as nice a beard as I've seen for a long time.

"That was over a month ago," Newton said. "I had a word with him about it. I own that I didn't say anything to Colonel Brende. The Colonel rather saw red when Benison's name was mentioned, and I didn't want Wissler upset. The truth is as I've already reported privately, that Benison approached Wissler. He wanted him to give a lecture at his Institute. Wissler isn't conversant with our—well, subterranean movements. He acted in quite good faith. I think he even considered himself very flattered And he thought the lecture would be one in the eye for the Hun, so to speak."

"And he hasn't seen Benison since?"

"Come, sir, come," Newton said with a quick dignity. "I'll not be questioned like that. Professor Wissler was free to go out, or to use the telephone, as I was. I'll enquire into no man's private actions unless I see very good cause."

"I'm sorry. You're quite right," Hush said, and that appeared to be all that was wanted from Newton, whose face was rather red as he went out.

The next to be called was Penelope Craye. When she came in she interchanged little smiles with Gunner and Hush, who seemed to be old friends. She was wearing that same demure grey, and anyone who hadn't known her would have seen the perfect secretary; quiet, competent, but still very much a woman. As for that last, I'd often been aware of her good looks, but I don't think I'd ever so realized what a handsome and attractive person Penelope Craye could appear. But when she went over the events of the Saturday night as far as concerned herself and Brende, I knew her little speech had been well rehearsed.

"You are still definitel of the opinion that he had discovered something big?" asked Air, speaking for almost the firs time.

"Oh, yes," she said unhesitatingly. "I'm sure by his manner it was something very important indeed."

"Did he flouris his note-book at you?" smiled Hush.

"Note-book?" She looked rather blank.

Hush explained, and she said she hadn't seen the note-book— at least not lately. She knew it, of course, but the Colonel had never shown it to her or discussed it.

"You're a relation by marriage of the Colonel?" Home said to her.

"Oh, but very, very distant," she protested, though somewhat archly.

"Still, shall we say there were private relationships and business ones? I mean that the Colonel might have chatted to you in private about things which he wouldn't mention in his office

"Oh, no," she said. "The Colonel never did that. I'm afraid he was rather a martinet." A shake of the head had accompanied that statement, and then was at once adding a rider. "Very nice to work with, of course. But perhaps I oughtn't to have said all that."

"But certainly," Home told her. "That's the very sort of thing we do want to know. And you yourself didn't go out at all on the Saturday night, I believe?"

I didn't see just what he was driving at, but when she had gone, the point was clear.

"That's the central point of this extraordinary business, gentlemen," Home told the conference. "The fact that Colonel Brende should disappear just when he'd made some vital discovery or other. Everything was so apposite. I can't help feeling that there's the solution of the whole thing—and more."

That was something which had occurred both to Wharton and myself. Indeed, it was a fact that stood out yards.

"When I say ' more '," Home was going on, "I mean that if espionage or worse is going on, the people concerned have been responsible for things in the past, and, unless they're caught, will be responsible for more in the future. But about Miss Craye. She never left this building on Saturday after she'd heard from Colonel Brende that he'd made his discovery." He cast a wary look round, but not at Wharton. The old General's eyes were demurely on the papers before him. "I rather gather that Miss Craye hasn't always been famous for discretion. I say that not unkindly. Though she never left here, there was still the telephone."

He went on to elaborate the theory. Newton and his two assistants had said nothing to a soul, if only because there had been no one with whom to speak but themselves, and they were not the kind of people who would telephone to friends that Colonel Brende had made an important discovery. Mrs. Brende knew nothing, and there remained only the staff particularly the Service staff who might have overheard something.

Pattner spoke for the firs time.

"Might I ask, sir, why you think *anybody* would telephone?"

Home shrugged his shoulders. "Human nature is human nature. The public have been led to believe that the night-bomber problem is near a solution. The fact that Colonel Brende thought he'd solved it would be an event of terrifi importance, not only to those who've been bombed and are certain to be so again, but to the whole conduct of the war. Even Dalebrink's been bombed. I maintain that it would be asking a lot of self-restraint to keep Colonel Brende's news to one's self." He shrugged his shoulders again. "That's all very obvious. We want to know who passed out the news that evening. That will bring us to who received the news, and decided on immediate action against Colonel Brende."

Then he was looking at me.

"Major Travers must be asked to supply Superintendent Wharton with all the documents of the men under his command who've been loaned for work here." Then he happened to glance at his watch, and he smiled somewhat ruefully. "I'm afraid it's almost two o'clock. Perhaps we should adjourn for lunch. I don't think we need keep Major Travers."

So that was the end of me as far as concerned that conference, and Wharton lent me his car to get back to Camp. As to my own impressions, I will say only this. I thought the members were shrewd, and highly competent people in their various lines, but I made an exception of Gunner. My old prejudice against the War House, you may say, but I honestly think you are wrong. After all, Gunner did compliment me on the disposal and handling of the guard, and in himself he seemed likeable enough. What I did think was that he was not up to the job in hand. That he should have been sent down earlier to report on the progress of the work at the Hall, when he was admittedly no physicist at all and no great shakes as a mathematician, seemed to me yet another example of the mishandling of which the W.O. can be capable. Hush was the man who should have been sent down, even if the W.O. had to borrow him.

The only other thing I would say is that Penelope's evidence was given with an adroitness of which I should never have believed her capable. To me it had the air of being a pack of lies from beginning to end, and yet if I had been challenged, I could not have mentioned a single lie. That she was a pretty good actress, I knew, but not up to the standard of that morning. I wondered too what the gentlemen of the conference would think if they ever saw Penelope with back arched and claws out, and listened to her command of language that would have made a commercial traveller blench.

After my belated meal, Harrison and I got to work on the records of those men of ours at the Hall, and we also called in the Company office   and colour sergeants concerned. The reasons I gave were the tightening up of hush-hush precautions at the Hall, and when the job was over we were all in agreement that every man would stand every possible scrutiny. By the time copies of documents were ready for Wharton, with the report, it was sixteen-thirty hours. I had had enough of being shut up in office   and as Harrison did not want to leave Camp, I thought

I'd run down to the town. Craye had left a chit to say he'd fixe
the carburettor and the car was now O.K.

There was quite a good library in the Camp, at least as far
as concerned the troops, but the books were somewhat grubby
from much handling, and far from being up to date. Bernice had
our subscription to the library in town, so I thought I'd join a
branch in Dalebrink. But fir t I was going to that special tea-
shop to stand myself a meal. As a matter of fact I didn't get as
far, and this is why.

As I got out of the car and cast the usual look round, I saw
Penelope Grave's little car just across the road, trying to cut
in between a bus and a horse van. It was going so slowly that
I clearly saw Pattner, and at once I remembered something.
Then her car had to dodge behind the bus to avoid an oncoming
vehicle, and it crawled as far as the turn. I shamelessly followed
on foot on my own side of the road, and I was level with the
turn when she shot her car into it. Past the garage it went, and
it was about a couple of hundred yards along the side road that
she drew it to a halt. She and Pattner got out, and went through
a gate and out of my sight. From what Wharton had told me, I
knew they were paying a visit to her flat

All sorts of things ran through my mind. In a highly guarded
way Pattner had stood up for Penelope by asking Home why
she should telephone the news about Brende's discovery to
any friends. Penelope had had that fla for only a week, and I
wondered why she had not hit on the idea before. Pattner's name
had also a foreign air, and then my finger went to my glasses.
But not because I had made a discovery; it was rather because I
knew I was making a fool of myself. Why shouldn't Pattner, or
any other man, be on friendly terms with so attractive a woman
as Penelope? As to thinking a man with Pattner's record guilty
of double-dealing or worse, that was sheer idiocy. And yet, I
couldn't help thinking that Pattner might be the guileless piece
of plasticine in Penelope's tricky hands.

Then happily I became aware that I was disgracing His
Majesty's uniform by standing in the middle of the pavement,
polishing my glasses and blinking like an idiot. But as I was

almost at the library I decided to walk on the few yards and have tea later. There were few people in the shop, and the library part upstairs was deserted except for one woman client. She appeared to be waiting for the assistant to fin her a book, and suddenly I knew who she was.

"What are you doing here, Annie?" I smiled at her.

"Collecting books for the mistress," she told me. "I always come in on Mondays by the bus."

"A nice little trip for you." I said, and then the assistant came out of the inner sanctum with a couple of books.

"Two for you," she said to Annie. "And will you tell Mrs. Brende that her list is getting rather low."

I've already told you I'm a curiosity-ridden busybody, so you won't be surprised that I looked at Annie's books. One, to my surprise, was a detective novel. Annie must have seen my lift of the eyebrows.

"The mistress likes those, sir," she said. "Mr. Howard"—it was young Howard Craye to whom she was referring—"lent her one and she told me she would never read it. Then she did, and she's been reading them ever since."

"Good," I said. "Even bishops read them, they tell me. And tell Mrs. Brende you saw me, will you?"

No sooner had she moved off than the girl was asking me if I was Major Travers. Then she was giving me a message. I had told Harrison where I was going, and he had got hold of the shop. Wharton, it appeared, wanted to see me, and would be at the Camp. Since he would probably be there by then, I apologized and bolted.

Wharton was at the Camp, but his business was not so urgent that I couldn't have had a cup of tea. Still, we had tea of sorts in my offic and I never saw two cups disappear so quickly as those that went down Wharton's throat. The conference had not closed down till after four o'clock, he told me. Home was staying on for the night, and he was to have a further conference with him later that evening.

Meanwhile what was being done was this. Every police-station in the country was being given confidentia news of the disappearance of Colonel Brende, with a photograph and a description both of the man and the clothes he was wearing. There was also being circulated a description of the tyre of which Wharton had taken the plaster cast, for that particular section, which had run across a handy molehill, showed certain recognizable peculiarities. But Wharton said frankly that he expected no results. A very minute fraction of cars could be examined with any care, and as for Colonel Brende, he was doubtless where the eye of the law would never run over him.

"Do you think he'll ever be seen again?" I asked George.

"Don't know," he said, and looked pretty serious. "Personally I very much doubt it. What might be discovered, and soon, is his body."

He also told me that he might be seeing very little of me for a day or two, as what with receiving and collating the reports of his men and having to be at the end of a telephone, he might be kept to the house. If anything important happened he would keep me informed, he said, and meanwhile he would take with him the report on those men of mine at the Hall. Nothing new had arisen out of the conference, and I had nothing to tell or suggest. I did think of mentioning Penelope and Pattner at the flat but since George had told me he was having her watched, I knew the information would reach him in due course.

Well, the next day went by, and the next. I saw nothing of George and heard nothing, though I did learn in a roundabout way that he had conducted a night experiment at the window of Colonel Brende's bedroom. Later I learned that it was one I'd thought of trying for myself—to discover whether the man with the fishing-ro could see the bed in the dark, and therefore hold the chloroformed wad in the right place.

It was not in fact till the Thursday night that I saw Wharton again, and before then things had happened to myself.

CHAPTER XI
MANY MYSTERIES

MY job at Dalebrink was not to assist George Wharton, even if it may have seemed that I was spending a considerable time in his company. But practically all that arose out of my duties as Commandant of Camp for which I was being paid. Mind you, I would not in the least have minded being on loan for a week or two, even instead of leave, for nothing so intrigues me and gnaws away at me as a mystery unsolved. When I had to spend the best part of three days without hearing from Wharton, I was worrying my wits over the affai whenever I had any leisure, and I was hunting for ways of tackling that case from the various angles that would keep occurring to me from time to time.

There was only one thing which I actually did do, and that seems too unimportant to mention. I had been thinking of the three experts at the Hall—the three who had been so carefree when I had fir t seen them, and so nervy and apprehensive after the disappearance of Brende. For Newton's worries I thought I could account, as I had already told Wharton. Wissler was different unless he was worrying about having to leave the Hall and work that must have been congenial. He might also have been scared about his dealings with Benison coming to Wharton's notice. But what had Riddle to be scared about? My firs impressions of him had been that he was resiliency itself. That red head of his was an oriflamm of optimism, and his grin a perpetual tonic. Could it be, I thought, that Master Riddle had a yellow streak? If work at the Hall were closed down, might not Riddle, who had been specially released for that research work, be reclaimed by the Army? And since the last place to put him was the firing-line wouldn't that be where he would be sent? Did Riddle apprehend all that, and was he dreading the recall?

Then I remembered another individual at the Hall who had gone all apprehensive and nervy too—Lance-Corporal Ledd. There was another example of high spirits and cheerfulness suddenly giving place to their opposites, though Ledd might also be genuinely worried about Colonel Brende, and still more about having to return to duty at the Camp. But thinking of Riddle and Ledd made me recall something they had had in common: each had left the Hall on the Saturday night, and for what had been stated was merely a walk.

Now I had the means of checking up on that, if only to a certain extent. At every guard hut at each prohibited area under our charge a record book was kept, giving the names of all owners of passes who entered and left, with times, and also the times of the visits of all inspecting office   including, of course, the orderly office   I take no credit for that admirable system which had been instituted by Harrison and my predecessor. Everything also that had happened at a post, including the above, was incorporated in the daily guard report. I did not therefore have to institute special enquiry to discover what had happened on Saturday night; all I had to do was consult the file of guard reports. What I read was this:

Booked out—Ledd 21.0 hours	Front Gate
Riddle—23.0 hours	Rear Gate
Booked in—Ledd 00.15 hours.	Front Gate
Riddle—00.45.	Rear Gate

Ledd had told Wharton he was not seeing his girl. What had he found to do then for three hours and more? Had he friends at the City? There were no buses at that hour to take him to the town, and Ledd hardly struck me as the sort of person who'd wander about alone on a dark night. Then who were his friends at the City? And, more to the point, had he told those friends about Colonel Brende's discovery, which he had overheard when Brende had spoken of it to Penelope? In any case, there was something that might be referred to Wharton, if he had not already thought of it himself.

As for Riddle, his tale seemed true. He had gone out and returned at the times he had given, and that rear gate led to open country. That guard report also showed that Penelope had not left the Hall that night, and that led me to look her up for previous nights. What I ascertained was interesting. Until the time of the taking of that flat she had rarely been absent from the Hall at night. During the week she had been in possession of the flat she had been out for the whole of three nights, and had returned at about eight-thirty in the morning. I confess I attached no particular importance to all that. After all, the fla was a new toy, and there would probably be work to do—curtains, decorating, and so on—that would keep her too late to return to the Hall.

And so to the happenings of that Thursday—the day I was to see Wharton again. The firs was an urgent chit sent from local headquarters. It was really a circular sent to all units, and it reached us, therefore, as no special orders referring to us alone. Special look-out was to be kept, it said, for three Germans who had baled out of that plane at about twenty-three-thirty hours on the Saturday night, and had not yet been apprehended. Before I had read that chit a second time, I was having the most fantastic theory. There had been no mention of the crashing of the plane from which the airmen had baled out. Why then should they not have been dropped for a special purpose? The crew of the plane had surely numbered four. If three baled out, then the pilot carried on and returned the plane to its base. And if three picked agents had been dropped, why not for the purpose of contacting home agents? Why not for the express purpose of sabotage or other action against the Hall?

Fantastic it may sound, but things far more fantastic have happened since. My measure of belief in my own theory is shown by the fact that I nearly grabbed the phone to submit it to Wharton, but when I actually saw him I didn't even have the temerity to mention it at all.

It was just before lunch-time when a call came for me from the Hall, and to my surprise it was Mrs. Brende. I was even more surprised when she asked if I were alone.

"The telephone's perfectly safe," I told her laughingly, and it rather struck me that she had absent-mindedly forgotten that we were using the phone.

"People sometimes overhear," she said. "I want you to do something for me, and I'd like you to keep it just to ourselves. Could you possibly put a guard over my bedroom?"

"But"—I'm afraid I rather stammered for a bit—"I don't quite follow. Look here. May I come round and see you about it? Confidentially of course."

"Oh, no," she said promptly. "I'm not going to have you laughing at me to my face. I can be much more bold and persistent over the telephone."

"You're really serious?" I said. "You want a guard posted over your bedroom?"

"I do. I know I'm a silly, nervous old woman, but I'd be happier."

I gave a grunt or two while I collected my thoughts. There had been no humour in her voice to show that that self-deprecation was some sort of joke, and Mrs. Brende was the last person in the world to be put in the categories in which she had just placed herself.

"Then I'm frightfully sorry," I said, "but it can't be done. I have to account for every one of my men, and I simply daren't put one over your room. What I can do is this," I hastily went on, "I can have a man outside your window. Your room has a sound lock to it?"

"I think so," she said.

"Then everything should be all right," I told her. "And— you'll pardon my suggesting it—you might have Annie or someone sleep in your room with you."

There was quite an interval before she spoke. Then she said, and she sounded enormously grateful, that she was now much easier in mind.

"You'll have the man put outside to-night?"

"Yes," I assured her. "I'll see to it at once. And will you pardon another personal question. Just why are you so alarmed? Or aren't you?"

"Well, after what's happened," she began lamely, and then broke off "I told you I was foolish and nervous."

"You've been reading too many detective novels," I laughed at her. To my relief she laughed too.

"I expect that's what it is. Annie told me she'd seen you yesterday, by the way."

"Oh, yes," I said. "I caught her in the act of aiding and abetting. But you do as I say from now on and there's no need to be alarmed."

"There's no news, I suppose?"

"Not a thing," I said. "If I do hear anything, I'll let you know. Good-bye, then. And no more worry."

There was a peculiar sound in the phone as if she were clearing her throat or half-formulating a word. Then she did speak.

"Are you still there?"

"Yes."

"I wonder if you'd do something else for me. Very confidentially You won't laugh at me?"

"Why should I?"

"Well, it's this," she said. "If you have a spare revolver, would you lend it to me?"

Once more I was taken pretty considerably aback.

"A revolver's a dangerous lethal weapon," I managed to say. "Are you sure you can handle it?"

"Oh, yes," she said confidently "When we were in India I did quite a lot of shooting. We had a little indoor range, you know."

I did a grunt or two to make time.

"I have got a little automatic of my own," I said. "What I'll do is send it along unloaded, and a dozen rounds. By the way, you'd better send me a confidentia receipt."

"You *are* good," she said, "and I'm really very grateful. Whoever brings it, let him ask for Annie, and I'll have the receipt ready."

"Fine," I said. "And when am I coming to tea with you again?" She gave a little laugh.

"I'm not going to let you make fun of me—just yet. On Sunday perhaps. You're not busy on Sundays?"

As I hung up I was doing some hard thinking. Why Mrs. Brende should have these sudden alarms was beyond me, and as for her claims that she was a foolish old woman, nothing was further from possibility. Absolute coolness was one of her characteristics; moreover, she was definitel trying to avoid me for fear I should ask awkward questions. And yet I hardly knew. When all was said and done, she was a very lonely woman who must have suddenly become more lonely, and no loneliness can be more frightening than that of the dead of night.

After lunch I found that little automatic, cleaned and oiled it, and sent it by my batman together with a further confidentia note and a dozen rounds of ammunition. I also pencilled a draft amendment to the standing orders of the Park guard, and submitted it to Harrison with an explanation that seemed to convince. It was soon after that when a telephone call came from Holby and Caddis. The speaker said the name would probably convey little to me. I admitted it was unfamiliar.

"I'm John Holby," he said, "the senior partner. Our fir have handled Mrs. Brende's affair for a good many years now. What I want to do is to see her at the Hall to-morrow morning, on private business, and I understand I must have a pass."

While I hesitated he was going on again.

"I can give you every possible reference, Major Travers. I'm in the Home Guard myself, and so is my boy. I think you've run across him, by the way."

"It wasn't references I was thinking of, Mr. Holby," I said. "What I can't do is get you a pass through by the morning. What I can do is this. I've got a certain discretionary power to issue special passes. In other words, if you call here on your way tomorrow morning, we'll see what we can do."

"I understand," he said. "I'm very much obliged. Will about half-past ten suit you?"

"I shall be here," I said. "But I ought to put one question to you, even if I am anxious to oblige both yourself and Mrs. Brende. As I said to a recent applicant for a pass, why shouldn't the mountain come to Mahomet?"

He laughed. "I'd rather not put that to a client. Too much competition these days. But seriously, you're sure it will be all right?"

I assured him it would, and then I was once more beginning to theorize. Important business with Mrs. Brende might mean alterations to her will. No sooner did I think that than I was seeing various implications. Was Mrs. Brende of Wharton's opinion that the Colonel was dead? Or was it that her will was not up to date, and she was realizing, after the raids, that life was an uncertain business these days? Or was there some connection with her requests to see me that morning? Did she know something that she had not revealed? Did she really think she was in some personal danger, and was that why she was putting her affair in order?

Then, as usual, I began to hedge. Having given theory a free rein, I pulled in. And I decided I ought to say nothing to Wharton. After all, he had a habit of making himself conversant with most happenings, and his own men would doubtless make him aware of Holby's visit to the Hall in the morning. After that, one so manipulatory with women as Wharton boasted himself to be, could fin   out from Mrs. Brende direct not only the reason for the lawyer's visit, but also what lay behind her alarms.

Wharton rang me up to see if I could meet him at that tea-shop in the town. I duly turned up, and while we were waiting for the order to come, asked him if it wasn't rather too prominent a rendezvous. Some of his friends in the City must surely use that tea-shop.

"That City business is all over now," he said, and then was leaning forward mysteriously. "Have a look in your paper to-morrow."

"Why shouldn't you tell me now?" I suggested.

He thought for a moment and then was leaning forward again.

"Old Dove has just been collected."

"No!" I said. "What have you pinned on him?"

"Mustn't tell you," he said. "General subversive activities is good enough. Nothing to do with this other affair unfortunately."

"And what about John Knox?" I said, using that camouflag because the waitress had suddenly popped up with our tea and toast.

Wharton didn't reveal much, but he did say that Benison was only a stool-pigeon. Harking back to the subject of the danger of the tea-shop rendezvous, I instanced Penelope, one of whose favourite haunts it seemed to be. Wharton shelved the question.

"I was with her just now," he said. "Had some business at the Hall. She's worried, that young lady."

"Perhaps she knows she may lose a cushy job," I said.

"How do you make that out?" he fire   at me. "You're always talking about logic, and where's the logic in that? I wouldn't have called that job of hers cushy? Long hours and loafin   about and not much company."

Before I could mention possible compensations, he was hauling out his wallet, and making fina   comments on Penelope while he looked for some paper or other.

"Besides, she was worried before this affai   cropped up. Those anonymous letters upset her I expect. I saw some sleeping tablets in her bedroom that morning. And now what do you make of this?"

He handed me three photostats, and I spotted them at once as salvage from the burnt note-book. Wharton said they were all that the experts had been able to treat, for the charred paper he had sent them had been in a bad state of disintegration. The three photostats I was given represented about an eighth of a page from each of three pages of the original, and they were reasonably distinct considering what those originals had been through. In one of them could be seen a portion of a diagram. The rest of it, and the whole of the others, was mathematical fomulae, which naturally began nowhere for me and ended nowhere. I told Wharton as much. My mathematics went no further than a sixth form at school, and I had done nothing in that line at Cambridge.

"And I thought you were one of these brainy ones," Wharton said reproachfully.

"You did algebra at school, George," I said. "Could you have solved a problem if you had no idea what x and y and z and all the rest of it stood for? Look at this," I said. "About half the letters of the Greek alphabet, and every sign from cube root to sigma. I don't know where Brende was starting from or what he hoped to arrive at."

"Can't you guess?"

"Oh, yes, I can guess," I told him. "Taken in conjunction with this fragment of diagram, I'd say he was working on the curvature of curves."

"And what the devil's that?"

"Well, in simple terms it's this. Assume he was working at interception or detection of enemy planes at night. A plane takes avoiding action by diving or climbing, and its course is a curve. He was working on such curves. Sorry I can't be more helpful, but why don't you tackle Newton? He's the one to see daylight. I'd even be ashamed to mention the word mathematics in his presence."

George began putting the photostats back in his wallet, and he was pursing his lips. When he spoke again his tone was that gentle, conciliatory one which I well knew.

"As a matter of fact I gave him three for himself."

"The devil you did!" I said. "And what did he say?"

Wharton chuckled. "Asked me if I hadn't any old Egyptian hieroglyphics and things so that he could start on them and work his way up. Very sarcastic he was."

"I see," I said, and nodded heavily. "Newton had no more idea than I have, and yet you had the nerve to question me."

"What've you got to grumble about?" he asked me, and glared. "You ought to be damn pleased I had such a high opinion of you. But talking of Benison—"

"We weren't," I said. "We were talking about your nerve in expecting me to know what Newton didn't."

"You're too touchy," he told me. "But listen to this. I got something out of Benison about that picket. While they were there a big car came from the Hall direction at about midnight. His men were on the qui vive, and as this car went by, one hollered that the rear light was out. All the car did was to shoot on as if it had been stung."

"Which way. City or town?"

"The town. And a woman was driving it." Up went his hand. "Don't ask me what woman. I know nothing about it. All I know is that a man thought the car was slowing down, so he ran after it to say the rear light was out, and he said all he could see was a woman driver, and he wouldn't swear on a stack of Bibles even then. No one knew what the car was either, except that it was a big one. Rather wide, he thought, like a big Austin or a Daimler. It was a dark night, you remember, and that picket wasn't worrying about cars."

I understood all that, and that the car might have been one of no interest to us, in spite of the fact that George's deductions from the tyre cast were that a big car had been used to carry Brende away.

"How're your bloodhounds getting on?" I asked.

"Ah!" said Wharton. With wide sweeps of his handkerchief he wiped his moustache and mouth, and pushed aside his plate. Then he was leaning forward again.

"Your friend Passenden's not having too good a time in Scotland."

"Oh?" I said. "And why?"

"Because he isn't there. Where do you think he went to from here? Up to that Sowdale place where Mrs. Brende's people used to live. He stayed a night in a pub there, and then we lost him."

"Lost?"

Wharton shrugged his shoulders. "That's it—lost. He paid his bill and off he went to the local station with his luggage. My man got there in time to fin   out he'd left the bag at the booking-offic   which does for a left-luggage offic   and then he simply disappeared. That's all there is to it. My man's still hanging around."

"Why shouldn't he go back to his old haunts?" I said. "Or perhaps Mrs. Brende asked him to do something for her. Also he may have spotted your man and been a bit annoyed. Passenden's just the man who'd take a delight in throwing him off the scent."

Wharton agreed so readily that I knew he had something more up his sleeve. Also he changed the topic and began telling me what he was doing generally. To my relief he was interested in the three Huns who had baled out before the raid on the Saturday night. At least I thought he was interested. With Wharton you never could tell, and he might have been throwing dust in my eyes for some obscure reason of his own. He also said everything was very difficu on account of the secrecy required. No use to search for Brende when there was all England to search in, or at least an area as large in radius as that big car could have travelled before dawn on the Sunday, or even later. All he could do was to hope for something from the police, or for a stroke of luck.

I couldn't tell him about Mrs. Brende, so I kept things going by asking what he thought about Pattner. I said, rather too lamely that I hadn't seen him till the day of the conference. Wharton shot a suspicious look at me, then said that Pattner was a very good chap. He had been very thick with Penelope Craye at one time, he added, and they still got about a lot together, though there was nothing serious in it. I guessed that one of Wharton's men had seen me snooping round that side street and I changed the subject.

"By the way, George, did it ever occur to you that our lady friend might have composed those anonymous letters herself for some obscure purpose? I do think it was rather fish that yarn of hers about not showing them to Brende in case he'd be worried?"

Wharton was getting to his feet, and nodding enigmatically.

"I've got it in mind," he said. "I've got a lot of things in mind."

He paid for the tea, or the taxpayers did, and out we went. Once more he said he'd not be seeing me for a day or two, and then he said he'd be glad if I'd have a word with Newton about those photostats.

"You can manage that all right," he told me cajolingly. "Don't tell me you're ashamed of your ignorance, and all that bosh. You worm out of him what he knows."

"Then he does know something?"

"I didn't say so," he put in hastily. "Perhaps I didn't make myself clear. You and he go over those photostats together." Some hopes, I thought amusedly as Wharton drove off I'd just as soon call on Einstein and say, "Here's a little paper I think you've dropped, Albert. A prolongation of that little relativity business of yours, by the look of it. What about us two putting in a half-hour on it?"

What else I thought doesn't immediately matter, and I probably forgot most of it because things again began to happen. After dinner that night I was called to the phone.

"Call coming for you, sir," orderly told me as he gave me the receiver, and in a few moments I was talking to Passenden.

"What a surprise!" I said. "And how's Scotland?"

"Not too bad," he said. "Still standing where she did. What I'm worrying you about is to know if you can tell me if there've been any developments over you know what."

"Nothing that I know," I said.

"Not a word or anything? No demand for . . . hush-money shall we say?"

"Not a thing," I said.

"Right," he said. "I'm much obliged to you. Just thought I'd get the low-down if I could, being a bit worried and so on. Ringing from a friend's house, by the way, so I'd better ring off before the pips go."

As Passenden had said nothing about secrecy or confidence I got hold of Wharton at once. He wanted to know everything about the call—exact time, what exchange had said, and so on—so I knew he would be trying to trace its origin. He also asked if I were sure that it was really Passenden who had been speaking. I said I had no doubt whatever.

"Right," he said. "I may be seeing you in the morning. Or it may be in the afternoon. In the morning I may be busy."

George didn't know how busy he was going to be, neither did I. I slept rather badly that night as it was, but if I had known that in the morning I was going to survey a corpse, I doubt if I'd have slept at all.

CHAPTER XII
MURDER?

IT was just before breakfast when I was called to the phone. Wharton's voice came impatiently.

"Is that Major Travers? Am I through to Major Travers?"

"Speaking, George," I said.

I heard him let out a breath of relief, then he was asking if I could be at the Hall in a few minutes. Something pretty bad had happened.

"Mrs. Brende?" I blurted out before I knew I had spoken.

"What made you say that?" he was asking at once.

"I don't really know," I said. "She's a personal friend, the only one I have there."

I could hear him snort, then he was saying he'd expect me inside a quarter of an hour. I was asking for more news, but he had rung off

What I felt like I can't quite say. You might say I was knocked all of a heap, but there was more to it than that. I was genuinely fond of Mrs. Brende, and I believed she had a considerable liking for myself, so there was something personal about the shock. Then there was the worry about what she had told me the previous day, and all at once I was telling myself that she had committed suicide—*and with my automatic.* That put me in a further dither. I would have to own up to what had happened, George Wharton would think I had been holding back information, and he might even claim that if I had told him what was in the wind, Mrs. Brende would be still alive.

I swallowed some toast and a scalding cup of coffee and then was off An ambulance, and a private one by the look of it, was standing at the front door of the Hall. Ledd admitted me, and he looked lugubrious enough without having to act.

"What's the matter with you, Ledd?" I asked him.

"I'm a bit upset, sir," he said, and shook his head. "This way if you please, sir."

He evidently expected me to know what the tragedy was, but when we got to the top of the stairs he turned away from the direction of Mrs. Brende's room and past the Colonel's rooms, and it was the door of Penelope Craye's room at which he tapped. Someone spoke and Ledd was showing me in.

It was a much larger room than I had imagined. A curtain on stout runners divided it into sitting-room and bedroom, and each was ample in size. The sitting-room part had its fireplac and looked most comfortable. As for the other part, the curtain had been drawn back and there was the bed. Wharton and a stranger were standing by it, and when Wharton moved to meet me, I saw on the bed the body of Penelope Craye.

"She's dead," I said.

Wharton merely nodded. Then he was introducing the doctor. He had his own nursing home with a resident staff and the body was going there at once for a P.M.. I moved across to have a look at it.

I fin the examination of a corpse the most trying part of a case. The sight of blood, for instance, upsets me physically, and I can't help that overwhelming urge to turn away. Wharton is hardened enough, and corpses to him are twopence a bundle like radishes, but I had no reason to wince as I looked down at the body of Penelope Crave, for she might have been asleep. Her pyjama suit was unstained, and it looked as if she had died peaceably in her sleep.

"What was it?" I said. "Heart failure?"

The doctor shot a look at me.

"Major Travers is all right," Wharton told him. "All this is being kept dark by the way, till I get a ruling from the Powers-that-be. What we think from a cursory examination is that these caused it."

He was pointing to a small bottle of sleeping tablets on the side table. There was a wineglass too, I noticed, and then my eye caught a half-bottle standing on the floo close by the bed. It was almost certainly a champagne bottle. I also noticed her clothes neatly folded on an easy chair at the foot of the bed; except for a frock that hung from a hanger on the handle of the door of the wardrobe. Everything, in fact, seemed natural. The frock, a biscuit coloured semi-evening affair and not the offi garment of dove grey, had been put there when she had undressed, and—my wife does the same thing—she was intending to put it away in the morning.

There was a tap at the door and Newton looked in.

"Come in," Wharton told him. "Just witness these two statements, will you, and then the doctor can go."

The statements were lying on the open fla of a desk at the sitting-room window. Wharton, I thought, must have been at the Hall for some considerable time. Probably the body had been discovered by a maid or someone who had brought early morning tea. Probably Ledd had brought it, which was why he was upset. Just then Ledd looked in.

"Two men at the gate, sir," he said to Wharton. "The sergeant says are they the ones who're to be let through."

Wharton clicked his tongue annoyedly.

"Tell him to get 'em here quick. You bring them up at once."

Wharton and the doctor and Newton went on with the reading or mumbling over of the statements, and I had another look round. This time I saw the wet on the carpet by the bedside, where something had been spilt. Wharton had evidently considered it important, for he had drawn a chalk mark round it. I also noticed that on a shelf under the side table was a carafe of water and a glass. It looked as if Penelope had been accustomed to taking the sleeping tablets in water, but that night she had treated herself to a half-bottle instead. I gave my glasses a polish and had another look, and then I saw that Wharton had been testing the carafe and various other things for fingerprints

Wharton was coming over with the other two.

"Just witness this," he said to them, and was kneeling by that wet mark on the carpet. With his knife he cut out a rough circle of the carpet, then placed it in an envelope, sealed it, and the other two wrote their signatures across the flap Then his two men arrived, and one was carrying a camera. What happened then was something that utterly bewildered me.

First Wharton removed the pyjama jacket. It was of pale green material, I remember, and embroidered with little sprigs of flow rs. An expensive suit, it looked to me, but quiet and in admirable taste. But the trousers were perfectly plain. My wife doesn't wear them, and it was the firs time I had seen a woman's pyjama trousers, which was why I was surprised to see they had no front opening but were all of one piece, as it were, and with elastic round the waist.

But for that attitude of repose, what happened next would have been gruesome enough, for after a general photograph of the body and its position, it was held up and a photograph taken of the lower half. Then it was reversed and another taken of the back. Then there were two close-ups of something I could not see, after which all the plates were sealed, and again the two affix their signatures.

"Get these off at once," Wharton told his man. "They are expecting them."

"They" would be experts at the Yard, that much I knew, but for the rest I was in as thick a fog as ever. Then the statements seemed to have been completed, for Newton was asking if there was anything else. Wharton asked him to wait till the doctor had gone. Then he told me that according to Mrs. Brende, young Howard Crave was Penelope's nearest surviving relative. While under the circumstances it was not necessary to obtain his permission for anything, it might be as well to let him know what had happened—in strict secrecy, of course.

I didn't want to miss anything, so I made it pretty quick. All I did, in fact, was to ask Harrison to send Craye to the Hall. He wasn't to enter, but only to ask for me. As I left the phone the body was going through to the ambulance, so I sprinted upstairs to hear what Wharton might be saying to Newton. Nothing seemed to have been happening, but as soon as I came in, Wharton asked how Mrs. Brende was.

"She was very upset when I saw her," Wharton said. "How is she now?"

"Quite composed again," Newton said. "I don't wonder at her being upset. It upset me pretty badly too. And what makes it worse for Mrs. Brende, Miss Craye was having tea with her only yesterday, afternoon. She didn't often have time for that lately."

Wharton nodded consolingly, then brisked up.

"Now then, about things generally, and always in the strictest confidence Assume she was killed—murdered if you like. A wild hypothesis perhaps, but at my game, you've got to take no chances. Why should she be murdered? What did she know?"

"How can I tell?" Newton said with a shrug of the shoulders. "Didn't she claim that she knew nothing?"

Wharton smiled cynically.

"What she claimed and what she knew mayn't be the same thing. Would you call her a snooper, for instance?"

"Snooper?"

"Busybody, Paul Pry, Nosey Parker," gabbled Wharton impatiently.

"Well, she certainly was—" He broke off "I don't know how to put it. She used to come down, perhaps, and pass on certain instructions from Colonel Brende. I didn't like that at all, at first but I'm a man of peace and I didn't like to protest. Also she was so charming in her manner."

"You knew she was making the most of her position and you didn't like to interfere," Wharton summed up bluntly.

"Well, yes—perhaps."

Then Wharton was nodding mysteriously, and his voice lowered.

"Look here now, Newton, we're all three men of the world. Everything we say is secret as the grave, but just between our three selves, was there anything—well, romantic, between her and the Colonel?"

Newton's face went a rosy pink. Wharton's oily description of the Professor as "a man of the world" had tickled my fancy at the time.

"Well, I don't know," he said, and was nervously rubbing his chin. "After all, they were relatives by marriage."

"Marriage, my foot!" Wharton said. "He was a man and she was a woman, and I'd say she had a pretty coming-on disposition. I'm not calling her a tail-swisher, mind you, but you're a man of the world and you can put two and two together. Now then what about it?"

"I still wouldn't like to say," Newton said nervously. "There were times perhaps when I did have ideas of the sort, but, as you see, it wasn't really my business."

"But weren't you sorry for Mrs. Brende?"

Wharton had so hustled him off his feet with that, that he could only stammer. Then all at once he was assuming something of that dignity with which he had rebuked that too anticipatory questioner at the conference. Wharton mustn't put words into his mouth. The subject was a distasteful one and he would rather not discuss it. As far as he knew there was nothing improper in the relationships between the Colonel and his secretary.

"That's all I want to know," Wharton told him placatingly, and bestowed a surreptitious wink on me. "What I was driving at was this, as you've probably seen. If they should have happened to be close friends, shall we say, then he might have told her a good deal he never told anyone else. In other words, to get back to where we started from, we arrive at something serious. Suppose the Colonel's kidnappers can't make him talk, then they might have killed her so that she shouldn't talk. If they haven't got what they wanted, they're taking good care nobody else shall have it."

Newton had been nodding gently, but at those last words his face took on a sudden alarm.

"Then what about myself, and Wissler, and Riddle?"

Wharton shrugged his shoulders.

"An attack on you is feasible, of course. But not an attack, though. An attempt at attack. You'll all be far too well protected from now on, so you needn't have the least worry about that."

Except to request once more the most implicit secrecy, Wharton had no further immediate need of Newton. As soon as he'd gone, George was making exasperated noises.

"Where do they dig these fellows up from! No wonder you read about all these rags that go on with students and professors. Did you ever know a chap like him? Why the devil can't he give a plain answer to a plain question?"

"Because your questions were far from plain," I said. "Your technique isn't adaptable enough. You're getting careless. Newton won't be hot-stuffe by those old tricks of the trade."

He glared indignantly, then was nodding to himself and chuckling.

"What's it matter either way? The Colonel was too thick with her, and he knew it. Look at that bottle, for instance. Do you know that she had permission to go down to the cellar here and help herself? Do you know that she had the keys and she availed herself of it pretty freely? Are those included in the privileges of a secretary?"

"But, dammit all, George, what's it matter? He was a full-blooded specimen and she was what she was. We're not concerned with morals. Mind you," I said, just as he was about to cut in, "I saw what you were driving at. Did she know any details of his discovery or the lines on which he was working? If so—"

"She did," he said.

I stared.

"The proof is that note-book," he said. "He had lent it to her, or she'd taken it. When he was missing, she got the wind up and burnt it."

"You're right," I said. "I hadn't thought of that. All the same, if Newton thought that note-book stiff going, how could she understand what was in it?"

"Listen," he said, and held up an avuncular hand. "There's more to this case than meets the eye. Why shouldn't she have been in the habit of taking that note-book, and copying what'd been written, and then passing it on to someone outside."

"You mean she was a kind of spy?"

Once more he was shrugging his shoulders.

"You told me she was hard up. You couldn't guess how she'd ever got in here. Well, isn't that an answer? That, and her physical charms? And I'll go further."

He did, by coming nearer to me and breathing hoarsely.

"That Newton. Why's he all over the place? Why shouldn't that nervousness be for the same reason?"

"Good God, George! you can't imagine anyone of his standing and reputation—"

He cut me off at that.

"I've got to imagine everything, haven't I? And what about her standing and reputation? Two of those Big Bugs the other day were calling her by her Christian name. One called her Penny. Penny, my foot!"

I glanced at my wrist-watch.

"George, I ought to slip back to the Camp. But about this murder theory. What's in it? What was the carpet business, and the photographing?"

It was all very simple when he explained it. The pyjama trousers had been put on the wrong way round!

"The way I know is this," he said. "My wife wears the damn things, and night after night she'll say, 'Oh, bother it! If I haven't put them on the wrong way round.' I get fed up because I'm waiting in the cold to draw the curtains when the light's out, so that we can get some air in the night, and I have to wait while she changes them round. I asked her more than once why she couldn't put a bit of embroidery or something on the front, so she'd know at a glance. You know what women are? You couldn't do a thing like that. Couldn't be blowed! Then I had a look at them on my own one morning, and I couldn't tell back from front till after quite a time. But what I want to tell you is this. She knows at once, the very minute she has them on, whether she's been in too much of a hurry and put them on the wrong way round. Also she's said more than once, as part of the argument, that no woman could sleep if she knew they were on back to front."

"In other words, Penelope Craye didn't put her own trousers on last night."

"That's it. Mind you, she may have been very tired or in a great hurry. That champagne may have fuddled her, but I'm taking no chances. If someone slipped into that champagne enough tablets to send her to sleep for good, then that somebody undressed her and put the trousers on the wrong way round. And that somebody must have been a man."

"Yes," I said. "And I think I'm beginning to see about the carpet. Some of the champagne was spilt. If it has the drug in solution, then we're dealing with murder. If it hasn't, then we're back where we were."

Ledd looked in again to say I was wanted on the phone. I was surprised he didn't follow me downstairs.

"About Craye," Harrison told me. "We can't fin him anywhere in Camp."

"Can't fin him?" I said. "But he was Orderly Offic yesterday, wasn't he?"

"Yes. He came off duty at reveillé."

"Well, then, he shouldn't be out of Camp."

"I'm sorry—"

"Wait a minute, Harrison," I said. "I'm not blaming you. It's no fault of yours if these young office   dodge the regulations. You can't have your eves everywhere."

"That's true enough," he said. "What shall I do? Send him to you when he turns up?"

"Too late, I'm afraid," I said. "I'll see him there, later."

When I got upstairs again, Ledd was just leaving the room. Wharton gave me one of those peering looks from over the tops of his spectacles.

"Is that chap Ledd a drinker?"

"Probably," I said. "But he'd hardly start as early as this. Why'd you ask?"

"Something he just told me. He and the other batmen sleep in that barn place, just across the yard, as you know. He says they all get up pretty early, and he's the earliest bird of the lot. Now listen to this. Miss Craye used to be valeted by Annie when she firs came here, then the housemaid did it, and then Ledd. All it means is bringing early tea, and meals, and cleaning any shoes there are. The shoes are sometimes put outside the door as in hotels. Ledd says he asked her to do that so that he could clean them early. Well, up he comes this morning for the shoes, and he says it was about six o'clock. He came up the back stairs, and who should he catch sight of but Mrs. Brende. She was coming from this way, and carrying something. Ledd says he didn't want her to see him—he doesn't know why—so he ducked down. And what do you think he says she was carrying? A dust-pan and brush!"

"Good Lord!" I said. "What an amazing way for Ledd to talk about Mrs. Brende!"

"Of course it didn't come out quite like that," Wharton said airily. "I asked if he'd seen anybody about, then he said he had, and so on. What's more he says that yesterday morning he came up here early and just as he got to the top of the stairs he saw someone disappear round the far corner. He thinks that was Mrs. Brende. Just instinct, he called it."

"But a dust-pan and brush," I said. "What on earth should she want those for?"

"Probably couldn't sleep, came up here, saw them lying about, where a maid had left them, and took them away," Wharton said, but he was cocking a questioning eye as if he hadn't much faith in his own theory.

"Maybe so," I said, and wondered what he was really thinking. "But what about Penelope's overnight movements? Anything interesting?"

"No." he said. "She went out before dinner and came back here for a meal. Then she told Ledd she wouldn't want anything, and didn't want to be disturbed. He fille that water carafe, and that's all. Next thing was when he found her dead this morning."

"That tea with Mrs. Brende yesterday. Doesn't that strike you as unusual?"

"Why should it?"

"Now, George, don't be obstinate and mysterious," I said. "You know as well as I do that Mrs. Brende kept herself very much to herself. That's one reason why I sometimes wondered if there was anything between that other one and the Colonel, and she'd become aware of it. Mrs. Brende let Annie be her maid when she firs came here, so you just told me. Then another maid did it, and then that stopped. Doesn't that mark a gradual decline in relationships?"

"There may be something in it," he said. "But you don't think Mrs. Brende had a hand in—?" He waved a hand at the bed where the body had been.

"Of course I don't," I told him. "Mrs. Brende's the last person in the world to get up to tricks like that. But supposing it *was* murder. Was it done by the same persons who kidnapped Brende, and did they get in in the same way?"

Wharton merely shrugged his shoulders.

"Then was it an inside job?" I persisted. "If so, and the two events are connected, the last was an inside job too, and all that wisteria stuff was camouflage.

"How could it have been an inside job?" he said. "Colonel Brende was kidnapped, wasn't he? He went *out*. And those who took him, went *out*."

"But they might have gone out by the front door," I said. "Perhaps a sentry was nobbled. A man'd fin   it hard to resist heavy baksheesh." Then I was shaking my head. "I don't think that's likely though. But I still think it was partly an inside job. That car that Benison's picket saw was driven by a woman. It might have been the car with Brende trussed up inside and Penelope driving it. She might have handed him over to the people who paid her handsomely for extracts from that diary note-book."

"I've got all that in mind," he told me. "Rome wasn't built in a day."

"And too many cooks spoil the broth," I said, with a look at my watch and remembering that the lawyer would soon be at my offic

Wharton walked with me as far as main guard where I had left my car. I thought young Craye might be there, but he wasn't. Then I thought I'd have a look at the book and see at what times he'd inspected the guard during the night.

"The book, sir? Certainly, sir," the sergeant said, and far too briskly. He was an old-timer, red-faced and beery.

The book showed that Mr. Craye had been round the guards at twenty-one-thirty hours, which was pretty early. The next entry was at three hours fifteen I looked up to see that sergeant watching me in a most peculiar way, and I had a sudden suspicion. So I nodded to Wharton and then asked the sergeant to follow me outside. When we halted he was looking most uneasy.

"A straight answer from you, sergeant," I said, "or there's going to be trouble. Did Mr. Craye visit the guards at three hours fiftee this morning, or didn't he?"

He wouldn't catch my eyes.

"All right," I said. "I think I know the answer. That's all."

"What was young Craye doing? Playing the old game?" Wharton said.

"Looks like it. Writing the three-fiftee signature when he was here at twenty-one-thirty, and passing half a crown over to the sergeant. Probably did that everywhere and so wangled himself a good night's rest."

"He's the nearest relative too," Wharton said, and pursed his lips.

I said we oughtn't to jump to any conclusions till I'd seen Craye personally. Then as I got into my car I remembered Passenden.

"The man's a liar," Wharton said. "He was ringing you up from Buxton and pretending to be in Scotland. And he wasn't ringing from a friend's house. He was at a hotel where he'd called in for a meal. By the time my man had been warned, he'd disappeared again."

"Curious," I said. "What the devil's he up to? But suppose he rings again. Shall I mention what's happened this morning?"

"Wait a minute," Wharton said, and frowned in thought. "I think perhaps you might. I'd rather thought of putting an obituary notice in the papers. 'Suddenly, at Dalebrink Hall,' and all that. Just to throw somebody off the scent in case there was anything fishy.

"And what are you going to do now?" I asked.

"Going over everything in that room. When I've finishe there won't be a square inch I haven't run my rule over."

"Anything you'd like me to do?"

"Well, yes," he said, but none too heartily. "You might have one of those roving commissions. Have a talk with Ledd for one thing. You can do that better than me. Mrs. Brende too, perhaps. You know, just condole with her and so on."

Thank heaven I've no intellectual arrogance, but I had to smile at George's subtle hint that I should be lacking in artifice But my face straightened soon enough as my hand went to the brake. It was the sudden knowledge of what I was leaving behind. For the last hour and more I had been too close to things, and at the best of times a murder enquiry is callous work.

"It'll seem strange not having Penelope Craye here," I said. "And it's a damnable business, if it really is murder. What makes me feel so rotten about it is that I never had a good word for her."

"Ah, well," said Wharton. "But let me know what happens with that relative of hers."

"I will," I said, and my hand went down again. Then I realized that George had been working for three days and had given me never an idea of his progress.

"Made any headway, have you?" I said. "Got any real ideas?"

He had a quick look round and put his head inside the window.

"I don't know that I haven't got the key man. If I could make him talk I'd know as much as anyone."

"The key man? Who is he? Benison? Passenden?"

He gave a snort of disgust.

"Why don't you use your brains? You saw him this morning. Newton—that's the man."

"Good Lord!" I said, finger already at my glasses. "You must be—"

But Wharton had waved a cheery hand and was making his way back to the house.

CHAPTER XIII
WHARTON IS OBSCURE

As I drove back towards the Camp I was thinking of many things, but principally about Newton. That a man like him should be mixed up with anything treacherous and unsavoury passed the bounds of even my elastic comprehension. Yet Wharton had spoken soberly enough, though with him, as I have said many a time, you never could tell. One thing then did occur to me. If the incredible had really happened, and Newton was far from what he seemed, then the nerviness and fright of Riddle and Wissler could only mean that they too were mixed up with things. Riddle was a former pupil and protégé of Newton, and Wissler would be entirely under his orders. And yet, the more closely I looked at it, that triumvirate in treachery and crime seemed so fantastic as to be ludicrous. William Le Queux would have blushed if he had thought of that for a plot.

I also thought of Mrs. Brende, and I wondered why Wharton had introduced her name as a kind of afterthought. That was an old trick of his, to lay scant stress on anything important. Why should he want me to see her when he was on the spot and had every excuse for asking for an interview? Indeed, he had seen her already that morning. There was Ledd too, whom he had already seen, and then suddenly I began to feel just the least bit annoyed with Wharton. If he wanted me to do a job, why couldn't he give me details of what he wanted? In fact, but for that insatiable curiosity which would have led me to poke a finge in the pie, Wharton or no Wharton, I should have felt at that moment like throwing my own hand in.

Harrison happened to be out when I got back to Camp, but the R.Q.M.S. said there were two messages for me, and each of them made me think. The firs was from the local police and said that the Huns had been collared at last, two in some woods near Buxton and the third near Sowdale. It was curious how that word kept cropping up. It was Mrs. Brende's old home for example, and Passenden had gone there, and it was near there that he had shaken off Wharton's man.

"I see in the paper they've caught those Germans, sir," the R.Q.M.S. said.

"In the paper, is it?"

"In my paper, sir. I see how they reckon the plane they baled out of was one that came down right away over in North Wales somewhere. Looks as though they made a bloomer, sir, don't you think? Got the wind up and baled out."

"Maybe," I said. "Still, I expect they had a shrewd idea they were going to crash if they didn't jump."

So that seemed to knock one theory on the head. And when later I read what was said in the paper—that there had been a fourth airman and he had been overcome by fumes—I knew those Huns had never been landed for the express purpose of kidnapping Brende.

As for the second message, it was from Holby, the lawyer. Other arrangements had been made, he said, and he would not need to take advantage of my kind offer And that looked to me as if Mrs. Brende had changed her mind on account of the morning's tragedy.

I went to my own offi and signed some papers Harrison had left for me, and then, with nothing much to do, I naturally began thinking of things again, and whichever way my thoughts went, they kept coming back to Mrs. Brende. Finally I had to talk to myself seriously. Let there be no more furtiveness, I said. Mrs. Brende herself would be the firs to demand the fullest enquiry into anything that might place her under suspicion. Those who are innocent have nothing to fear, so why should I not be open in my own mind as far as concerned the case for and against Mrs. Brende? And if Wharton was suspicious, all the more reason why I should continue to be her friend. And how, I somewhat speciously assured myself, could I be her friend unless I arrived at the facts?

What was there against her? Well, if she still loved her husband, she might be prepared to go to extremes to figh to retain him. It certainly seemed to me that she had become aware of some sort of intrigue and therefore she would know that Brende had planted Penelope in the house in the role of secretary and that knowledge, acquired later, would be more than galling. For Mrs. Brende seemed to me to have accepted Penelope at fi st at her face value, which was why Annie had been lent her as maid. Mrs. Brende might also have become aware of those other activities of Penelope. She might have warned her husband and have been rebuffed Then when he was kidnapped she decided to take the law into her own hands. Once Penelope was dead, there could be no proof of laxity on the part of the Colonel.

What I thought might be disregarded entirely was that story Ledd had told Wharton. Ledd had not spoken in front of me, which might mean that he was trying to ingratiate himself with Wharton. I didn't question the story itself. Mrs. Brende, it seemed to me, would gladly get up at dawn. Why should she not walk round a house, which belonged to her, and which was virtually closed to her during the day? As for the brush and dust-pan, she had most certainly known that it had been forgotten and so was taking it to the kitchen. That was just the kind of thing a precise, tidy person like Mrs. Brende would do.

But when I came to state a case for Mrs. Brende, I was startled to fin how thin that case was. All I could say was that it was far from certain that a murder had been committed at all, but that was a flagran begging of the question. All, in fact, that I could produce was the bald statement that Mrs. Brende, from even my little knowledge of her, was incapable of murder. And that, I had to admit, was nonsense. In my time I have run up against murderers—and women at that—who looked like angels of light. And, as I also had to admit, that killing of Penelope Craye by the sleeping tablets was a woman's crime. No blow and no blood, but just a furtive business of a moment or two.

But instinct all the same is a tough thing to be up against, and I was still of the opinion that if Wharton had Mrs. Brende in mind, it must be for something other than murder. Also, there seemed a kind of treachery in my own hunt for premature suspicions, and I tried to keep Mrs. Brende from my mind. Then just as I thought of going to the Mess for a look at the paper, Harrison turned up.

"I've got Craye, sir," he said. "Had an idea he might be in the town, so I borrowed a car and took a cruise round. There his lordship was, walking with a girl too."

"He's here?"

"Outside waiting. I called him aside—didn't want to let him down in front of the lady—and he caught me up on his motorbike at the gate. That's another thing. Using Government petrol and property."

I told Harrison just what I suspected, and asked him to stay while Craye was questioned. Then he called Craye in. Craye's salute was impeccable.

Well, I put the question to Craye very bluntly. He must have guessed what was in the wind, for there was no start of surprise at the accusation. He admitted he was out of Camp that morning in defianc of regulations, and said he was taking a chance.

"I don't see how you could deny that much," I told him. "But about the other question. I want a plain yes or no. Did you or did you not inspect the guard at the Park at three hours fiftee this morning?"

There was a silence of a good minute.

"Will anything happen to the sergeant, sir, if I say anything?"

"That's no concern of yours," I said. "I'm not driving a bargain with you. I want an answer."

"Sorry, sir, then I've nothing to say."

I gave a Whartonian grunt and glanced at Harrison. He took up the running.

"Mr. Craye, it will be the easiest thing in the world to question the men themselves and fin out if any of them actually saw you this morning. The Commandant didn't wish to do that before he'd seen you. If he does do it, then the sergeant will most certainly be for it."

Craye thought that over.

"Very well, sir, then I didn't inspect the guards. But it wasn't really the sergeant's fault, sir, I told him it was something very urgent."

"And what was the urgent matter?" I asked.

He shook his head.

"Sorry, sir, I can't say."

"Can't say! But you must be mad. Do you realize what this means to you?"

His lips clamped together. I waited a few moments, then had a last attempt.

"Open confession, and a full one, may make things easier. This is my last warning."

"I know, sir," he said, humbly enough. "I'm grateful to you, sir, but it's something I can't talk about."

I let out a deep breath.

"Very well, Mr. Craye, consider yourself under open arrest. And Captain Harrison, I'd like a word with Mr. Craye alone."

I warned Craye again before I spoke. If he breathed a word to a soul other than his aunt, I said I'd break him if it was the last thing I did. Then I told him about his cousin. No details, of course, but that she had died suddenly during the night, and that he, as the nearest relative, had been wanted. Either he was a fin actor, or else he was flabbergasted

"When did you see your cousin last?" I wanted to know.

"I don't know, sir," he said. "To tell the truth, we didn't get on well together. I think I saw her in the town and just spoke to her about a week ago."

"Why didn't you get on well?" I thought he might think that a highly personal question, so I added that I had my reasons for asking.

"Well, sir," he said, frankly enough, "we had no use for each other. I know she told lies about me to my aunt."

"Why?"

His lip curled.

"I think she was trying to get me out, sir, and herself in. But it didn't work."

"I see," I said. "And you wouldn't care to reconsider your decision and tell me what you were actually doing when you should have been on duty?"

Once more he shook his head.

"Sorry, sir, I'd rather take what's coming to me."

And that was that. I had a sneaking idea that what he had told me was the truth—that, in fact, he had some highly confidentia reason for cutting duty and bribing the sergeant—but I couldn't let things stay put. So I rang for Harrison who took Craye to his offic   Then when Craye had gone, I knew I had been foolishly sentimental and I decided to get from Harrison a description of the girl with whom Craye had been walking in town that morning. Wharton could then take a hand, and if I found that Craye had been simply spending the night with a woman, then he would most certainly be for the high jump. If he had not, and Penelope had really been murdered, then Wharton would have a suspect. Penelope, I recalled, had taken tea the previous afternoon with Mrs. Brende. That seemed to me to indicate that she had succeeded in getting back to good terms with the one from whom young Craye had great expectations. In fact, a murder motive stared one in the face.

I got that information from Harrison before lunch, and gave it to Wharton over the phone. He seemed most grateful and said he would get to work at once.

"I shan't take any disciplinary action, other than what I've done," I told him, "because if you get hold of anything, I can use it as a lever to make him talk. It may be some common little intrigue when he does own up, and on the other hand it mayn't."

George told me guardedly that he'd had no luck at all in Penelope's room, so after a spot of lunch which Ledd was findin for him, he was going out for a breather. He was calling at the doctor's place for one thing, to hear what had happened at the P.M. Then he'd probably be at the City to take a call from the Yard about the carpet analysis.

"What about your key man?" I said. "Had any more conversation with him?"

Wharton gave a little chuckle, which seemed to me to indicate that much of that mysterious hinting about Newton was mere blether.

"Oh, him," he said. "He's peevish. Says he's got his own job to get on with, and Colonel B. wasn't the only one who might be on to something big."

"Serve you damn well right," I said. "I expect you've been asking for a snub. Why don't you bully someone as big as yourself?"

He seemed delighted at that, and promised off his own bat to let me know about the P.M., and the Yard expert's opinion on that wet piece of carpet.

Our Mess library was a ramshackle collection, but I remembered after lunch that I'd seen in it an old copy of *Who's Who*—that lovely garner of self-written epitaphs. Newton was in it right enough, and when I had read his staggering list of achievements and honours, I was more than ever certain that Wharton had been blethering for some deep reason of his own. Wharton hates Hitler worse than the Devil hates incense, but when it comes to the use of the lie, he has Hitler beaten to the wide.

One of his tricks, for instance, is this. He will suggest something which has some foundation of fact, and then proceed to embroider. When he has finished, you feel that there is still something vital which he has missed. But you have seen it, and you tell yourself that you will follow it up and surprise him. When you try to do so, you discover the fraud, and you go to him indignantly and ask if it is necessary to mystify or even double-cross those who are supposed to be his helpers. Then he guilelessly explains that in what you have just told him was the very something he had been looking for. He also repudiates scornfully the charge of misrepresentation. All he did, he says, was to put in your mind a certain view-point towards the suspect. When you try to pin him down, he asks triumphantly if the means haven't justifie the end.

Does that read a bit woolly? I hope it does, provided you've got the main idea, because you may feel how woolly and even pained I've felt in my time when I've been a victim of George's circumlocutions. But to get to the question of Newton. The suggestion was that Newton knew the truth about everything, and that I was the man to extract it. Now I was quite prepared to see Newton. I had my own interests in him, and I was certainly not going to the Hall to treat him as a suspect. I wanted to hear his views on those photostats, and—that overmastering curiosity again!—to get from him some definit hint of the lines on which he and his assistants were working, and the hopes they had of success. After all, I did have a wife working in a London hospital, and there would have been a personal ease of mind, if nothing else, to have a hint that the night bomber was on the way to being badly mauled if not mastered.

The trouble was to fin a good excuse for seeing Newton, and it was not till the middle of the afternoon that I found one. Off I went at once to the Hall. I had a short wait before Newton could see me, and while I was in the empty offic Riddle came in. He was in slacks and pullover, and came bursting in without seeing me at first

"We've busted the last ping-pong ball," he said grinningly. "I think there should be some here."

"Who's winning?"

"Oh, Wissler," he said. "He gives me fiv start and then beats me three times out of four. Were you waiting to see Professor Newton?"

I said I was, and he explained. Life at the Hall was erratic in the extreme. Sometimes one slept all day and worked all night, and sometimes it was a kind of half and half. Riddle said he and Wissler could do with very little sleep, but Newton liked more. As a matter of fact he was just getting up after snatching a few hours.

Off Riddle went with a couple of balls that he found, and I told myself that there was a young man who was much easier in his mind than when I had last seen him. So boyish and absolutely natural had he been that even Wharton could never have suspected him of subterfuge, let alone crime. What he had told me about Newton was useful too, for when the Professor did come in, I was all apologies about disturbing him, and he all protestations that he hadn't really been disturbed, and so we were on loquacious terms at once.

"Can I get you some tea?" he said, "or is it too early?"

"Just a bit too early for me," I said. "Besides, I don't want to take up your valuable time. What I really came about was Ledd. Strictly speaking, he isn't performing duties while Colonel Brende isn't here, so I ought to have him back. On the other hand, if you say you'd still like him here, that's good enough for me."

He seemed most grateful for what he called my consideration. He had got used to Ledd, and Ledd was used to the Hall, and so he'd esteem it a favour if he might remain. I said he could consider it as settled.

Then I decided to employ my own un-Whartonian technique. The room suggested mention of work; that suggested the admiration of the layman for the experts like himself and Hush; and then to my surprise he was volunteering information.

"As a matter of fact," he said, "Hush should have been coming down here on the very day he did come."

"Periodical stock-taking?" I said.

He smiled. "You might call it that. He's an exceedingly able man and it's a pleasure to talk things over with him. He's one of the few who know."

"Not like myself."

"Oh, I don't know," he said. "I know your civil life reputation, and I wouldn't put you among the badly informed."

"All the same," I said, "this work you're doing here is far in advance of most of what I could grasp."

"Don't you believe it," he said. "Of course I can't give you any hint of what we're actually doing here, but I can tell you of one idea. Highly confidential by the way."

I was most interested, though I couldn't for the life of me have told if what he was telling me was something on which he was really working. The idea was to make use of the sensitivity of certain metals like selenium, and he instanced television. Suppose, for example, that an enemy plane is in a pitch dark sky at an unknown height. Its vibrations affec an extremely sensitive instrument on the ground, and this instrument is co-ordinated, shall we call it, with a special gun. Then no matter how the aircraft twists, climbs or dives, the selenium records it and automatically transmits it to the gun.

I had to admit that the idea had tremendous possibilities, but that to transmit them into results was an even bigger business.

"By the way," I said, "Wharton told me he'd given you some rather interesting photostats. Was he pulling my leg as usual, or *were* they interesting?"

Never in my life did I meet a man who so closed down as Newton did at that question. Instead of being genial and chatty, he froze completely up. He did say the photostats were interesting only as examples of how modern science could read what would once have been called the irretrievably lost, and then he was changing the subject most pointedly. I even got the idea he was trying as gracefully as he could to get rid of me, so I said I wouldn't keep him any longer. A word with Ledd and I'd have to get back to the Camp.

He pushed a bell and another batman came. I said I'd see Ledd in the hall, and I shook hands with Newton and thanked him, and he thanked me, and that was that. Ledd came along to the hall at the double, and he was still buttoning his tunic when he appeared. I told him what had been decided, and he seemed very relieved. I liked Ledd, I don't quite know why, unless it was that grin of his and the perky snub nose.

"While I'm here," I said, "I'd rather like to have a look at the cellar. The wine-cellar, to be exact."

"Yes, sir," he said, and at once was leading the way. In a corridor just short of what various odours told me was the kitchen, he went through a door and into a small empty room which had a fligh of stairs going down from one of its corners. There was a light which he switched on, and it was necessary, for the steps were none too wide. The cellar itself was stone-floored and not as large as I'd expected, and very few bottles were in the racks.

Ledd said that Mrs. Brende had sent most of the wine to the local hospitals. I asked why the door had been unlocked, and he said that Wharton had been down there and had probably forgotten to lock it after him. There were only two keys, he thought, and Wharton now had one and Mrs. Brende the other.

"What the devil is that bumping noise?" I said. It had been going on ever since we had been down there. Ledd pulled a face. There was another cellar through that door, he said, and coal was just being chuted down from the back yard. Tons and tons of it, he said.

"But what's worrying you?" I asked him. Ledd had one of those faces that reveal pretty closely its owner's mood.

"I'm not worried, sir," he said, and his grin was sheepish. "The only thing is, sir, we had the coal outside up to now, and it was easy to bring in the house."

"I see," I said. "And now you've got to come down here and carry it up the stairs."

"Well yes, sir," he admitted.

We were on such friendly terms that I thought I'd talk to him like a Dutch uncle.

"Ledd," I said, "I've been wanting a quiet word with you for some time." I caught his quick, worried look. "Where were you exactly on that Saturday night when Colonel Brende disappeared?"

"Where, sir?" He coloured up to his scalp. "Out for a walk, sir."

"A pretty long one, wasn't it? You didn't get back till early morning."

"Well, there was the air-raid, sir."

"Oh, no," I said, "the real air-raid didn't develop till after you were in."

That was a slip on my part and he took quick advantage of it.

"It was that other one, sir. I hung about looking for the parachutists that dropped."

"Very thoughtful of you;" I said dryly. "You see, Ledd, I want to help you if I can. If you've got anything on your chest which you'd like to get off now's your chance."

"I've got nothing, sir."

"You certainly had on Sunday morning," I told him. "Still it's up to you. Mrs. Brende in, do you know?"

He said he didn't know, and I was wondering if I ought to force myself on her after all. As I looked back from the door, Ledd was still staring after me, and I knew more than ever that that young fellow had something on his mind.

It was a sunny afternoon and the wind had shifted a point more east so that it was less cold. As I stood for a minute admiring the young green of the trees and the flauntin colours of the rockery, I caught a movement by the summer-house, and I was just in time to identify Mrs. Brende. Just as quickly she disappeared, and I suddenly remembered again that Saturday evening when I had seen someone whom I had erroneously taken for Colonel Brende.

In a moment I was stepping off the gravel and making my way across the lawn.

CHAPTER XIV
UNEASY INTERIM

That was the first time I had walked towards the summer-house in what might be called broad open daylight, and I was noticing something of which I had previously been unaware. The lawn fell away much more steeply than I had imagined. That was natural, since the tennis-court, or part of it, had once been a bathing-pool, and would therefore lie in some sort of hollow. That tennis-court broke the line of descent, but beyond it the land still fell away, so that you might have said that it and the summer-house lay on the side of a hill, of which the Hall itself was the summit. It was not a real hill, of course, for the actual differenc in altitude between the end of the slope and the base of the house could not have been more than fift feet. As for the summer-house itself that overlooked the tennis-court, it stood on an artificia mound, the back of which was terraced away till it lost itself artistically in the level lawns beyond.

I came up the side steps and there was no sign of Mrs. Brende. As I came round to the back, there she was, just in the act of locking the back door. Then she turned and saw me.

Over her face came a most extraordinary expression. Let me describe it like this. Suppose you have told a young nephew not to touch the fruit on a certain tree, and then you come on him suddenly and catch him in the act of eating a stolen pear. That happened to me with a nephew of mine, and over his face came an expression which said: "You've caught me, then, uncle. I'm not going to attempt to argue. Here I am and I'll take my medicine." In his look and attitude were admission of guilt and, with never a sign of brazenness, a free acceptance of the consequences.

Mind you, that's what I knew later. At the moment two ideas flashe into my mind to explain that extraordinary look in quite other ways. I thought the firs quick confusion was at seeing me, and so suddenly, after having tried to avoid me. Then I wondered if I were on private or sacrosanct ground, and if I had not taken a liberty by wandering about the grounds.

"I'm so sorry," I said. "Perhaps I oughtn't to be here, but I thought I'd caught sight of you, so I came over to speak."

She gave a little smile, but it was one of relief.

"I was just taking advantage of the sun. Those cold winds kept one so much to the house."

"Yes," I said, still standing there awkwardly and feeling rather stupid. "And how are you?"

"Very well," she said. "Thank you enormously for everything you did for me."

"That was nothing," I told her. "I'm awfully sorry, by the way, about this last dreadful business."

She caught me up at once.

"She didn't die naturally?"

"Why should you ask that?" I said gravely.

Her eyes turned away. For a moment or two she was thinking hard, brows puckered, then she shook her head, and her eyes met mine again.

"She was very young to die. Only this time yesterday she was with me, and I thought how robust she was. She never ailed a thing in her life."

"One can never tell," I said. "These things happen, you know."

All the time we had been standing there, neither of us stirring an inch. I knew my presence was some sort of restraint so I decided to depart gracefully.

"Well, I must get back to the Camp," I said. "I just called here on business, that was all. Don't forget I'm to have tea with you soon. Or why shouldn't you have tea with me?"

She smiled. "I so rarely go out. You must come here. In a day or two, I hope. Perhaps you will let me telephone."

I left her there and puzzledly began making my way back to the drive. Then I had an idea, and it arose out of those last words of hers about telephoning. Then it got mixed up with what she had said about rarely going out, when I recalled that she had made an exception in favour of Passenden. And Passenden had been at Sowdale, her old home.

That was how the thoughts began to crowd in, and on the last heels of them was the remembering how Passenden, when he rang me up from what he hoped I should imagine was Scotland, had asked me if anything had happened at the Hall. So I turned back to the house, and luckily it was Ledd who opened the door. I went a few yards along the bare corridor.

"This is in strict confidence Ledd," I told him. "What are the telephone arrangements here now? Has Mrs. Brende asked for an extension to be put through to her room, for instance?" I saw I had scored a bull. Ledd said he had fixe that simple extension himself.

"Is it much used?" I said.

"Not a great deal, I don't think, sir. It was this morning, though. Mr. Newton wanted to make an urgent call and we were held up because they had a trunk call."

"They" in Ledd's vernacular would mean Mrs. Brende, which was all I wanted to know, so I cautioned him again and then made my way out by the back, and so through the shrubbery path to the drive again and the front gate. What had happened seemed to me to be reasonably clear. Mrs. Brende and Passenden were in telephonic communication and she had rung him up that morning to tell him of Penelope Craye's death. If so, she had doubtless told him that in her view that death had not been natural.

As I drove slowly back to the Camp I saw something else. When Ledd caught sight of Mrs. Brende that morning, she had been coming from Penelope's room. Perhaps something there— something she had removed in that dust-pan—had told her beyond all doubt that Penelope had been murdered.

But how was I to clinch that argument? I saw no possible way of proving a single suspicion, and it was no business of mine to cross-examine and question. Then I did think of some small proof that might present itself, even if negatively. I was expecting Passenden to ring again, and again to ask me if anything had happened. If he did not ring, then it might be proof that he had other sources of information.

It was not till almost dinner-time when Wharton rang me up that evening. He said he'd just had a call from the Yard to say that the champagne had a strong solution of veronal.

"Then it *was* murder," I said.

"I knew that in any case," he told me.

That was a surprise for me. George never made foolish boasts like that without reason.

"You knew! Good Lord, how?"

"Knowing and proving are two differen things," he said, and obviously to put me off "As a matter of fact I'm trying to make a start on the proof to-night."

"And what about the P.M.?"

"Confirm everything, and by the by, she was not a virgin."

I merely grunted at that. After all, what was there to say? Neither old scandals nor new seemed to matter much just then.

"Still, as I was saying," Wharton was going on, "I have to be away for a few hours. It may be a day or two. I happen to have been lucky enough to have overheard a certain telephone conversation."

"Going to Sowdale, are you?"

It was his turn to be startled.

"How'd you guess that?" he snapped at me.

"Guessing and proving are two differen things," I couldn't help telling him. "All the same, you seemed to have done the proving for me."

I could almost see him glare. A moment or two and there came a faint chuckle. George is in some ways an Oriental. Fond of duplicity himself, he can admire the little tricks of others. "Come on," he said cajolingly. "How did you know?"

"That's one of the things I'm not going to tell you—just yet," I said. "All I will say is that the conversation you listened to was probably between Mrs. Brende and Major Passenden."

That took the wind out of his sails. I was trying to put the question of what they had talked about, when George recovered first

"You've been to the Hall, have you?"

"I did just drop in," I admitted.

"What did you learn? Who did you see?"

"I'll make a bargain," I said. "You tell me what you overheard and I'll tell you what I learned."

"Come on, come on; I've got a train to catch."

I thought he wouldn't dodge the bargain, so I played fair Briefl I said Ledd was still frightened about something but wouldn't talk; Newton would talk about everything but the photostats, and Riddle was easy again in mind. George interrupted me.

"Ledd was still worried, you say?"

"He struck me as so. Mind you, he was in a bad humour about some coal."

Then I had to tell him all about that. He didn't seem any too grateful when I'd finished all he wanted to know was if I'd actually spoken to Mrs. Brende. Naturally I said I had, though by accident. Then again I had to tell him everything that had happened at the summer-house, and how she suspected murder

"Now your side of the bargain," I said. "What did you overhear?"

He had me, as I might have expected, though I must say I thought he was telling the truth.

"She told him the lady was dead. He said what sort of a death. She said she didn't know but she suspected the worst. He said it was the last thing that could have happened, and that was all, except that he'd be seeing her soon. She didn't ask what he was doing or where he was speaking from, or anything. He simply said he was grateful and then he rang off.

"And you discovered he was speaking from Sowdale?"

"He wasn't. He wasn't many miles away though."

Then before I could think of anything else he was giving me instructions. I had better keep away from Mrs. Brende unless it was she who approached me or requested me to call. I should not be able to get in touch with him, he said, because he would be here, there, and everywhere, but if anything turned up which I considered really important, I was to ring the local police and give the information to the Superintendent only. If Passenden rang me up, I was at once to inform the local people, who'd trace the call and pass the information on.

"Good luck to you, George," I said, just before ringing off

"I'll need it," he told me grimly. "That fellow Passenden is a regular will-o'-the-wisp."

Then I just caught him again in time.

"About young Craye and the lady? Do I have to wait till I see you again before I get any news?"

"I'd forgotten that," he said. "I'll arrange to get the information to you direct. I believe we've already picked up the scent."

Something else did happen as a kind of tail-piece to that conversation, and it was something that made me just a bit annoyed with Wharton. A night or two previously I had inspected the tunnel guards, and as a result I considered certain changes might reasonably be made. Harrison and I talked them over, and the morning after that telephone conversation with Wharton, I decided to have a daylight look round, so off I went and one of the Company Commanders concerned was with me.

It was about eleven hours when we drove slowly through the town, and while we waited at the traffic lights, whom should I see but Wharton, small bag in hand, and making for the railway

158 | christopher   bush

station. As we got well through the town, a train for Buxton and the north actually overtook us, and Wharton was almost certainly on it. I couldn't see why he had thought it necessary to lead me to think he was going to Sowdale or thereabouts at once when he had no such intention. Then it struck me that he really had intended to go the previous night, but something had cropped up to keep him till the morning. What did not occur to me was that that something might have arisen out of the report I made of my afternoon enquiries and experiences at the Hall.

And now if you are expecting things to happen, you will be badly wrong. Three days were to elapse before I was to see Wharton again, and then things did certainly happen, but those intervening three days brought for me what George Wharton once vulgarly but aptly told me was a diarrœa of theories and a constipation of ideas. What I did think does not matter because you have probably been thinking too, and have ideas of your own, and since nothing happened there is nothing to relate. But there I am wrong.

Something did happen, though it had no bearing on the main case except for the purpose of elimination. The morning after Wharton actually left Dalebrink, the post brought me a tiny package from—of all people—Benison, and inside a note.

Dear Major Travers,

I have been thinking the matter over and, as there are no other troops in the immediate neighbourhood except those under your command, I will turn a certain matter over to you, and if nothing comes of it, then nothing more need be said.

You will remember that when you were good enough to see Dove and myself, we both harped on the kind of men you had at your Camp. This, I can now divulge, is the reason. The morning when that burglary was discovered, I picked up the enclosed button from the floo of a room at the Vicarage. Perhaps it will convey something to you. I recognize it, but naturally can take no action.

I should be grateful if you will let me know results of your enquiries. As a man of peace, however, I would not like any action to be taken against the offende or offenders

> Very many thanks,
>
> Yours sincerely,
>
> L. Benison.

ps.—The Government have made a great blunder over Dove, and one they may live to regret.

That button did set me thinking, and that same afternoon found me at the Hall. Ledd admitted me as usual, and I asked him to find Riddle. When the two came I mooched along the corridor mysteriously till I found an empty room. Then I produced that button, bearing the crest of a famous London regiment.

"This is yours, I think, Ledd. You dropped it at the Vicarage."

He shot a quick look at his tunic, and then at Riddle.

"Don't deny anything, either of you," I said. "You two raided the Institute and the Vicarage. One of you left Camp by the back and one by the front, and you came in the same way. Why did you commit that crime?"

Ledd opened his mouth first, then Riddle was butting in and saying the idea had been his own. He had been fed up, he said, with the Negger activities and how the Government were letting them do as they damn pleased, so he had talked the matter over with Ledd and they had agreed to try and get their hands on something definitely incriminating, which would force the Government to take action. If they *had* found anything, Riddle had intended to make a clean breast to Hush, who, you may remember, was due at the Hall in a day or two. Nothing had, however, been found. And nothing had been said because both he and Ledd were of the opinion that the affai had been forgotten.

I cursed several kinds of hell out of the pair of them. I don't often let myself go, but honestly, what I told Ledd would have been well worth bottling. Riddle's tail was specially well twisted.

"You," I said, "doing a man's work, and work of vital importance, and endangering it and your whole career for a bit of so-called patriotism. What action I shall take I don't know. What I do know is that if either of you ever lets out a word, I'll break you both."

There was more to it than the above well-censored reprimand, and the two crawled off with tails well down. When I had cooled off I had to do a furtive smile. Boys, the pair of them, and with never the foggiest notion of what their prank implied. And I could feel a certain furtive admiration for the fact that they had at least done their nefarious work in first-clas style. Perhaps I shouldn't have felt that way if Benison had caught them red-handed.

I rang Benison that same evening, thanked him and said that suitable action had been taken. He thanked me and that was all, but as he was nothing of his ponderously loquacious self, I rather gathered that the loss of Dove had chastened him considerably. In other words, it was Ichabod for the Neggers.

Then the afternoon before I saw Wharton again, something else happened. One of Wharton's men called at the Camp, and he had quite a lot of information for me. Craye's lady friend had been traced, and she was living in furnished rooms under the name of Mrs. Rawlins. Her so-called husband—Mr. Rawlins — was none other than Craye.

"Looks to me, sir, as if he's installed her there," the detective-sergeant said. "Probably one of his fancy pieces he used to run before the war."

"What's she actually like?" I said.

"You never can tell with that sort," he said. "I must say she struck me as superior."

"You actually questioned her?"

He hadn't done that, he said. He had followed her into a shop and heard her talking to the assistant, that was all. His questioning had been done with the landlady who occupied the rest of the house. The young woman had passed muster with her; there wasn't any question about that.

"Mr. Craye spent the Saturday night there?" I asked.

"He came in at about half-past ten," he said. "The landlady saw him and he told her he'd been on duty, visiting some guards. She said his wife had a hot meal ready for him. I reckon she'd been poking her nose in to see what was going on."

I didn't like to ask the sergeant just how much he knew of the Hall happenings, so I thanked him and off he went. Then I prepared to see Craye. What he had obviously done was to visit all the guards by twenty-two hours or thereabouts, and to arrange at each to have the later times put down as already done. I was not prepared to say he'd been able to bribe every N.C.O. in charge, for he had probably produced specious reasons or even said he had permission to make such arrangements.

I told Harrison I would prefer to see him alone, so in he came to my offic   He looked both washed-out and worried. I said I was giving him a last chance to spill all the beans, but once more he said he had nothing to confess.

"You arrived at a house called 'Silverglade' at twenty-two-thirty hours on Saturday," I said, "and you spent the night there with a woman known as Mrs. Rawlins. I'm now about to make close enquiries into what arrangements you made to set you free from visiting the various guards. From now on you are under close arrest."

His firs surprise had given way to a kind of stupor. I gave him a look as if inviting him to speak after the eleventh hour as it were, but he had nothing to say.

"Now I must tell you something much more serious," I said. "It is believed that your cousin's death was not a natural one. To put it bluntly, somebody may have killed her. By your own admission she was a rival of yours for your aunt's money—that's putting it crudely, but the police, you'll find are crude people who call spades. Do you honestly think the evidence of this woman will be good enough to give you an alibi for the whole of that night?"

"Evidence?" he said, and stared. "You mean there'll have to be an enquiry?"

"My dear Craye, use your common sense. If there's an inquest both you and the woman will have to give evidence in public."

He was shaking his head and breathing a bit hard. Then he asked if it would be published in the local papers.

"It most certainly will," I said, seeing no reason to tell him that peculiar secrecy which the case demanded would almost certainly mean that there would be no public or other inquest.

"That you'll have ruined your career is another matter."

His eyes were on the floor and he was still shaking his head. So utterly wretched did he look that I was already feeling some sneaking sympathy.

"If I tell you something, sir, will you keep it a secret?"

"Pretty late in the day, isn't it?" I said. "Still, say what it is you've got to say!"

"Then it's my wife I was with, sir. We were married when I had that long week-end leave."

"This is the truth? Not made up for the occasion?"

"The absolute truth, sir." I'd known that already since he had taken no offence

"Why this secret marriage? That's against regulations, as you know."

It all came out like a penny novelette. His aunt had a wife in her mind for him, and he was afraid to risk offending her. The girl he had married was twenty-two, like himself, and a games mistress at a private school near Buxton.

"You priceless young fool," I said. "I don't mean about getting married, but all this hole and corner work. Has she any money? Have you?"

Neither had a bean beyond his pay and allowances, and, as I told him, his story was no mitigation of his military offence In some ways it aggravated it.

"As for this other business," I said, "you're in a more parlous case than ever. As your wife she can't be asked to give evidence for or against you. There's also obviously no value in any evidence she might give for you. What you've been trying to avoid by keeping your mouth shut, is what you've achieved. Your marriage must come out."

"All right, sir," he said. "I'll take what's coming to me. And may I ask a favour, sir? Might I see my wife? I'll give you my word of honour, sir, that I'll come straight back."

"You give me your word now that you'll stay in Camp till I give you permission to leave it," I said. "Then I might leave things as they are at the moment. After that, we'll see."

First I thought he was going to blubber and then that he wanted to grab my hand, but out he went in any case. I'm several sorts of a fool, as you've doubtless gathered, and now all this sentimentality had landed me in a hole. I had begun by hating the sight of young Craye. Then I had gradually realized that he had the devil of a lot of good qualities. From that I had come to have a bit of a liking for him, and now I was being the world's worst disciplinarian. I could even say, when he left my room, that there, but for the grace of God, went Ludovic Travers. I could even begin wondering if his career could be saved after all. Soon I was going further and wondering if I could anyhow smooth over the situation between Craye and his aunt.

But I could see no way of doing that, and then I began to feel the obvious reaction, and be furiously angry with young Craye for the mess into which he had landed both himself and myself. Nor did I see why I should lose the friendship of his aunt for the sake of one who had behaved so badly. Then, of course, I began wondering what sort of girl the wife was.

That evening I did something else that only a fool would have done. I saw young Craye and took him down town in my car. I saw his wife and I liked her enormously; indeed I had the idea that that marriage would do the pair of them an enormous deal of good. What I didn't see was how I could smooth things over with the aunt. Later on a way was to present itself, and the circumstances were some of the strangest in my brief career.

On that eve of Wharton's return something else happened. I caught sight of Passenden in Dalebrink. There was no mistaking him, but I couldn't stop my car as I was taking young Craye back to Camp. That night it slipped my mind that I ought to have informed the local superintendent, and then we had an air-raid which kept me up half the night, and in the morning I slept late. When I did get in touch with the local police I was informed that Wharton was already on his way back.

CHAPTER XV
THE FINDING OF BRENDE

IT was in the early evening when Wharton turned up at the Camp. Not only did he look worried but he was just the least bit peevish.

"Any luck at all?" I asked him.

"Yes," he said. "Damn bad luck, and nothing else. Couldn't clap my hand on Passenden, even though I had him as near as dammit. All over the place he was, and when I thought I'd caught up with him, away he'd be. Then yesterday morning I lost him altogether. Couldn't hang about there all my life, so I thought I'd come back and try another tack."

"When you say you lost him, what do you mean?" I asked.

"What I say," he told me grumpily. "We'd follow up a trail and fin where he'd spent the night. He'd be away and gone and by the time we'd found out which way, he'd be gone again. Devil of a country to get lost in too. Like wandering about in the Alps."

Well, I had to get it over, so I took a deep breath and blurted out.

"I saw Passenden in Dalebrink last night," I said. "When I rang the local police they told me you were coming back here. That was at about noon to-day."

You never saw such a look as he gave me. At firs it fairly blasted me, then it turned to the most pitiable reproach. At my excuses and explanations the look became merely more reproachful.

"Saw him last night," he said, and clicking his tongue. "Where did you see him?"

"He was walking," I said. "Just as I caught sight of him he turned down some side street or other. I couldn't even be sure of telling you which."

There was another click of the tongue.

"Every theory knocked to blazes," he said, and then all at once his eyes were popping. He raised a finge as for silence, and then was helping himself to the phone. It was the local superintendent to whom he spoke, and he wanted to know if Major Passenden was staying at the same hotel as before. The information and anything else relevant was to be sent at once to the Camp number.

"Why are you so anxious to get hold of Passenden?" I wanted to know.

"Why?" he glared. "Because he's in all this right up to the neck, that's why."

"But how?"

Then he was shuffli again.

"Isn't that what I want to fin out? Besides—"

Then his face went into contortions of agony and he was almost literally tearing his hair. There was another dive for the telephone. When he got what he wanted, I was pretty sure he was talking to the detective-sergeant.

"Any more messages? ... I see. . . . You're sure! . . . At the hotel yesterday, at tea-time. . . . No, no, no. . . . Yes, I'll meet you there. . . . Yes, in a quarter of an hour."

Once more he was giving me that look of reproach.

"For God's sake don't keep looking at me as if I'd sold the pass," I said. "I've apologized and explained, and if it comes to that, there're the devil of a lot of things I might look reproachful about myself."

"Oh?" he said, but that look went from his face all the same. His voice took on a honeyed smoothness. "You gathered what I was talking about? Mrs. B. had tea with Passenden yesterday afternoon. That's upset a little scheme I'd come back here for."

The telephone went and he grabbed the receiver.

"Ah, yes. . . . He is, is he? I had an idea from something I just heard. . . . Really? . . . Yes? . . . Yes? . . . Trains for Scotland. You surprise me. . . . Good. . . . Well, thanks very much. Good-bye."

"He's at the same hotel," he told me, "and he's talking of leaving to-morrow morning. Been working out trains to Scotland."

"You're going to let him go?"

His eyes puckered in thought, and he was giving that Colosseum smile.

"I might as well. Let him have all the rope he wants. I'll know where he is this time. Soon as I want him, my hand will be on his shoulder, like this."

He had got up to go, but as he was squinting at the set of his bowler in the offi   mirror, he remembered he was being too precipitate.

"Anything been happening with you?" Then he gave a little complacent laugh that rather got my goat. "But of course not, or you'd have let me know."

Well, I told him about Ledd for a beginning. He looked at me rather perkily throughout, and when I'd finishe   he gave a little chuckle. Then I told him all about Craye. He looked pretty serious during that story, but at the end he merely shrugged his shoulders. He'd never really considered Craye seriously as a suspect, he said.

"I won't call you a liar, George," I said, "but you've got some devilish queer ideas of what constitutes the truth. Also, you're decidedly ungrateful. I've eliminated three suspects for you—say what you like—and all you do in return is to keep your own information to yourself."

"You're too touchy," he assured me in his best Chadband manner, "And who keeps back information? Listen to this. I've eliminated a suspect too—that fellow Wissler."

"How?"

"Doesn't matter how," he said. "There're always ways and means. Know what he's always been scared about? Well, he was in Prague when the Nazis marched in, and he hung on there as you know. Then he foolishly tried to compromise with the devil, and actually got himself accepted for membership of the Party. Then he found he was expected to act as stool-pigeon, and he bolted. Ever since then he's been scared stiff He never owned up over here that he'd been a Nazi in name. He says it would have queered his pitch with the authorities. Ever since then he's been scared stiff Every offici   who turns up he thinks is someone who's found out and has come to lug him off to an internment camp, or worse."

I grunted.

"And what about the principal suspect?" I asked guilefully. "You haven't eliminated Newton?"

George was moving off to the door at once.

"All in good time, all in good time," he said. "Rome wasn't built in a day, was it? He'll be talking soon, or my name's Robinson."

I warned you that after Wharton's return things began to happen. And they did happen. The following morning, soon after breakfast, he was ringing me up, and his voice had a tremendous impatience.

"Is that Major Travers? Am I through to Major Travers?"

"Speaking, George," I said with a bit of a grin.

"Ah!" he went on. "News for you. Brende's been found!"

"Good Lord!" I said, finger at my glasses.

"I'm just going there. If you'd like to come, be outside your gate in ten minutes' time."

"Yes, but where is he?"

"A good way off and in pretty bad shape," he said curtly, and slammed his receiver back.

It took me less than no time to arrange things with Harrison, then I grabbed my British warm for it was a cold morning even if the sky was clear. George was on time and he had borrowed a car with one of his own men driving. He and I sat at the back, but it was not till we were through the town that we did much talking. My questions were not much use, for he knew little more than what he had told me.

He had been rung up, he said, by the police from a little place called Cumberforth. A man had been found in an

168 | christopher   bush

exhausted condition by a shepherd among the crags, and they
had recognized him from that confidentia circular issued to all
police. The sick man was now in the local cottage hospital.

"Once he can talk we'll be all right," George said. "Don't you
think so?"

I wondered why he should ask so obvious a question.

"Naturally there'll be a lot of new information," I said. "The
question is whether or not you'll be able to use it. I don't like
these hush-hush cases where your hands are tied. You mustn't
question this person and you mustn't do something else because
it might let out secrets. It's fightin with your hands tied."

"Don't I know it?" he said, and changed the subject
surprisingly to Mrs. Brende. She ought to be relieved, he said,
to know the Colonel was safe. What with his disappearance and
Penelope Craye's mysterious death, she must have been badly
alarmed.

I don't know why, but I suddenly had the idea that I wouldn't
like George to know that I had done so foolish a thing as to
furnish Mrs. Brende with a gun. It wasn't that I was afraid of
that automatic ever being traced back to me, for I had bought
it once on a holiday in France and had then forgotten it till the
outbreak of war, when I had taken it with me not knowing that
I should get a service issue. What I didn't like was the thought
that I had been concealing from George something which he
might consider as really vital.

"Mrs. Brende's a woman of very strong character," I said.
"She isn't likely to lose either her nerve or her head. But one
thing's just struck me. Everything to do with Colonel Brende
may still have to be kept as secret as the grave, but that can't
apply to Penelope Crave's death. Murder is murder, and the
murderer's got to be brought to book."

"I don't know," he said mildly. George was in one of his mild,
argumentative moods that morning, which made me suspect
that he was on good terms with himself. "I'll lay a five the Big
Bugs consider it all part of the hush-hush. No announcement
will ever be made beyond that one about her sudden death."

That twenty-mile journey was through some of the wildest and loveliest country I have seen for some time, and the narrow lane through which George had directed the driver wound an always ascending way among the ragged hills. In the distance George pointed to a church spire and said that was Sowdale. It was lost almost as soon as we saw it, and about ten minutes later, after a particularly steep rise, we suddenly came to the head of a dale. Its church stood clear about a mile away, and the houses hugged the sheltered slope. That was the tiny town of Cumberforth.

Our car left the lane and turned into a wider road. In fiv minutes we were drawing up in front of the police-station, and just as we did so, a motor-cyclist drew in behind us. It was the detective-sergeant. George told him to stand by, and into the station we went. George produced his credentials and introduced me to the local inspector, and then was asking for details of the morning's news. George, by the way, had already told the inspector over the phone that any local newspaper must be warned not to print a word about the exhausted man.

Well, this is the complete story as the inspector told it to us in the privacy of his room. Just after dawn that morning a shepherd thought he heard a cry. Then he caught sight of a man on all-fours, making a slow way across some rocky ground, and he ran across at the best speed he could muster. By the time he got to the man, the man had collapsed. The shepherd at once got in touch with the Cumberforth police. The man had been brought in and then a search was made, the shepherd helping, to discover from where the man had come in case there should be anyone else in his company. They had then discovered a cave in which the unfortunate man had been kept.

I should say, by the way, that the inspector was guessing a lot about Brende. All the circular had told him was that Brende had lost his memory, but he was a shrewd man and more than capable of putting two and two together. Sometimes he would cock a sparrow-like eye at Wharton, as if asking for confirmatio of a bit of guesswork, but Wharton let him run on and gave no hint or sign.

At the moment Brende was in the local cottage hospital, the inspector confirmed He had seen him there only a few minutes before our arrival, and had the latest report. The doctor was sure that the man had lost his memory, but though he had obviously been through a very bad time indeed, he was in mental rather than physical danger.

"What clothes was he wearing—if any?" Wharton asked.

"The same ones as published," the inspector said. "That was one way we identifie him. He smelt a bit, by the way, as if he hadn't had a wash for days."

"Right," said Wharton. "You get a report typed in triplicate, and we'll look in at the hospital. Make it as quick as you can." Then he was at last giving one of his peering looks. "Keep that report to the actual facts. Those it's going to are rather like me— they don't like people who know more than they ought."

The hospital was in the level bottom of the dale, about a couple of hundred yards away. The inspector had nevertheless been warned to let the doctor on duty know that we were coming, and he was looking out from the door as we walked along the short drive. He was one of three local practitioners who did duty at that small hospital which served quite a large rural district. A pleasant, elderly man, and well up to modern methods was how he appeared to me.

Wharton had a confidentia talk with him before he asked for information. He had various methods of imposing secrecy and hinting at the consequences of loose talk, and the one he now worked was so effectiv that he had the doctor in something of a dither. Nothing should be made public, he assured us. A trustworthy resident nurse was already in charge of the patient, and certainly he would exclude all mention of that patient from the hospital records.

"I shall inform higher authority that you can be implicitly relied on," Wharton said imposingly. "And now to business. Tell me all about the patient."

The doctor said he had obviously been kept in close confinemen for some days, and for most of the time he had been drugged. The pricks from the injections were plainly visible, and his condition tallied with them.

"Pupils of the eyes dilated or otherwise?"

"Of course not," the doctor said. "As soon as the effect of the drug wore off and he recovered consciousness, the dilation would automatically go. I put it that way to you."

"That's right," Wharton said heartily. "Medical jargon's as bad as any other. I understand, by the way, that his memory's gone.

The doctor said that was undoubtedly so, and he could give no opinion on when it would return. Recovery might be hastened by visual and other contacts with familiar scenes and people.

"Ah!" said Wharton. "Now we're coming to it. What I want to do is to have him removed to Dalebrink. To his own house, in fact, where I'll make every arrangement for medical supervision and treatment." His voice lowered and he was nodding mysteriously. "If he should start to babble indiscreet things, for instance, the fat would be in the fire Also I shall have to have some trustworthy man of mine at his bedside. You know the procedure, and you remember what I told you about the special importance of secrecy. So what about it? When can he be moved?"

The doctor did some quick but heavy thinking. Then he would go no further than saying it all depended. If care was used and everything went well, then he might possibly be moved the following afternoon.

"That's good enough for me," Wharton said. "I'll let his wife know and I'll make all arrangements. Meanwhile I have a man of mine here and you might let him stay handy, in case the patient does any talking. Now what about us seeing him?"

The doctor left us for a minute or two, and when he came back he said the patient was sleeping. It was a rambling, single-storied building, and a few yards took us to the room. The doctor whispered to the nurse, who withdrew, and Wharton and I approached the bed. If I hadn't known from other evidence that the man was really Brende, I could never have recognized him.

The growth of beard, of course, made the great difference but there was more to it than that. I think I told you that he was of the lean, restlessly active type, and almost as thin as myself. Now the beard accentuated the leanness and made an effec of almost emaciation, while the comparative pallor of the face and the dark pouches under the eyes so added to that effec as to make it something frightening. I felt a sudden fury. The thing for the ones who had kept Brende in that cave was not the justice of the law, but a few rounds clean in the belly, where it would hurt most and linger longest.

Wharton whispered to the doctor, who carefully drew down the sheet and revealed a bit of Brende's left arm. The pricks of the syringe were clearly visible. Wharton nodded, had a last look at the sleeping man, then was motioning to the doctor to lead the way out again.

"Now then," he said officiall when we were back in the reception hall again. "You've seen what powers I have and what I can override and not override. What I want you to do is to get an immediate sample of his blood. Pack it, or whatever you call it, how you like, and have it ready within an hour. Seal it and write your name across the seal. I'll collect it and one of my men will rush it up to London."

The doctor had been nodding in an agreement that had much of doubt.

"I can do that," he said. "But pardon me if I ask something. If you're after the drug that was used, I think it will be a waste of time. The amount of blood in the human body is so enormous compared with the amount of drug used, that the drug will have been dissipated in the blood stream."

Wharton's smile was courteous and even deferential.

"I agree—with one little reservation. Modern methods of crime detection aren't always made public. Believe it or not, a blood sample *will* reveal the drug, provided it's been used within forty-eight hours or so. That's why I'm rushing the sample up to town."

Well, that was that, and off we went back to the police-station.

"Were you telling the doctor the tale, George," I said, "or can they really discover what drugged Brende?"

"I was serious," he said. "The method's been out for only a few months, but I'm told it's infallible."

"Right," I said. "Then what use is it to you to know what drugged him? Suppose at this very minute you know it was morphia, how does that help your case?"

George shrugged his shoulders.

"Sometimes I wonder what happens to those brains of yours," he told me sadly. "If we know the drug we might manage to trace it, couldn't we? Suppose there was morphia kept at the Hall, and it's now missing, wouldn't that narrow things down?"

I made no reply, because we were entering the police-station, not because there was no reply to make. It struck me, for instance, that the Hall, or any other private house, would be extremely unlikely to keep in its medicine cabinet a drug that was capable of being used as a stupefying agent. Still, I supposed, one never knew.

Wharton did a lot of telephoning, and I took a stroll outside. When at last I saw him at the station door he was making urgent signals of recall. The inspector was findin a guide, he said, and we were making a quick visit to the cave. He had made arrangements, he said, for the doctor to hand over the blood sample to the sergeant, who would take it to town by motor-bicycle. Wharton's other man, who had driven us to Cumberforth, was already on duty at the hospital.

The guide Wharton had mentioned turned out to be a driver too, and this time we took the local inspector's car. There was only a mile of drive, and then about a quarter of a mile on foot, and Wharton said that was lucky for he wanted to get back to Dalebrink at once. As for the mile of drive, we went back to the narrow lane by which we had come, and it soon became ruttier than ever where the spring rains had gullied it.

Suddenly Wharton was asking the driver to stop, and then he was getting out and going back to examine the track, and, as I judged, for tyre marks.

"This road used at all?" he asked the driver when he got in again.

The driver said it was used on market day at Cumberforth but not much on other days, for outlying farms were too busy these days for gadding about, and there was the petrol rationing. At night he doubted if it was ever used. By the time he had told us that much he was bringing the car to a halt again and saying that we had better get out.

The lane now overlooked a rocky gully, but there was no roadside hedge and it was easy enough to make our way down. What we did then was to circle more gullies, and take twisted paths through scrub and undergrowth, and all the time I noticed that Wharton's eyes were on the ground. Mine were too, but it was safety of going that concerned me, and not foot-prints.

The guide stopped and pointed dramatically. There was where the shepherd had been, and that was where he had found the exhausted man. Wharton lugged out his note-book and took details about the shepherd, then on we went. When we did finall halt it was dramatically once more. We were making our way along a round bit of land under a kind of cliff from the face of which grew stunted trees and shrubs. Then the guide all at once stopped, and Wharton almost collided with him. A straggling bush was drawn on one side, and he was announcing that there was the entrance to the cave.

"Just a minute before we go in," Wharton said. "A lot of caves in this part, are there?"

The man smiled. "Absolutely honeycombed with 'em."

"And did you know this particular cave?"

"I didn't," he said. "They're so common, you see, that we don't take much account of caves. I reckon you'd fin some of the old codgers in these parts, though, who knew all about it. If they didn't, they'd swear they did."

Wharton produced as by magic a torch from his trouser pocket.

"No gas or anything?" he said.

Before the man had time to do anything more than smile, Wharton was making his way in.

CHAPTER XVI
PASSENDEN TELLS

THE guide had remained outside and Wharton and I made an examination of the cave by the light of the torch. But the cave was not altogether dark. Light penetrated in two places from its roof, and where the rain had come through those wide fissures in the rock, the walls were stained and the rocky floo was still moist.

How large was that cave? Well, of the size of the biggest room in a suburban villa perhaps, which would be about sixteen feet by twelve, though I did not measure it. What particularly struck me about it was that it was amazingly well chosen, for it could have been made quite snug and warm. I won't say that an illicit distiller could have concealed the worm of smoke that would have come from the roof, but an oil-stove would have warmed the place and a primus could have cooked. As a matter of fact the firs thing I smelt on entering was paraffi and almost at once we found the oil-stove that had been used, and a petrol tin with paraffin in it.

But Brende had been given no comfort. All he had had to lie on was a heap of dry litter in the corner farthest from the entrance. He had evidently been kept drugged and allowed to recover for two things—to be questioned and to be given enough food and water to keep him alive. Two cups and two dirty plates were there, and Wharton said they all came from Woolworth's. One of the cups had tea stains, and the plates had grease marks which Wharton said was butter or margarine.

The following traces were found of the person or persons who had been with Brende in the cave: a few cigarette-stubs of common brands, match-ends and a small heap of charred paper. The last description was not absolutely correct for the heap had been reduced to the fines ash. There, as we thought, lay all Brende's private papers and, but for the burned note-book, the results of all his private researches. Wharton got to work looking for finger-prints Naturally there were plenty of Brende's, of which he provided himself with a specimen, but of any others there was never a trace. Then he began a most careful examination of the litter of the bed, but in fiv minutes was giving it up.

"I'll get the place sealed," he said, "and send a man or two to go over it at leisure."

But he flashe a torch once more over the floo as if loath to leave the place, and then we stepped outside again. While we were in there we had grown so accustomed to the queer light that for most purposes we could have dispensed with the torch.

"What now?" I asked Wharton.

Just a scout round, as he put it, for a good ten minutes. I thought he was looking for feet-marks, but when I suggested that the ground, made rock-hard by the draught, would show no marks, he explained what he was looking for. In the cave there had been no signs of urination or excretion. Brende, drugged or not, couldn't have resisted nature, so something of the nature of the chamber-pot must have been used, and emptied somewhere outside. Well, to cut the story short, we did come at last on a couple of such spots, and about a hundred yards from the cave entrance among some bushes. Wharton seemed to think that the captor wouldn't have taken the trouble to go so far;

I thought that the farther the better, so as to avoid the eyes and nose of chance wanderers like the shepherd.

Our guide was a local constable who had helped fin the cave and was now on duty. Wharton said he had better stay there, and we would take the car and arrange reliefs and so on with his inspector. Off we went then, back to the station, I driving the four-year Morris.

"One thing I'll own up to at once, George," I said. "In my heart of hearts I never thought it possible for Brende to have been kidnapped from that house. Though that riflema of mine and the R.S.M. made an entry, I know it wasn't a fair test, because they knew all the ropes. Now I'll own up that that cordon of mine couldn't have been effectiv after all."

"We all make mistakes," Wharton said with smug generosity. "By the way, we'll get off back to Dalebrink as soon as we can. I want to get those men of mine to work."

"You want only one or two, didn't you say?"

"Don't know," he said. "Ten or a dozen will be more like it. That means I'll have to borrow some."

"But why all that number?"

"Don't know," he said again. "We were lucky over findin that tyre mark outside that side gate at the Hall. We might have a bit of luck like that here."

"You've discovered the car that brought Brende here?" I said, and with a touch of indignation that he had not told me so.

"Well, no," he said mildly. "I was just giving that by way of illustration."

We were nearing the station or I might have told him a few things. Then he was doing more telephoning and I was feeling uncommonly hungry by the time we got away, for lunch-time was already past. But I was driving the car, which was that much nearer the Camp and a meal.

"One thing you do know for a certainty," I said to him. "The kidnapping was under the direction of someone who knew all about that cave beforehand. There's the local touch, George."

"You can't be sure," he said.

"Why all the Dismal Jimmy business?" I asked him. "You ought to be thunderingly well pleased with yourself. And why can't you be sure the job wasn't planned locally?"

"This land's all open," he said. "Everyone knows the hills are riddled with caves. All anyone planning a kidnapping had to do was to survey the ground for a likely spot."

Specious, wasn't it? There are times when I think that George's mental light filte excludes everything likely to be informative to the very ones who ought to know, and for the reason that at the very last moment he can discard the filte and have a grand display of illumination and colour presided over by himself.

"You're a brain-picker," I said. "You're a user of talents. What you want round you, George, are strong silent men who sweat blood for the good of your cause and ask no questions."

He looked startled, as if he'd been suddenly savaged by his pet rabbit.

"For instance," I said, "what about Passenden? Where does he come in? Don't tell me you were looking for him for two days to ask him to tell you the story of the Three Bears?"

"Passenden!" he said, with all his old contempt. "Any fool knows where he comes in. Soon as the Colonel disappeared, Mrs. B. had a talk with him, didn't she? She thought the Colonel had lost his memory and he'd be wandering back to the scenes of his childhood, so she asked Passenden to look for him."

"If you wait a moment while I repress a tear," I said, "I'll compose myself sufficient to ask why you wanted to see Passenden. That yarn doesn't fit.

"Oh, yes it does," he said, and gave a little chuckle. "If he did make a discovery, I wanted to be Johnny-on-the-spot. Couldn't have clues obscured, and so on."

But I wasn't listening at that particular moment. He was still babbling on, but I remembered something, and it sent my finger to my glasses.

"Wait a minute," I said, "and listen to this. The word Passenden. A common name, do you think?"

"Well, not uncommon. You'd expect to fin it in the telephone directory."

"Granted," I told him. "But suppose you're picking up the receiver and asking who's speaking. The voice says, 'Passenden speaking.' Would you spot the name firs time? Wouldn't you ask to have it repeated or spelt out?"

He pursed his lips, then admitted grudgingly that perhaps I was right.

"I'm damn sure I'm right," I said. "One proof is the day when Passenden rang the Hall and Ledd tool the message. Ledd's used to taking messages and yet he told us that Major Passenham was on the phone."

"That's right," said Wharton, cocking a more attentive ear. "But what's the moral?"

"This," I said. "Penelope Craye made a slip, though I don't know why. When Passenden firs called to see me I tried to get Brende for him, but Penelope answered."

"You told me all that," he cut in. "She looked for Brende but he'd gone out."

"True," I said. "But I told her that a Major Passenden wanted to speak to the Colonel. I didn't give the name emphasis, or speak specially clearly. But she didn't say, 'Who?' or ask me to repeat or spell. As soon as I'd said the name, she knew it, and therefore—though, mark you, she pretended ignorance of Passenden—she knew his name. Therefore he must have been expected."

"She'd seen that notice about Passenden in the paper," he said. "He was a friend of the family and that's why she knew he'd ultimately turn up at the Hall."

"Agreed," I said patiently. "But Penelope and I weren't exactly strangers. Here are some of the things I'd have expected her to say to me under those circumstances. 'How *is* Major Passenden? We've been expecting him. The Colonel will be awfully sorry to have missed him. Do send him along to see us.' That would have been normal conduct, so I claim. Everything she did was abnormal, according to your arguments."

"There may be something in it," he admitted, and then we stopped talking, for I was driving through the town and the traffic needed watching. Then in less than no time we were at the Camp and he was taking over the wheel.

"You'll be in Dalebrink from now on?" I asked.

"I very much doubt it," he told me. "A spot of grub and I'm off back to Cumberforth. May be there a day or two."

He waved a hand and was off I nodded cynically at the back of the car. If George still considered it necessary to be secretive, my withers would be unwrung. I had my own work at the Camp, and since no one could bar my entry at the Hall, I had my own sources of information if I felt so disposed.

I was busy enough during what was left of the afternoon, but no sooner was tea over and time on my hands than I began thinking about things again, and in spite of my self-assurances that the case was Wharton's affai from now on, and that if he didn't want me to play in his yard, I wouldn't be fretting. What I did think, as I laid aside the cross-word at which I had been spasmodically working, was that it might be exceedingly gratifying to work out at least part of the case and put it to Wharton as beyond all question.

I am not going to bore you with lengthy arguments or abstruse deductions. All I want to do is to sum up things briefl and, I hope, clearly, and see if you agree. And we start off with what seemed to me to be the clearest thing of all, that the killing of Penelope Craye was the central point of everything. In it would be found the master clues, and it was upon it that I might reasonably concentrate, since Wharton apparently was thinking otherwise. If then I could gather anything from what I had already seen and heard and from Wharton's scanty hints, the following facts stood clear:

(*a*) Brende had been kidnapped for obvious reasons.

(*b*) Penelope Craye had been killed because she could not be kidnapped too. To use the same method would have been too dangerous.

Why had she been killed? Because

(*a*) Brende's captors had gathered from him or otherwise that she knew things.

(*b*) They had been unable to get anything from him at all, and hoped for better luck from her. Connected with both (*a*) and (*b*) is Brende's note-book, which P.C. did have and which she burned.

(*c*) She was a member of the gang and her mouth had to be shut once and for all. Also she would have served her purpose.

Now it couldn't be denied that the killing of Penelope Crave was an inside job. But all suspects, except Newton, had been removed. That, you will say, is all to the good. Didn't Wharton boldly state that Newton was his key man, and that if he could be made to talk, then the case would be over in its entirety? I admit it. Wharton did. So far, therefore, so good. Newton killed Penelope Crave, at least if we follow the arguments to their logical conclusions.

But when I had got so far, a personal knowledge of Wharton and his idiosyncrasies began to cut across things. If Wharton stated that Newton was the master mind, it was all the more reason why I should not believe him. In ordinary cases he was secretive, doling out information as a last resort. What then might I expect on a hush-hush case like this, where he had every reason to keep everything important from the faintest risk of disclosure? In other words, why had he told me something so conclusive, so staggering and so dangerous as that Newton was the man behind it all? What did he want? Why had he put the thought in my mind? One reason only could present itself to me. He wanted me—without committing himself—to hint to Newton that we were wise to him, and he hoped that Newton would then let something fall for which he—Wharton—had been waiting, and which he had not been able to obtain by his own methods.

Very well, I told myself, I would call on Newton again. I would scheme to bring back the topic of the photostats, and I would pin him down. In fact, on the old principle of no time like the present, I would see Newton before dinner, and as soon as I'd planned the precise lines of attack.

Mind you, there was something else of which I had not lost track. The killing of Penelope Craye might have been an entirely independent thing, or only remotely connected with the kidnapping of Colonel Brende. Bluntly, she might have been poisoned by Mrs. Brende for reasons already argued. If so, Newton was Wharton's master mind only as far as concerned the kidnapping.

I wanted to see young Craye, so I went to my offic   and while I was waiting for him to come, I thought I'd fin   out if Newton was in. Ledd said he'd just gone out for a walk. That rather surprised me, as I'd never thought of Newton as taking open-air exercise, and it was decidedly salutary as showing how slovenly my thinking had recently been. It was also extremely lucky for me that Newton was out, for if I had gone to the Hall and tackled him along the lines which I had prepared, I should have made several additional kinds of a fool of myself.

Craye came in and I asked if he wished to go to Penelope's funeral, which was the following afternoon at the local cemetery. He said he ought to go, and he was grateful for the favour. He had heard from his aunt, who had sent him letters of condolence arising out of the announcement of the death. He also told me that the solicitors whom Penelope occasionally used in town, had no knowledge of a will. That, though we didn't mention the fact, seemed to make him principal heir to whatever she had.

"You still don't feel like making a clean breast to your aunt?" I asked him.

He said he didn't. He'd rather move cautiously. He also wanted to know when he was coming up for judgment. I refused to commit myself. A considerable deal of anxiety would still do him no harm.

Out he went. I stretched my legs and wondered if I should see Newton after dinner. Then the phone bell went. Passenden was asking if I were busy, and might he just pop in for a moment. He was going away in the morning, he added, as what struck me as an afterthought. I said I'd be glad to see him, and straightaway I was wondering how I could bring the conversation round to the subject of Sowdale, and the time he had spent there when he had led me to think he was in Scotland. What I particularly wanted to do was to test that absurd theory Wharton had put forward, about Passenden helping Mrs. Brende to fin a husband who hadn't been kidnapped after all, but had lost his memory.

I couldn't help wondering too, why it should be me in particular whom Passenden wanted to see, and, being a suspicious cove, I was soon having the idea that there must be something he was wishing to find out. Then all at once I realized how little I really knew about him considering how closely he had been connected with what one might call the fringes of the case. He had turned up in Dalebrink at just the right moment, which was strange when you take into account those months of wandering through France and Spain and Portugal. He had been in the vicinity of the Hall on that Saturday night, and he had led us into thinking he was in Scotland when he was actually in the vicinity of the place where the kidnapped Brende had been found. No wonder, then, that I began to be more and more interested as the moment of his arrival drew near. What I actually was to hear from him was so amazing that if I had been given a hundred guesses I could never have come within a mile of it.

Passenden was looking just the same. A bit more tanned, perhaps, and with much of the newness gone from that civilian suit, but as quiet in manner as ever and utterly unperturbed. As he was going away in the morning he had come to say good-bye and to thank me, so he said.

"I don't think there's anything to thank me for," I said. "And where're you bound for this time?"

"Oh, town," he said. "Scotland's none too good at this time of year."

"I suppose not," I said, and passed my cigarette-case, and then flicke the lighter for him.

"You've heard about poor old Brende?" he was suddenly asking.

"Yes," I said. "Wharton let me know, as I was interested. How did you get the news?"

"Through Mrs. Brende," he said unconcernedly. "They're bringing him to the Hall to-morrow, I believe."

I gave a Whartonian grunt, and ventured the opinion that it had been a queer business all round.

"Does your pal Wharton think so?" he said.

"Hallo!" I said to myself. "Now we're getting down to things. Here's where I'm expected to give the show away."

I said I didn't see how Wharton or anybody else could help thinking it a queer business. Kidnappings were virtually unknown in this country.

"And that other business, of Miss Craye," he said, as if it had just occurred to him. "Wasn't there something fish about that?"

"Why do you think so?"

"Mrs. Brende gave me that impression. I know her well enough to read between the lines." His eyes switched from his cigarette and he was giving me a quizzical sort of smile. "I suppose you know the facts?"

"I'm sorry," I said. "You can't expect me to talk of confidentia matters. I might on certain conditions, of course."

"Such as?"

"Well, if we both talked frankly and laid our cards face upwards on the table."

"Aren't we doing that?"

"Now, now, now," I said. "I'm too old a bird to be caught like that. You give me your word that anything that's said here and now goes no further."

"Why not?" he said. "You begin."

"Right-ho," said I. "I'll begin with a question. Why did you lead us to believe you were in Scotland when you were actually in the neighbourhood of where Brende was found?"

He smiled amusedly. "Just change of plans. Weather a bit cold for Scotland, you know. Also the north of the county was one of my old stamping grounds."

"A mere coincidence that Brende was found there?"

"My dear fellow, how could it be anything else?" Then he was looking down at his cigarette again and shaking his head, though still with something of amusement. "I expect I rather worried your friend Wharton?"

"What you've got to think about is the other side of the question," I told him grimly. "You watch for the time when Wharton begins to worry *you*."

"I'm a suspect?"

"Haven't you behaved like one?"

He shrugged his shoulders. "I suppose that's one way of looking at it. But do you hint that I'm suspected of kidnapping, or murder, or both?"

"I'm not in Wharton's counsels," I said. "You'll know when he tells you that you're not to stir without keeping him informed of your movements."

"He's done that already."

"The devil he has!" I said, taken considerably aback. "Well, there we are then," I added lamely. "I don't see there's much more to add."

He was getting to his feet.

"Well, I must be pushing along. I'm sorry I can't confess that I'm worried about being a suspect, because I'm not."

"You mean that if you'd been involved, Wharton could never prove it?"

He shrugged his shoulders again. "Take it that way if you like." That amused look came into his eyes again as he put the question. "Honestly, do you think I look like a kidnapper or a murderer?"

"I shouldn't make that your trump card with George Wharton," I told him earnestly.

He nodded, face a bit more sober.

"I like you, Travers. I'm perfectly frank when I say that. I think you're a good sort and I know Mrs. Brende thinks so too. She had every reason. We're talking in strict confidence isn't that so?"

"Yes," I said. "Even if neither of us may be telling the truth, the whole truth, and nothing but the truth."

"Maybe. But you've forgotten something. It's my turn to make disclosures. You'd like to know more than Wharton will ever know about these happenings?"

"Yes," I said calmly, "if it's good for my health."

He looked me straight in the eye, and I'd never thought those brown eyes of his could be so chill.

"Your word of honour that you'll never speak a word of this, or hint it?"

I hesitated, wondering to what I was about to commit myself. Then my damnable curiosity got the better of me.

"Certainly I'll give it, if you think it necessary."

"I do think it necessary," he said. "And this is why. By the way, don't bother to see me out. I know my way pretty well. But what I was about to say was this. I was responsible for the kidnapping of Colonel Brende."

"Good Lord!" I said, finger already at my glasses. "You can't be serious."

"I never was more so," he assured me.

My eyes were suddenly narrowing.

"And that other business—the murder of Penelope Craye Did you do that too?"

"Well—yes," he said slowly. "You can take it that I was responsible for that too."

He had been moving towards the door, and all at once he was looking back. His look was gravely courteous and his manner unperturbed as ever.

"Good-bye, and thank you again. And don't forget I trust your word."

The door closed behind him, and there I stood polishing my glasses and blinking away like the frightened idiot that I felt.

CHAPTER XVII
WHARTON IS READY

That evening I felt like a deflate tyre. Every interest had gone out of the case, just as it would have gone out of a detective novel, if I had read the last two chapters first Then as I lay in bed that night, and on the borderland of sleep, my old inquisitiveness began to move back into its accustomed quarters from which Passenden's statements had shifted it, and I was puzzling my none too active wits over many things, and findin no very satisfactory answers.

Above all I wondered just why Passenden should have seen fi even under strict secrecy, to make those astounding and damning disclosures. Though I must own that I had always liked the man, I could not but regard his protestations of liking for me a very much in the nature of calculated flattery We are much better informed about our virtues than our vices, and, mildly please though I momentarily was, and true as Passenden's statement appeared to ring, I knew of no favours received or of sufficie judgment on Passenden's part to make such an appraisal.

It was not till I woke next morning that I hit on some solution Passenden's call on me was something in the nature of a criminal return to the scene of the crime. He had, in other words, to tell to somebody or bust. But that led to something far more serious. Had I actually been talking to a kidnapper and murderer? Was he sane and was he serious? Had those experiences of his a last taken toll and had he cracked under them? Frankly I did not know. At the time I would have sworn he was both sane and most damnably serious, but now, out of the presence and hearing of the man, I was not so sure.

But it seemed to me there were two ways in which to test him. Why had he done what he did, and how had he done it? Then I was bang up against it. Unless he was blindly on Mrs. Brende side and wished to end a possible affai between Brende and Penelope Craye, I saw no reason at all, for it wasn't sane on my part to think of such a man as an enemy agent out to stop at all costs that work at the Hall.

As to how he could have done it, I was more than ever beaten. Even if he had arrived in Dalebrink a day or so earlier than he had pretended to me, he could not possibly have had complete knowledge of the night disposition of my men, and such knowledge was the essential to slipping through the cordon. But according to him he had done it twice, and that passed the bounds of reason. Then, too late, I knew I could have asked a question which would have proved a good deal. "Do you know anything about cracking anyone on the skull, and if so, how and where did you do it?" A frank answer to that would have proved a good deal, as I said, but now it was too late and I could have kicked myself for not having thought of it.

As for my future attitude to Wharton, I thought that would not be difficul for I could still simulate interest. What would be hard would be to see the dear old General heading the wrong way, with me unable to tell him so and head him back. But I admit that that part of the business did begin to worry me, and after lunch I rang his City address. His landlady, when she was sure of my identity, said she thought he was in London, but he would be back late that night. As I replaced the receiver I was thinking not of Wharton but of the City itself. Now that old Dove had gone, one had ceased to think of the City at all. All the local fury, gossip and scandal had gone into the thin air, and doubtless war-time suspicion and the urge to talk were being directed against other Fifth Columnists compared with whom the Neggers would be pitiful creatures deserving even of a certain sympathy.

Later that afternoon I rang the Hall, with a view to sympathetic enquiries about Brende. Who should answer my call but Mrs. Brende. From her voice I could never have imagined that anything had happened.

"How are you?" I said.

"Keeping very well," she told me. "I don't like the weather to-day. I hate a drizzle."

"So do I," I said, "especially when it's cold. And the Colonel—is he with you?"

"Oh, yes," she said. "You must come and see him. He may not know you."

"Thanks," I said. "I'd love to come. And I hope I'll fin him much better."

One word in that brief talk intrigued me much—*may*. If Colonel Brende *might* recognize me, then he was recovering his memory, and that opened possibilities.

So I went to the Hall almost at once. Ledd admitted me, and I expected him to ring for Annie to take me to Mrs. Brende. What he said was that Mrs. Brende had told him to take me straight up to the Colonel's room. I expected to fin her there, but she was not.

The bedroom was on the far side of the house and appeared to me to have been specially furnished and prepared. Some of its contents had come from Penelope's room, and that seemed to me to be rather strange. A uniformed nurse was sitting knitting by the window when Ledd showed me in, and she came over at once.

"How is he?" I whispered.

"About the same," she whispered back.

"I can see him?"

She nodded and smiled. "Do you wish me to go?"

I shook my head and moved over to the bed. Brende had been shaved, and I must say he already looked his old self. What was different and strangely repellent, was his eyes. As I stood by the bed they ran idly over me, as if something had come between him and the light. Then his head turned on the pillow again and his eyes closed. I gave a shake or two of the head, and then there seemed nothing else to do but go. The nurse followed me out to the corridor.

"What's the report on him?" I asked.

"He's all right in himself," she said. "They feared pneumonia at first but we're not worrying now. To-morrow, if he shows any desire, he may be allowed to get up."

"Has he recognized anybody at all?"

She smiled. "He recognized Ledd for a minute or two and then forgot him again. But nobody else. Nor Professor Newton, nor Mr. Riddle, nor even Mrs. Brende."

"They've sat with him alone?"

She seemed surprised at the question.

"Oh, yes. That's much the best way."

"And what're the prospects of recovery?"

"Very hopeful," she said. "It may be a long time or it may be at any time. These cases are very erratic."

I smiled a good-bye and made my way downstairs. There seemed no reason why I should thrust myself on Mrs. Brende, so I went straight to my car. Then I had a sudden idea. Was it Brende who had been the traitor? Brende and Penelope Craye together? Had Passenden abducted the one and disposed artistically of the other because he considered it a national duty?

My thoughts went further. Was Passenden an agent of the Government? Was all that France, Spain and Lisbon business a fake? Had he been sent to Dalebrink months before to check up on what was going on, and had that disposal of Brende and Penelope been considered the best way? I shook my head, but not in doubt. It was war-time, I thought, and desperate expedients are needed to meet desperate situations.

But I could do no clear thinking that afternoon. That dull, unseeing look in Brende's eyes was beginning to haunt me, and to put me further in the grip of a tremendous depression was the clouded sky and the drizzle that made me flic on the screen-wiper. Ichabod was the word, I thought. Everything had changed at the Hall from the day when I had firs seen it. Then it had been a vital, friendly place, and now it was somehow moribund, and something to avoid. And there seemed too an infinit of things to regret. So gloomy indeed were my thoughts that I could almost have wished for the sight of Penelope Craye, or to have been back at that night when I sat by the summer-house and someone—Passenden almost certainly—had given me the crack on the skull.

That night went by, and the following morning, and I hear nothing from Wharton. Then just after lunch he rang me. H voice was so mild that I thought he was droning away at script.

"Are you busy these days?"

"Why? What's on?"

"Like to be at the Hall at fiv o'clock sharp this afternoon?"

"What's in the wind?" I asked, guessing from the placidity of his tone that something mighty serious was about to happen.

"I'm hoping for a show-down," he said.

"Really?" I gaped a bit, then told him that Passenden was in town.

"Oh, no, he isn't," he said. "He'll be with us at five.

"Anyone else?"

"Newton—perhaps."

"For heaven's sake cough it all up, George," I told him patiently. "You're not paying instalments on the piano. Who have you got new?"

"One or two oddments. I saw a Big Bug or two in town and we talked things over."

I remembered something.

"That drug test. How did it turn out?"

"None too good," he said. "Negatively, as a matter of fact."

"Too late in getting it to the analyst?"

"Maybe. Also there're drugs we don't know too much about." He gave a little cough. "See you at fiv o'clock then?"

"I'll be there," I told him, and before I'd time to add, "if it's the last thing I do," he had rung off

I can't recall when I was in such a state of general excitement and dither. How to pass the time till fiv o'clock was my problem, so I concentrated on the cross-word, frowning away as if had a missing five in the accounts. But it was no use, so drifted along to the offi and sent for Craye, about whom I'd had a long talk with Harrison.

"Well, Mr. Craye," I said, "I've decided that you may carry on as if nothing had happened. I don't promise the matter won't be reopened, and reopened fully, but that may largely depend on yourself."

"Thank you, sir," he said. "You shan't regret it, sir."

There seemed to be something else on his mind, so I told him to get it off

"Well, the sergeant, sir. I oughtn't to let him down."

"He returns to his Unit to-morrow," I said. "The least you say about sergeants the better for you. And about everything."

"Yes, sir."

But he was still fidgeting

"Well, what else is there?" I asked him.

"My aunt, sir. I was wondering if it would be trespassing too much on your generosity if I asked if you could do anything for me."

"Be a man and do it for yourself," I said. "When you can come to me and tell me that, then we'll see."

But, of course, I didn't see, at least what I'd so airily promised. What I did see was that it would be pretty presumptuous on my part if I butted into the private relationships of aunt and nephew. Then something occurred to me. There are occasions when mild blackmail—or pressure, shall we call it?—is both useful and salutary. There might come a time when Mrs. Brende—who had been in close touch with Passenden—might wonder if I knew too much for her future peace of mind. In that case I might exercise a little diplomacy, always provided young Craye was really on the straight and narrow lane of reform.

Well, the time came at last and into my car I got. I was early, but I preferred to dawdle on the way rather than be any longer inactive. Ledd opened the front door to me and he was looking lugubrious. It would be a pity, I thought, if that grin of his was lost to the world.

"A nasty day for a walk, Ledd," I said, and his face coloured as he spotted at once at what I was hinting. Then I indulged in a Whartonian look over the top of my horn-rims, and a faint smile came to his face. Perhaps I was not so fearsome after all.

"No, sir," he said, and then pulled himself together. "This way, sir. Mr. Wharton's expecting you."

This time he took me to Brende's old room, and there Wharton was, and Passenden and Newton already occupying chairs. Newton smiled most tentatively. Passenden nodded, and his smile was definitel cynical. Wharton's manner was that of an undertaker's head man.

"Here you are, Major Travers. Take a seat there, will you? Make yourself at home. Smoke by all means, gentlemen. Just a small matter which shouldn't keep us long."

A table, folded flat had been rigged up, and Wharton took a seat at it. Then he put on his antiquated spectacles, and fussed with some papers he took from his wallet, and I knew he wanted to let us think it was all very preposterous and red tape, and the fault wasn't his. Then he coughed gently and took a look at us.

"Well, gentlemen, I said I shouldn't be keeping you long, and that really depends on yourselves. Not on Major Travers, exactly, but on you other gentlemen. All you have to do is to talk."

"What about?" Passenden asked. "Just anything?"

"Yes," said Wharton unruffledl "Just anything, provided it's to do with what's been happening here recently."

Passenden looked up from fillin his pipe. He shrugged his shoulders, looked at Newton with a raising of eyebrows, then was stoking his pipe again. Newton looked most uncomfortable

"You, Major Passenden," Wharton said. "Perhaps you'd like to begin. I assure you, and everybody, that what's said here this afternoon will never be made public. All you two gentlemen have to do is to tell the truth and then forget all about it."

"Personally I'm in the dark," Passenden said. "I haven't the foggiest notion what I'm supposed to talk about."

Wharton peered at him over his spectacle tops, then fingered the papers that now lay spread on the table. He found one and handed it to Passenden.

"Anticipating such a move, I've prepared a list. You can either talk about them here in private, or we'll both talk about them very much in public."

"Here comes the iron fis out of the velvet glove," I thought, "or else Wharton is trying a bluff. But my eyes were on Passenden. He read what was on that sheet of paper, and without moving a muscle. Then he handed the paper courteously back.

"Sorry," he said, "but I'm afraid it's all Greek to me."

"You prefer the alternative?"

"That's up to you," Passenden told him, and his eyes were steadily on Wharton's. "One thing I will say. No man ever made me talk when I didn't want to. What you care to say doesn't interest me."

Wharton let out a breath and gave a mournful shake of the head. Then he was looking at Newton, and never had I seen a man look more uncomfortable than the Professor.

"Perhaps you'll start then, Professor Newton."

"I?" stammered Newton. He gave a sort of titter. "I'm afraid I'm the same. I don't see what there is for me to talk about."

"Ah, well," said Wharton resignedly. "Here's your little paper. Just read it and make sure I know all about things."

Newton's look was a quick one, and he was still shaking his head as he handed the paper back.

"You know, like Major Passenden, that this may considerably hamper your future career?" Wharton asked him.

Newton shook his head again, but the hand that produced the cigarette-case was rather shaky. Wharton's tone changed. It was brisker and just a bit hard, but I knew it to be nothing compared with what might come in a minute.

"I see. Neither wants to talk. Well, there're more ways of killing a cat than choking it with cream. I propose to tell you one or two." The tone hardened and there was a perceptible sneer. "By the time I've finished gentlemen, you'll both wish—"

There were quick steps in the corridor, and a tap at the door. Wharton said, "Excuse me, gentlemen," and went to the door himself. I just caught Ledd's excited voice, and then the door closed behind Wharton. In less than a minute he was looking in again.

"Pardon me, gentlemen, please. I'll be back in a moment or two."

Well, there we sat, nobody saying a word. Passenden was sitting arms on knees, and interested in nothing so much as his pipe. I looked at Newton, half caught his eye, and then he was being solicitous for the ash of his cigarette. I gently cleared my throat.

"I'd like you to know, Passenden, I said that this meeting is very much of a surprise to me."

I hoped he'd take it as a hint that I'd kept my word. He apparently did, for he smiled.

"My dear fellow, you needn't tell me that."

Then we were all cocking an ear, for steps were heard approaching in the corridor. They were Wharton's, and he looked grave enough as he closed the door. But he took his time about things.

"Well, gentlemen," he said at last. "I fin   I shan't need the thumbscrews after all. You can both talk. Colonel Brende is dead."

"Dead!"

It was I who spoke.

"Dead," echoed Wharton. "And by his own hand. Five minutes ago he shot himself."

CHAPTER XVIII
THE SHOW-DOWN

Passenden's first words were really directed at me, even if the eyes were on Wharton.

"I suppose I was responsible for all this, even if it wasn't my fault entirely. It arose out of that discovery I made. It was when the Huns were just breaking through and my A. A. guns were red hot. I'd been soldiering for twenty-fiv years and it had come to me out of the blue, just at a time like that. A pretty good idea it was, though I say it. I was so full of it, I went and told Brende, even if it was just a bit above his head.

"I did keep a bit back, I don't know why. Perhaps because I felt differen about him, though I never had trusted him entirely. You see, I knew he was having an affai with the Craye woman. Oh, yes, I knew her long before I came down here. And I knew that Mrs. Brende was being kept very much in the dark. But about that scheme of mine. I told Brende to his face that there was one little bit I was keeping back. I'm rather sorry about that now.

"This is why. The Bosche broke through and we thought we were cut off I don't want to go into details but he and I were the last to leave our little headquarters. We were burning documents and things, and all at once he said to me that neither of us knew if we'd ever get out alive, so oughtn't I to tell him the rest of my idea. I agreed, and I did tell him, and I gave him my rough notes, and his eyes popped out of his head. A few minutes later a man came running in to say that Hun tanks were coming over the ridge. Brende told him to hop it on the pedal-bicycle and leave the motor-bike for us two. I can see him now, looking out of where there was once a window and I can see the man pedalling away like hell's hammers. Then he drew my attention to something, and the next thing I knew was that I'd been shot."

"He shot you?" asked Wharton.

"Oh, yes. He shot me all right. And he damn near made a good job of it. I just seem to remember him standing over me, as if he was findin out if he'd done the job well and truly. I even think I can hear the sound of a motor-bike which was him getting away, then I passed out and the Huns must have taken me for dead. But I wasn't, and the rest you probably know. I ultimately got to England and I made enquiries at the War House. Brende had got them enthusiastic about my idea and Dalebrink Hall was working at it with Brende in nominal command. I also discovered that Penelope Craye was installed as his secretary. Those are a few of the reasons why I wanted a quiet word or two with Brende."

"And why he didn't want them with you."

"Exactly. But what I couldn't understand was how Brende, who, frankly, never had the brains for that sort of thing was able to act as head of research. Either he must have modifie the idea, or simplifie it, or picked somebody else's brains. At any rate, it puzzled me. What didn't puzzle me in the least was when Major Travers rang the Hall and that woman swore he wasn't there. They must have known I would soon be in England — there was a paragraph in the papers—but they hadn't expected me so soon. Now you know why I took a stroll round that way that very firs night, when I was unlucky enough to get caught by the police. But I was lucky in another way, because it was that that brought me to Major Travers' offi where you told me about the kidnapping. I smelt a rat at once. I knew that kidnapping was a fake.

"The next thing I did was to get in touch with Mrs. Brende. I was glad she had got wise to Penelope Craye, and finall we talked freely, and we had to agree that the kidnapping was a put-up job. Her view was that he mustn't be allowed to bring more scandal on the name and that between us we must straighten things out as best we could. I guessed he'd gone to somewhere near Sowdale, and I hoped I'd be able to fin him. I did fin him, and in the cave which we'd both known as boys. He was having a good time, but I had a gun and I scared the life out of him. If he hadn't told me everything—or nearly so— and agreed to do what I told him, I'd most certainly have shot him and buried him where he'd never have been found. What I told him to do was to fake loss of memory, let himself be found, then resign his appointment and leave the service, and then to disappear for good. That was the only way to save scandal, and his neck."

"Why his neck?" I asked.

Passenden looked at Wharton.

"Tell him how he killed Penelope Craye," Wharton said.

"Well, that's rather involved," Passenden said, "and I'll tell you why. I got the idea that one of the reasons why Brende disappeared was to give himself an alibi for the murder of his wife. I honestly think his original idea was to get rid of her, come into her money, and then marry the Craye woman. I got Mrs. Brende of the same opinion, and I induced her to take special precautions. But Brende knew that Penelope knew too much. She was the one he decided to get rid of. Mind you, I even believe the Craye woman had an idea that he was going to kill his wife. That woman was capable of anything, even murder. Still, as I said, Brende made up his mind to kill her first and he did. He didn't kill her at her fla because that wouldn't have given him quite so good an alibi. When she was dead, I think he would have killed his wife next, or else he'd have tried wheedling her into some sort of reconciliation or money settlement."

"Just a minute," I said. "You're travelling too fast for me. How was that fake kidnapping done? How could he get through my cordon?"

"He didn't," Wharton said. "You told me about coal being put into a cellar. I discovered that that coal had been ordered on the morning of Penelope Craye's death and Mrs. Brende, who ordered it, insisted on immediate delivery. That coal concealed a door. But you go on, Major."

"It concealed a door to a passage that led to the summer-house," Passenden said. "It played a great part in the wicked days when there were high old goings on at the pool. Then it was more or less of a family secret. I knew about it, though Brende didn't know that. Mrs. Brende and I guessed he'd gone in and out that way, right underneath your cordon, Travers. As for the actual night, my arrival hurried things a bit. They'd planned it for a night or two later, perhaps, because there were other reasons for the disappearance besides my arrival. After all, he could have given me the lie direct and his word was almost as good as mine."

"What other reasons?" I asked.

"Well, about killing his wife. Also I think Professor Newton may have a few things to say about some other reasons."

"And how was the faking done?"

"The Craye woman hired a car," he said. "I can tell you where. While Brende was doing the faking of the room, for which everything was ready beforehand, and announcing to all and sundry that he'd made a colossal discovery, she fetched the car and had it outside the side gate after dark. She also used the passage, of course. She drove Brende to Cumberforth and brought the car back to where it was hired from, and then walked back into the house through the summer-house passage again.'

"And she had a look round to see everything was set," Wharton cut in. "She'd discovered he'd left the note-book behind, so she thought she'd better burn it. And both of them had been so hurried that they made slips. Breaking open drawers, for instance, when a real abductor would have helped himself to the drugged man's keys."

"Just before midnight, was it, when Brende got away?" I asked.

"That was about the time," Passenden told me.

"Good," I said. "I know at last who gave me that crack on the skull. I was sitting on the summer-house seat when Brende wanted to make his exit. He probably hit me with a croquet mallet. But about killing Penelope Craye. He didn't own up to that, did he?"

"He certainly didn't," Passenden said. "That's one thing he strenuously denied."

Suddenly he was getting to his feet and whipping open the door. He smiled rather sheepishly as he came back.

"I'd rather not have this known, except to ourselves, and I'd be glad if you'd forget it. We had another angle on that murder. Mrs. Brende, as cool as they make 'em, wasn't going to let herself be done in without taking precautions. Also you may not know it, but she's something of a detective-novel fan. She didn't tell me till later, but she had the idea of sprinkling something at night both in the cellar and outside Penelope's door, and she'd be up at crack of dawn to see results. Even before Penelope's body was discovered that morning she knew a man had entered the house, and the room. That, with what I could tell, would have been enough to hang Brende." He looked down at his cold pipe and shook his head. "And that, I think, is about all I know."

"Just one thing more," I said. "Why did Mrs. Brende have Penelope to tea the day before she died?"

Passenden smiled. "Just some idea about picking her brains. Cat and mouse business, and so on."

"Well, you've certainly cleared a good few things up," said Wharton, and was peering amiably at Newton over his spectacles. "And now what about you, Professor? What's your angle on things?"

"Well," said Newton, stammering as usual, "most of what Major Passenden has said is news to me, but it does confirm a lot of other things which used to puzzle me. Of course I didn't really know there was any illicit affai between Colonel Brende and his secretary. I did have suspicions at times, but really their manner was usually most proper."

"Exactly," said Wharton. "But how did you get into all this originally?"

"It was queer from the start," Newton said, gathering more speed and confidence "I should have met Colonel Brende at the Ministry and we were going into things with Hush." He didn't call him that, though I still prefer to leave him anonymous. "Then a sudden message came that Colonel Brende was unwell, and a typescript came instead. I saw the idea was excellent, the most promising I'd had in fact, but it had some gaps. I didn't tell Hush so, but agreed that there was every chance of ultimately putting the idea into working, and effectiv working. Later I was told to come down here, and in the interim I'd supposed that Colonel Brende was still unwell. But I found him down here, and he was nominally in charge of research.

"But that wasn't the only surprising thing, gentlemen. When I had to approach him about details of his idea, he would put me off He'd say I knew more than he did, or if I puzzled it out I'd hit on some improvement, or that he hadn't worked out that particular detail himself. Then there was that business of his working at another great idea by himself, upstairs here. Frankly I was puzzled. Believe me or not, I arrived at the only possible conclusion—that he had presented us with a scheme which wasn't his own at all. Either that or he'd got the glimmering of a notion and hadn't the faintest idea how to work on it further.

"Then Gunner"—and again he didn't call him that—"was coming down, and I was seriously alarmed. I didn't see how Colonel Brende could possibly get himself out of an awkward fix but he did. I'm afraid the General wasn't much better informed. At any rate, Colonel Brende satisfie him well enough."

"With the note-book?" asked Wharton.

Newton shot a look at him.

"Well, yes, with the note-book."

"You arrived at the conclusion that there was a lot of humbug about that note-book," Wharton prompted helpfully.

"Yes, but not at first As a matter of fact I hardly like to tell you this. It doesn't redound much to my credit."

Wharton gave a chuckle. "We're all rogues and vagabonds if the truth were only known."

Newton smiled. "I don't think it's quite as bad as that. What did happen was that I went to Miss Craye's sitting-room at her invitation and she didn't happen to be there. I was going to have tea with her, as a matter of fact. That note-book was there, and I wondered what on earth Brende was thinking of to be so careless. Then—well, my curiosity got the better of me and I had a look at it. Shortly afterwards Miss Craye came flyin in, full of apologies, and when she saw the note-book, she was very much perturbed. The Colonel had been in on business just before, she said, and must have left it there, so she took it back at once."

"And what did you see in it?"

Newton smiled down his nose, and was shaking his head as if at some reminiscence.

"Perhaps I might explain this way. In my early days as an examiner for various Boards I had to mark many thousands of examination papers. One day I came across a very long-winded answer that quite perplexed me for a moment or two. I thought for a second that I'd come up against some mathematical genius whose brain was functioning in spheres far outside my experience, and then almost as quickly I tumbled to what had been done. Later on I contrived to interview this candidate.[1] He owned up quite unblushingly. I should say he was quite a clever fellow at many things, but mathematics, after a certain point, were merely a blank as far as he was concerned—a very common occurrence, I assure you. What he'd done was to try to hot-stuff me, as he called it, by fillin a page with the most ingenious series of formulæ and gibberish. I assured him he'd probably land up in gaol if he carried that kind of dexterity into ordinary life. He was most cheerful about it all. I remember he said he'd hoped I'd allow him some marks for his ingenuity."

I had to laugh at that story. As a matter of fact I had an idea I knew the very bloke who had tried that bluff

"The note-book was something of the kind," Newton was going on. "A great deal of genuine stuff of no particular value, but very much more of the kind I've described. I couldn't help but conclude that it had been compiled for the benefi of Gunner. Mind you, I'm casting no aspersions on him. That book wouldn't have deceived the very elect, but it would certainly have convinced the half-informed."

"And the photostats?" Wharton asked.

"Well, naturally they were three brief extracts from what I've been trying to describe. One series of formulæ had been lifted straight out of a fairly well-known book on the Calculus."

"I don't know when I've listened to a clearer exposition," Wharton told us. "And you see what follows, gentlemen. Hush was due down, and all that eyewash and humbug wouldn't get by him. Brende had to do something about it. That's why he had planned to get out in any case even before you turned up, Major Passenden. But you must have been in a very queer position here, Professor?"

"A most painful position," Newton said. "When he came down that Saturday evening with his note-book and began talking of a big discovery, I hardly knew which way to look. And all the time before that, I was most uncomfortable. I knew the man was a charlatan, but what could I do? I couldn't rat on him. I didn't want to throw up the work here, which is definitel achieving results. Then when he disappeared—well, I didn't know where

202 | christopher bush

I was. I didn't know what to say or do, so I determined not to
think about things at all, but to get on with my job. When I
told you, Superintendent, that we should manage to get along
without him, I really thought I'd given the whole thing away."

"Only some of it," Wharton told him. "It was your manner
that gave you away. I knew you had something to say if only I
could get you to talk."

There was a moment's silence, and I managed to cut in.

"As the sole idiot of this pleasant meeting, I think I ought to
be allowed to ask a question or two."

"Why not?" said Wharton, waving a hand round.

"About that cave, then. I suppose Brende had it prepared
well beforehand?"

"You bet your life he had," Passenden said. "I don't know what
you fellows found, but when I stepped in he had a camp-bed and
a deck-chair and plenty of grub, and a primus stove."

"My men have unearthed some of them where he hid them,"
Wharton broke in. "And they're still scouring the district."

"But why did he look so ill?"

"He simply had to keep awake for twenty-four hours,"
Passenden said. "That's what I advised him. No grub and no
sleep and then that beard on his face and his natural thinness,
and a few pricks on the arm to show he'd been drugged, and
there you are."

"I begin to see things," I said. "There were marks of tyres
outside that side gate before Penelope drove up the hired car
that night. Those were the tyres of her own car, and she and
Brende used to pop out at night. That's why she took that fla in
the town. She and Brende could have got back to the house all
right through the passage, but she couldn't have brought in the
car without it being noted at the gate."

"One thing about the syringe marks on Brende's arm,"
Wharton said. "You didn't prime him well enough, Major. He
was right-handed, so he made all the marks on his left arm. That
set me thinking, or rather it confirme   certain ideas I already
had. Genuine marks would have been made anywhere and
everywhere."

He was getting to his feet and stowing his spectacles away in their antiquated case.

"That seems to be about all for the moment, gentlemen. Later on I must ask you for a confidentia report, but we'll fi that later. I rely on you two gentlemen to be at my disposal all tomorrow."

"One thing I've got to say," added Passenden. "My opinion is that Mrs. Brende ought not to be brought into all this under any circumstances. I'd hate to be truculent, but I'd strongly object to mentioning her name in any report of mine, however confidential.

Wharton raised a placatory hand.

"I agree. You needn't worry about that in the least. I assure you all that this whole affai is over and done with when certain formalities have been complied with." His voice hushed suitably. "Colonel Brende's death will be suitably announced, as was Miss Craye's. Professor Newton will go on with his work—under entirely new management, which will be his own. And you, Major, can do what you've been trying to do for days. Visit Scotland."

Passenden took the hit very well. Wharton peered roguishly at him, forgetting that the spectacles were no longer on.

"Taking what I've said into account, there's just one last question I'd like to put myself. Colonel Brende shot himself. You suggested that to him, Major?"

Passenden smiled wryly but said nothing.

"It was your gun?" persisted Wharton.

"The palaver's finished, Passenden told him amiably. "Even if you prove it's my gun, I'll still disown it."

Wharton nodded.

"Now I'll surprise you. Perhaps I agree with you. And between ourselves, I'm not sorry everything *is* finishe with. I think all the Big Bugs will be very much of the same opinion. Oh, and just before we part, gentlemen, there's one thing I ought to acknowledge. Major Travers won't be asked for a report, so as we may not all be together again, I'd like to thank him in front of you for the way he's helped in this unpleasant business."

"Hear, hear!" cut in Passenden. I sat polishing my glasses and wondering where George's latest hypocrisies would lead him.

"He's often had to be left in the dark," Wharton went on, "but that didn't damp his enthusiasm. Many a time he was giving me vital information without being aware of it." He cleared his throat and I had a sudden fear that he was about to fake a breakdown, but I needn't have been alarmed. He was merely bringing the meeting to a definit end. "And that's all, I think, gentlemen. I'll let you know the time for to-morrow."

So George had done it again. I'm not referring to the solving of the case, but to his blandishing of myself, for I had been fool enough to feel something of a glow come over me at those words of heartfelt gratitude, even if I knew somewhere deep down that they were only a part of his technique. Or weren't they? Had I really done anything, and was he genuinely grateful?

Those very questions show how he had had me fooled as ever, but there was something with which I was not disposed to let him get clean away.

"After those few comforting words of yours, George," I said, "I'm sorry to come down to earth. Give me a plain answer to a plain question. Did Colonel Brende die when you claim he did?" All I received was that look of pain and reproach.

"That business of Ledd coming along was far too apposite," I said. "You'd tried a bluff to make those two talk, and it hadn't come off Ledd saved your bacon. When did he actually shoot himself? Or hasn't he shot himself at all?"

"Now, now, now," Wharton said upbraidingly. "Of course he's shot himself."

"But when?"

"Well, as a matter of fact it was just before I rang you up and arranged that meeting. Nobody knew but myself and the nurse."

"I knew it," I said, and clicked my tongue. "My God, what an old humbug you are! How you can do the things you do, and get away with them, absolutely gets me down."

"Just tricks of the trade," he said, and chuckled. "I hoped they'd talk of themselves, but I took the precaution of having something up my sleeve."

"And you really think Passenden made him shoot himself?"

"Yes," he said, and soberly enough. "I think Passenden saw that that firs way out which he'd suggested at Cumberforth wasn't going to work." He shook his head with a certain lugubriousness. "As a matter of fact, I made a slip. I hinted to Passenden that I could pin the Craye murder on to Brende, and I'd take action at the right moment. I think Passenden used my name or yours and came here this morning through the guards, and had an interview with Brende, after squaring the nurse." He raised a quick hand. "Oh, no, I'm making no enquiries. I don't give a damn whose gun it was or what was done. Brende's death was a godsend, and I'm leaving it at that. But that doesn't prevent me knowing what happened. Passenden gave him the gun and said if he didn't use it, it'd be a question of a cold morning and a quick drop."

I agreed. George stowed away his papers and made a move. In the corridor he said he had to go to Brende's room, and would I care to see the body? I said I'd go with him, and I certainly wouldn't. The body, it turned out, was covered with a sheet, but the sight of that was enough for me. And something rather got me when I thought of the waste and tragedy of it all. What Brende might have been and done, for instance, but for that kink that twisted all his life.

"Here's the gun that did it," Wharton was saying. "Into my pocket it goes and that's the last that will be seen of it."

I said nothing because I was thinking, and I had never thought so clearly in my life. I knew who had been rung up by Passenden, and who had whispered those dreadful alternatives in the ear of Brende. I even incongruously knew that a certain young married couple might be forgiven, and get a start off in life. And how did I know it? Because the gun that Wharton put in his pocket was my little French automatic.

the end

Printed in Great Britain
by Amazon